'DIED' ON PINAS CREEK

'DIED' ON PINAS CREEK

& Other Stories

JACK WEST

ISBN: 978-0-578-57549-0

Dedication

This volume is dedicated to those who have encouraged me to write and publish this work and other works currently in progress. I have and am enjoying the labor of it.

Thank you, each and every one: Eugenia Nakamoto, Vince, Sarah, Cheryl Burress, Ken Rudin, 'Wild Bill' Cody, Steve & Pat Rolling, Harold and Ruth Anne Stephens Tom Trent, Gale Brown. Last, but in no way least, Paul Jokilehto and Hito. Two great friends I would gladly call my brothers if I could have more. Also, my Mother and Father, sadly, both long gone—Both are my Heroine and Hero. Also to my wonderful brother and safety-wire, James West. Rest in peace, Jim, I miss you, brother, every single day. And my daughter, J. Tara (West) Quale, whom I love dearly.

TABLE OF CONTENTS

SWEET SLEEP

I.

The serene weight of her body
as she sleeps
lies
sleek and brown
in and around
crisp white sheets
A dark and wonderful nipple
still erect, points and stands
above its full breast
and peeks from behind
rumpled white clouds of sheet
The other
a dot beneath a corner
rising in rhythm to find its way free only to fail and fall
and again
to begin again
and again
and again

II.

A flash of thigh
like a satiny
sea-glazed dolphin
caught for a moment bowed in

and out above the white
water sheet
smooth
and full and
having caught its breath and my eye
dives again
for cover

III.
I will miss
the wonderful sensual scents of her
as she sleeps among
the hills, swells
valleys, troughs and
fields
of wild flowers
printed on heavy
cotton
sheets.

THE TOLL

"Cob, we've got a visitor down by the jeep! He's with four armed men, standing beside two trucks with holding tanks mounted in their beds. He's holding a rifle over his head, walking toward our gate."

"Okay, Janet, toss me the binoculars," Cob says. "Mal! Get out here! Where's Dave?"

"He's here with me. We're comin' out." Dave takes the steps two at a time up into the tower. Janet hands him the M1A.

"Where's Tomiko and Trillya?" I ask.

"Inside, making bread," Cob says. "Janet gave Trillya a break from overwatch. They needed to talk."

"Do we know him?" I said as Cob checks him over.

"Looks like Cotton from the cul-de-sac a week or so ago. By the look on his face there's a problem."

"Ya, bet it concerns water," says Janet.

"What's up?" Tomiko climbs the steps with Trillya in tow.

"Nothing to worry about, ladies," I say.

"It's Cotton, from that cul-de-sac," says Trillya. "He seemed okay at the time, at least he didn't try to shoot you and Cob. He was concerned that I was taken against my will. If I'd made a fuss, the three of them would have shot both of you full of big holes."

"I'll talk to him across the fence. I don't want to open it till I know what his problem is. This is our first get-together without pointing guns." Saying that, I look up at our tower where Janet and Dave are sighting—it's just a small inaccuracy.

Cotton is holding his AR across the back of his neck. A very frayed ball cap is perched on his head. Both man and cap have seen better days. The material covering the bill of the cap is tattered and a portion of the plastic bill is showing. He's wearing a worn-out gray shirt with a frayed collar. His jeans are patched, and his tennis shoes are in worse shape than the hat. He is limping badly. His face is deeply lined, and his beard is nearly all white.

He looks up at our simple tower and sees scoped rifles pointing at his companions near the trucks.

"Seems the shoe's on the other foot this time," he says. "It's only fair. We mean no harm to you. Speaking of shoes, I gotta sit and pull stickers out of my foot. There's cactus everywhere. These sneakers are gettin' thin." He looks over the pea gravel of the drive where he's about to put his fanny.

"What size shoe do you wear?" I ask.

"Ten and a half. Why?"

I look back at Cob. "Those boots we took off Marco a while back, they ten and a half?"

"Ya, I think they are. I'll get 'em. They're hanging in the shop."

Cotton pulls the needles from the thin sole of his left sneaker, grimacing all the while. He removes the sock and inspects his foot. There are several smears of blood at the arch, but the needles weren't in deep.

Cob tosses the boots to Cotton who catches them neatly. He looks them over, then pulls on his sock and the left boot, then strips his right foot, slips it into the boot, zips both up, stands and stomps 'em good and proper. He does a little jig, grinning all the while, a happy lad, a happy older lad. "These are mighty fine. What can I give you for 'em?"

"No trade, friend," says Cob. "They're a gift from a someone who has no need for 'em 'cause he isn't walking around anymore. We kept 'em to pass on, happens to be you." We all grin at Cotton's excitement.

"Now that that's settled, what up?" I ask.

"We went to Saguaro Lake for water, and it's now a toll lake. A very big guy, with what I think are prison tats on his arms, and a bald head, has a half dozen guys with rifles and poles blockin' the bridge. There's one shooter on the high rock face above the bridge entrance. He wants ten dollars in junk silver for passage, and then for only 200 gallons of water. We don't want to pay, cause water in the desert belongs to everybody who's thirsty, human and beast. There is no humanity in any of 'em. No one should have the right to own water during hard times."

"If they can hold it, I guess they can own it," says Cob.

As much as I hate the idea, Cob's right. "Okay, 'Boots,'" I say. Cotton grins at his new nickname. "Go back to your vehicles. We need water to top off our main tank too. We'll bring some firepower. This is the second time a fool is pulling this stunt. There was a group out of Tucson that claimed ownership a while back. One of the Sparrow Units went for water and objected. After the disagreement was settled, the Unit piled the bodies and burned 'em. The barbeque pyre is on the south side of the parking lot. You can see the crisp remains off to your right, once you cross the bridge. We'll put an end to this right now."

I hope, I said to myself. "Time's coming when we're gonna have a major showdown with all of these dipsticks. As long as there are more than two people on this planet, there will never be peace. This beautiful little speck in the cosmos is a battleground!"

At my nod, Tomiko opens the gate.

Trillya touches my arm. I turn to her. She looks concerned. She hugs me around the waist and lays her head against my chest. I hug her close and welcome her warmth.

"We gotta go," I whisper. She steps back. I take her face in my hands and lightly kiss her lips and then her forehead. "I'm looking forward to eating whatever you're making," I say. "We'll be back before you know it."

Dave is looking at Janet from the passenger side. He's touching her arm and she his hand. She too looks worried. Cob is holding the driver's side door open for me. I pull it closed.

"You two kick ass." Says Cob.

Cob slaps the door in emphasis. I nod at my brother, shift into gear, and we're off, pulling our 300-gallon transport tank on its trailer.

Dave and I set up about 200 yards from the sniper above the bridge. It's mid-morning. Through my binoculars I watch the merry band drinking something and bantering back and forth, up and down. I count six on the road and one sniper above. The sniper is pulling a Thermos up by a rope. We hear it clang as it bumps against the outcropping on its way up to the heavyset shooter. The bipod of his rifle rests at the edge of the rock face. From its position, he'll have to fold the bipod to shoot directly down on anyone attempting to run the barricade. The distance from the barricade to the bend in the road, where we're holed up, is about 150 yards. Dave carefully positions a sandbag on the rocks and slowly, to escape observation, lays our M1A across it, then adjusts for distance, elevation, and windage to the sniper.

"Dave, I'm gonna pull our rig to the barrier to make sure our body count is accurate and how they're deployed. We don't want any surprises. Hold tight." He nods while removing the top of his canteen and taking a swallow. I crawl back to the road. "Cotton, I wanna make a reconnaissance. Come with me. Four eyes are better than two. Tell your crew what we're doing while I bring up our rig."

"You want water, you pay for it. There ain't one drop fer free. I want $10.00 in junk silver an' you can take 200 gallons, not one drop more." The tattooed man holds out a hand the size of a maple leaf, rubbing thumb and fingers together, sign language for "give me money," right out of an old gangster movie.

"Geez," I say, "I didn't know it was a toll lake now. Hell, I don't have that much junk! Never did and probably never will!"

"Well, go get it from someone who has it, and don't come back without it. I see you again here and you don't have it, I'll tear your fuckin' arms off. And I can do it. Now pull into the parking lot, turn this thing around. Don't come back without coins."

He waves an arm and two older guys, dressed in soiled khaki pants and gray sweatshirts remove the poles. We drive in and turned around. We are covered all the while by two men behind an older Toyota truck parked broadside in the parking lot. I point off to our right and Cotton sees the burned Tucson group. They are still a close-knit group, but not walkin' an' talkin' anymore.

I'm six foot two and 195. I am lean and strong. But this "Tat Man" is all of six-five and close to 300 pounds. It looks like he was born strong. Prison weights no doubt added more strength to natural strength. Whatever or whoever authorized weights for prison inmates needs to join the Tucson pyre party.

We reposition the truck and trailer. "How many'd you count Cotton?"

"Five at the bridge, one on top, and two in the parking lot—and of course, Jumbo. His arms are larger than my thighs!"

"That's a nightmare if there ever was one." I climb up to Dave.

"I'm dialed in, Mal, but he keeps movin' around. I'll wait for him to hold still for a bit. It might take a couple minutes."

"You see the Toyota in the lot? There are two more behind it with long guns."

I hand him the binoculars. "Okay, I see the truck and the rifle barrels sticking up. They're not moving around much. They're staying out of sight."

"Take out the high guy first and anyone else you can get to easily by the bridge. Send rounds to the Toyota. Keep them worried. I'll give a whistle when we're ready on the ground. We'll begin after you finish Mister Thermos."

I climb down and stand with Cotton and his crew. Two of them were with Cotton back when they confronted Cob, Trillya, and me at the cul-de-sac, after the Pinto became our plow blade. Tim Sims and Charles Bishop from the cul-de-sac are the only two I'm familiar with. Tim is about the same age as Cotton and dressed much the same. Charles is younger, about my age, and uses a lever gun, similar to the Winchester Cob uses. I saw Cob eying Charles's rifle while we were waiting in the cul-de-sac, several weeks ago. Charles is clean shaven and has a serious limp. I'll ask him about it one day, assuming we live through this one.

We're all very nervous about what is about to happen here. It's too bad reasoning is out of the question. All of us need this lake for our survival. I guess I'd rather die from a bullet in the head than from thirst. As for killing another person, for this reason, I have no regrets, none whatsoever. I'll leave regrets to Tomiko. Good, bad, or ugly, we all need water.

It's kind of strange: we are going to kill this group of bad folks, if we can, to allow other enemies to have water. Maybe we should control the water, force our enemies to the negotiating table. The only problem I see would be that we'd be fighting a huge force every day and all night, assuming we could even last one day. Can we trust our enemies? History teaches that in war time, they must be killed to the point where the few remaining give up.

Cotton holds up a thumb to indicate we're in position. I give a light whistle for Dave to signal that we're all set to assault the toll trolls and take the bridge.

I watch the sniper through the binoculars. Seconds pass. He keeps moving out of sight, then he leans over the barrel of his rifle with the Thermos in hand and is saying something to those on the road below who are slapping their legs and laughing. I feel the recoil of Dave's shot. I see the head of the sniper nearly explode with the strike of the .308 bullet. A head shot at about 200 yards is not what I expected, then I realize the head and shoulders were all the target Dave had.

The sniper's head rocks back with the force of the strike. Pink mist and dust fan out behind him as his body falls forward across the barrel of the rifle. Both fall from the rocky point. The body lands in the talus, head first, or what's left of it, and the rest of him folds on top of itself like an accordion. The rifle lands barrel first, the stock separating from the receiver. At the sound of Dave's shot, Cotton and his five friends fire away, and two of the revelers go down. Dave shoots another one lying behind several large rocks. In seconds, the big guy with the tats sees four of his crew go down.

One behind a large boulder is making a fight of it, mostly shooting up at Dave. Cotton sees the man's leg from behind the boulder and shoots it. The man screams and pulls the leg away. Dave shoots the leg again from his position. Still the man is making a fight of it, but after a minute or so, he is not shooting anymore.

Rounds from the Toyota pepper us with rock fragments, causing stinging cuts. Pieces of cactus imbed themselves in Charles Bishop's back, shot from a cholla cactus near him. I hear more rounds striking the rocks at Dave's position. Tat Man is making a run for the parking lot and the Toyota. He's followed by the fifth man from the bridge. Our bullets skip off the road around them. We're still taking incoming fire from the two in the parking lot.

I'm watching the Toyota as Dave sends rounds into and across its hood. The man following Tat Man goes down with a bullet in his backside. He commences squirming all over the road. The big guy just keeps running flat out in a zig-zag pattern toward the Toyota. "New Boots Cotton" and I are in pursuit, Cotton ahead of me, showin' off his new treads.

The two behind the Toyota are trying to sight us, and we're running in a zig-zag pattern also. One of them stands and holds for a moment, aiming at Cotton. Dave's shot takes the standing guy down and his shot goes off into the air. Cotton changes direction and rounds the far end of the little truck. He shoots the remaining rifleman, anticipating toward the wrong end of the truck, by which Tat Man just ran.

Cotton continues after Tat, who has reached the pier and a moored dinghy. He loosens the tie rope and jumps into the small boat. It drifts away from the pier. He stands at the transom trying over and over to crank the Johnson motor to life. The transom end of the little boat is bobbing up and down with his 300 pounds of urgency, but his attempts are futile. From about 20 feet Cotton aims his AR at Tat, who stops cranking and dives into the water over the Johnson motor. He barely makes it over the outboard as Newton's third law reaffirms its accuracy: "For every action there is an equal and opposite reaction." The force of his jump pushes the boat away from him and he sort of hangs in the air, then his feet clip the transom on each side of the motor and his belly lands atop the motor. The bow lifts from the water from his 300-pound belly flop on the motor.

Cotton stands on the pier, waiting for the diver to come up for air so he can finish the chase and add fresh corruption to the lake.

I stand to the side of the pier on dry land behind Cotton. Tat Man's artistic skull quietly breaks the surface behind Cotton. The tattoo on the back of his head is of a spider's web, complete with a large spider. Instead of swimming out into the lake, he's swum beneath the pier, surfacing behind Cotton. It was a smart move, I'll give him that.

Tat Man stands waist high in the water, pointing his pistol at Cotton, who is still searching for him off the end of the pier. I raise my 22/45 from about twenty feet. We pull our triggers at the same instant. His weapon does not fire. Maybe water soaked the primer. Water and powder don't mix. Could be the primer was not seated properly or not sealed against water. I double tap Tat Man, missing the spider with the first shot but scoring a bull's-eye on it with the second. His pistol makes a kerplunk sound as it drops from his dead hand. He falls forward and floats, momentarily buoyed by the air trapped by his shirt.

Cotton spins around at the sound of my .22. He looks startled then relieved and waves his thanks at me. I am shaking from adrenaline—the big guy was quick. But for the misfire, "Boots" would not be standing in his! I am once again reminded of the mistakes possible when reloading ammunition.

I wade out and grab a fist full of shirt and haul the dead man to the edge of the lake, out of our potential drinking water. Too much of a bad thing is never a good thing. Cotton helps me drag him onto dry land. We barely get his feet out of the water, he's so heavy. I notice that he is wearing Adidas high-tops. Another pair to pass along to unhappy feet? They are huge. If we can't pass them on, they will make great flyswatters.

We are not the police. We cannot arrest anyone. There are no courts, lawyers, judges. No ACLU advocates doing their work. There are jails, but no jailers. There is only survival or death, and the survivors do not always escape unscathed. We don't have food enough for captives in any case.

We walk back toward the blockade. We walk past the guy we shot in the butt. Now I see he's got a couple of holes in his head. A major portion of his face is fanned out toward the lake. The lone fighter that was leg-shot had bled out. His leg above the knee is attached only by skin. Our water trucks are coming toward us.

We back down beside the bridge to the lake's edge and begin filling our 300-gallon tank using one of our two submersible 12-volt pumps. I look back toward where we've left that human debris. He is not wearing his Adidas high-tops any longer. I look at the shoes I'd tied together and remembered the ads about those basketball shoes. "When you wear 'em you'll run faster and jump higher…" No mention was made of jumping against Newton's third law, and certainly not of running faster than a couple of speeding, subsonic .22 bullets.

Timothy Sims runs up and hands me our handheld ham radio. "There's a problem at your compound. Cob has been trying to get you. I said I'd find you. I told him our problem here at the lake is solved. And that you and Dave are okay. Told 'im we're all okay except for minor scratches and bruises.

"Cob?" … No answer. "Cob? Tomiko? Janet? Trillya? Anyone, pick up."

"Mal, get here fast!" It's Cob, his voice staticky and anxious. "We've got trouble. We've got one down." I hear weapons fire in the background.

"They're scattered all across our perimeter. I count six. Can't see their transportation from here. We're holdin' 'em but don't know for how long. Come quick!"

"We're on our way! Who's down, Cob?"

But the link is already dead.

"Cotton, have your folks rope the bodies to the bridge railing. Strip 'em and take what you can use. Anyone harboring similar ideas can see where it'll get them. If that Toyota works, haul the three of them up here. It'll take three or four to load the big guy. Here are his shoes, pass 'em on or string 'em around his neck. Our place is under attack. Dave and I gotta go, an' right now."

"I'm comin' with you!"

"Thanks, Cotton, but no. Stay here and finish loading your water and fence these bodies as a warning. If you don't want to fence all of them, dump the remaining with the Tucson group. If the Toyota is useable, keep it."

Dave has loaded our pump beside our near empty tank and put the M1A in the gun rack. I thought of taking a rifle, but I prefer a pistol. We take off in a cloud of dust. I see that Dave has fresh cuts on his forehead from rock shards.

Ten minutes later, we stop a quarter mile from our drive. I'm carrying our suppressor for the M1A. It's heavy and slips over the barrel and locks on to the front sight. There is a single person watching their vehicle. Unfortunately, it's a woman. I twist the silencer on. Dave lays the barrel on my shoulder, and I cover my ears, my right arm over the barrel, not blocking the scope. A suppressor on a large caliber rifle will not completely silence the sound, but it will reduce it some. Dave sights the woman and shoots her in the back. She's knocked flat to the ground and is still.

The echoing sound of gunfire has helped obscure our shot. We trot to their vehicle where I open the hood of the van and rip out the wiring, and all the while we hear gunfire. They may be leaving, but not in this. I lower the hood quietly as Dave checks the woman's pulse and shakes his head. His shot has severed her spine and she's dead. I shove her pistol behind my belt and we move closer to our drive and behind the burned jeep and wooden crosses. We have a very clear view of the attackers from here.

One shooter is about seventy-five yards in front of us. Next to him is another, lying on his back and not moving. There is a lot of blood on his shirtfront. Beyond him are two more with rifles, about 150 yards away. Further are two more firing at our compound. Both are clear targets for Dave. He shoots the farthest in quick succession because they have a better view of our compound. One of the two beyond the closest to us spots us and shoots too quickly. It's a miss, but the Jeep takes the hit. It's a long shot for my .45, but resting on the Jeep, I aim a foot above his head and squeeze off a round. I hit him, and he goes down. Meanwhile Dave has drawn down on the guy's companion and shoots him in the chest. The shooter in front of us stands and throws down his rifle, surrendering. Tomiko opens our gate and strides toward him, oblivious to the shooter drawing down on her with his rifle. Dave shoots at him. He's the one I knocked down with my pistol. Cob from the tower shoot at the same time. Thrice shot will not get up again.

As Tomiko gets closer I see the look on her face and it is not pretty. It's not the face of restraint and disgust with killing that I'm used to. She's angry and is holding Cob's Governor in her left hand and Hitoshi's katana in her right. I can almost see Hitoshi, her samurai warrior ancestor, in ancient Japanese battle dress, hovering beside her. I know that parched blade is about to quench its thirst for blood. A head is going to roll.

I wonder which of us is shot. Dave and I suddenly look at each other. Our eyes open wide in fear and near panic. Understanding hits both of us in the same instant. Cob's in the tower. Tomiko is striding down our drive. The volume of blood on her T-shirt cannot be hers.

It's either Janet or Trillya.

Dave and I begin running toward our open gate.

I cradle her head in my lap. We've put pressure on the wound, low, through her ribs on the right side. We're hoping pressure will cause the clotting agent in her blood to kick in. Her breathing is a rough panting, a choking inhale and explosive exhale, as though normal breathing is beyond her control. Blood is coming from her mouth and nose. Her eyes are closed. I feel that her breathing can stop at any moment. Trillya opens her eyes and looks at me. Her eyes are wide and bloodshot. My smile is stiff and fearful.

"Am I going to die?" she asks in one breath cycle.

"You've been shot in a bad place."

"Is everyone okay?" she asks in a weak voice.

"Yes, we're all fine. The attackers are no longer a threat to anyone."

I look up at Tomiko who has returned with a damp cloth. She kneels and wipes Trillya's face free of blood spatter.

"I don't want to die an' leave you." The hand that grips mine is weak but shaking with urgency.

"Then don't. Just close your eyes and focus on breathing. Relax your body. Let it do what it knows how to do, to fix and repair. If it can slow and stop the bleeding, you'll have a good chance to recover. Just think over and over, I want to live, I want to live. I'm going to live."

"You really believe…?"

"I do. So should you. Sherry Wilbur was a nurse with the hospital. She's with Cotton's group, and she's on her way here. Janet and Cob are escorting her. Just breathe, relax, and repeat positives. You're a strong woman. If anyone can fight through this, you can. I want you back, Trillya. We all want you back. We're here for you, pulling for you. You're not alone. We are your family. You have always been welcomed here."

"Did we get water?" she says weakly.

"We did." It's a small lie. "Don't worry about a thing. We are secure. Just breathe and relax. I hear a truck coming now. You'll be making flatbreads before you know it."

A faint grin and she drifts off, her breathing still labored. Her body relaxes. I check her pulse. It is very faint. Her heart is not circulating much blood; it's just pumping it onto the desert. The distance between each breath grows longer.

I feel my throat tighten around the lump of emotion there. I glanced up at Tomiko and Dave. Concern and sorrow are written clearly on their faces.

The nurse, Sherry Wilbur, rushes up with Cob and Janet. Cotton has come also. Sherry opens her bag, removes her stethoscope and listens to Trillya's heart, examines the wound, checks her pupils, watches her breathing then looks at me and shakes her head. The space between Trillya's breaths cycles increases until the last exhale. The next inhale does not come, and she's gone.

"There was devastating internal damage," murmurs Sherry. "She lost too much blood. I don't know how she lived as long as she did. She was a fighter. She needed immediate surgery, and even then…"

"I'm so sorry, Mal," Tomiko says. "The shot from one of those two at the entrance of our drive was meant for me. She shoved me away and took the bullet instead. Cob shot one of them. I don't know which one did it. I went down and cut that bastard slowly into pieces with him whimpering and screaming all the while that he surrendered… and I didn't care one stinking bit."

She examines her blood-spattered right hand and arm in a curious manner, then adds, "Trillya liked you a lot, Mal. She asked me about you and your family and what happened to them. That's the reason we were making flatbreads together. Remember when she asked to be part of our family? She told us her mom was a barmaid at The Bitter Root, and about her time in that gang. Janet and I gave her such a grilling that night. We were suspicious of her intentions. We were completely wrong. Remembering what we said really hurts. It will be a long time before I… we recover from that."

Janet nods at Tomiko's words, then with tears streaming, she bends and gives me a quick hug. She's too emotional to speak. She sobs as Dave holds her.

The weapons and ammunition from the attackers are collected. Cob gives them to Cotton who is living with a group of ten like-minded families in a small gated mobile home park. Weapons in their group are in short supply. Several other families near Cotton's MHP are in need also; the weapons from the bridge fight will be passed on to them. Janet keeps a second rifle, a scoped Russian SKS rifle. In the right hands, many of these are extremely accurate. They police all the empty brass at our compound for reloading. Cotton gives a bag of brass from the bridge.

While my family and friends are doing that, I just sit beside her. Every part of me aches. She died with her eyes partly closed. This is just her body,

I remind myself; her spirit, her energy is gone. Looking at her eyes, part of me expects her to glance at me and smile. I caress her cheek and look at the blood-caked earth beneath her. Except for the pain, I feel empty and hollow inside. I remember the warmth of our last hug.

We buried Trillya on the rise near our water tank. We buried her deep. I didn't want hungry critters sensing where we put her and disturbing her resting place.

The view from there, with her, had been peaceful. The lights, when there were lights, from A.J., Mesa, and Phoenix were even promising, considering what we were living through. She was quiet and soft there, unlike our first meeting at that Walmart parking lot.

We made love there and took care of each other. We were to each other an oasis in this barren, violent desert.

I don't go there anymore. It's too painful. I'm reminded of her, a hundred times a day, I feel yet another chunk of my heart has been ripped away. The women I've loved and cared about, Sharon and Melissa, my wife and daughter, and now Trillya, have all been ripped violently from me. Maybe I'm the kiss of death to any woman I care about during these times. Maybe these deaths are payback for the lives I've taken. More likely it's just the luck of the draw.

Whatever the reason, if reason is involved at all, it's painful. Could Newton's third law apply here also? "Live by the gun, die by the gun." In destroying others, we are destroying ourselves at the same time—inside and outside.

I wonder if intimate relations are worth all the pain, the anguish of loss—for all of us. I'm beginning to feel I cannot do this anymore, that my heart and vital juices are drying up, that I am becoming a reflection of this vast, and now dry, empty desert. I feel there's nothing left. Our oasis has become an empty place, a mirage, an unattainable shimmering in the distance...

Not real at all.

The End

'DIED' ON PINAS CREEK

"You ain't gonna make it, Penny," came Bob Tisdale's voice from among the rustling, trembling aspen leaves. Tisdale, darkly clothed, stepped to the edge of the aspen grove, holding his 1873 Winchester nonchalantly across his body, the business end not far off from Marcus Penny.

Bob Tisdale was a narrow-shouldered man of 25, nearly as tall as Penny's five foot ten. Tisdale's knee-length black wool coat covered a gray, pinstriped wool shirt, tucked into gray wool pants, which were stuffed into black, blunt-nosed boots with trailing Jingle Bob spurs. Peeking from the edge of the coat was his .44-40 cross draw Colt.

"Maybe I'm wrong," Tisdale continued in a mocking tone, the grin on his face reflecting his arrogance. "Maybe you can get away down this side of the ravine and up the other. I seen how fast you can run. But you can't outrun what I've got for you right here," Tisdale said, patting his blue baby with a hard, calloused hand. "Now step out from behind that there boulder to where I can see all of you!"

Penny shivered at the sight of the rifle, glanced around again and, seeing no way out, licked at his lips, swallowed, and stepped from behind the granite boulder. His legs were trembling so badly that he kept a hand on the boulder to steady himself.

Penny's Levis were faded and ragged. His patched and sun-faded shirt, two years and two sizes too small for him, was stretched to nearly bursting across his shoulders and chest and hung freely about his lean waist. His eyes were dark brown—nearly black—and wide open as he moved carefully. The smooth skin of his 17-year-old face was browned from the sun except for the pale, shaded hat line across his forehead. His dark auburn hair was very short.

Facing Tisdale, his lips were quivering, and his teeth were chattering. He was shivering all over, as much from the crisp, high mountain air as from what Tisdale was about to do to him. His heavy jacket was back in his night camp with his horse, his old .44 Henry rifle with its stock shot to splinters by Tisdale, and the rest of his kit now full of holes. He'd lost his hat back among the pines, while hastily pulling his rundown boots over his pine needle-garnished socks. Tisdale had rousted Penny from his sleep and driven him from his camp to this impasse, an abrupt drop to Pinas Creek. The ledge fell away abruptly to the creek 30 feet below. There was no cover to his left, down along the rim for a hundred feet. The area to his right was also free of any cover. He could run no further.

"I'm going to die right here," Penny mumbled to himself. The notion that he could die had never really occurred to him. It was a sobering shock. This can't be happening, he thought. Will he just shoot me dead, or will I roll around in agony and bleed to death? I don't want to be gut shot! I wish I could stop shaking. Was what I did so bad that I need to be murdered?

He glanced nervously behind him at the ravine of angry talus that fell steeply away to the creek, flowing with icy, spring snowmelt. It was flanked by brush and new growth that extended out over the water like a canopy. In places, the stream's movement was stifled by dead limbs and branches—nature's dams, formed without the aid of the beaver by spring thaws and gully washers.

Two images flashed to his mind, one of a chunk of hot lead punching a thumb-sized hole in the front of his head and ripping a terrible ragged hole exiting, and then of his swollen and rotting corpse, with the back of its head missing, fouling fresh, clean water all the way to the lake.

Tisdale's dispassionate eyes reminded Penny of a mountain lion measuring its next kill. They kill for survival. Only man kills for reasons beyond pure survival… revenge, greed, and for some, just the fun of it.

"You ain't going to murder me, are you, Bob?"

"Killin' a damned coward ain't murder, you Jack Sprat. It's like killin' a mangy, rabid critter." Tisdale grinned and poked back his black, wide-brimmed, flat-crowned hat, revealing his pale forehead and freeing a shock of brown hair to splash against it. His eyes were wide, with a hint of madness that Penny hadn't noticed before. He'd never stood in front of an angry Bob Tisdale. At this juncture, their supposed friendship counted for nothing.

Although Tisdale held the rifle loosely, Penny knew that nothing Tisdale did with that rifle could ever be mistaken for unintended.

"I never coulda guessed you was yellow, Marcus, knowin' your pa and brothers as I do." He paused, and a brief grin showed off his yellow teeth as he observed the change in Penny's expression. "But I knowed you was a yellow-belly when you wouldn't back me in that hard-rock miner's camp." Tisdale stared at Penny's face and continued. "They was easy. It was two on two. They took gold from the ground an' we was takin' it from them. We had the high ground and the drop on 'em, if only you'd stuck! You wheeled that nag you ride an' left out of there—left me to cover 'em both, while you, you horse's ass, left with that nag's tail between your legs. Left me holdin' the two o' them. Them two dirt scratchers looked at each other an' spread further apart, fixin' to flank me. I backed my pony up and faded into the night. I was damned lucky to get out of there with all my pickle, you gutless puke!"

"I ain't no thief, nor a murderer. You know me, Bob. I couldn't rightly do it!" Penny pleaded. "Maybe I am a coward; maybe not." Penny's voice trailed off as he gave Tisdale a forlorn glance.

"They was easy for two of us," Tisdale continued, ignoring Penny's plea, while pointing a finger at the ground between them in emphasis. "Them pack saddles looked heavy. It was gold, I'm thinkin', or silver! It was easy pickin's! Wouldn't have cost us one drop of sweat—just a coupla bullets, an' we coulda been set for a long time. Damn you, Marcus! Damn you to hell! I thought we was pardners! I can't stomach the sight of you!" He paused then added, "Well, you can't run no further, cause there ain't no place left to go—except ta hell, an' I got your ticket right here." He shook his Winchester at Penny with one hand.

Shame at being called a coward had turned Penny's neck red, and the color moved up to his face and ears. He'd hoped that going west with his friend would give him the opportunity to discover what he was really made of. A fair chance was all he'd wanted, and he'd failed at it. He realized that if he survived the day, he could never escape himself. His aspirations had only been pipe dreams. Suddenly he bent over and retched several times, though little came up. Now he was even more embarrassed by his body's betrayal.

Bent over, hands on his knees, Penny raised his head and wiped a short, frayed sleeve across his mouth. Death was probably the best thing, after all. At least his brothers and sister would never suffer from the terrible truth, and his brave and honorable father would never be shamed. Them knowing about his cravenness would be worse than being gut shot. He wanted to sink into the ground and disappear.

He searched for the words that would justify his existence—but there was nothing. All he could do was shrug his shoulders, for he knew the only option left him was to die.

"I ain't no thief nor murderer," Penny mumbled again weakly.

"You're a damned coward!" With one hand Tisdale punched the Winchester toward Penny's feet and pulled the trigger. The booming report echoed across the ravine and back.

The heavy bullet showered Penny with debris and he recoiled.

Tisdale stepped toward Penny while racking another round. The rifle boomed again.

The bullet slapped Penny's pant leg above his boot top and burned his shin. He flinched, his feet went out from under him, and he slid boot-first on his belly, 30 feet to the bottom of the ravine, with his legs set stiff and his fingers cutting furrows all the way down. Sharp rock fragments ripped off a fingernail during the slide.

It took him several seconds to realize that the fire on his belly was not from being gut shot, but because his shirt had rolled up, exposing his stomach to the succession of abrasive rocks during his furious descent.

Tisdale swaggered to the edge, sniggering, still holding his rifle in one hand. He stared down at the spread-eagle Penny. A breeze tugged at the edges of his knee-length coat. Pebbles continued to clatter and dance down to where Penny lay. They skipped and rattled about his head, shoulders, arms, and furrowing fingers.

Tisdale jacked another round, pulled the weapon to his shoulder, and put the front sight on Penny's head. He held it there for several seconds, and then shifted aim to a flat rock up tight between Penny's outstretched legs and squeezed off another round. Again the sound echoed. Smoke rushed out like a black tongue licking at the pitiful figure below. Then, as if repulsed, it curled up and away. The heavy bullet exploded the rock, stinging Penny's legs. Rock fragments bolted and skipped across the icy snow melt, splintering thick brush.

Penny winced but kept hugging the slope. He was numb clear through. He couldn't look up at Tisdale.

Tisdale allowed long, silent seconds to pass. Penny held himself ready against the shock of the heavy bullet and the eternal darkness that he hoped would release him from this wretched life. His body was still trembling and cold.

But a bullet did not come. It did not come! "Get it over with!" Penny finally yelled, unable to suppress his anxiety.

With two deliberate moves, Tisdale racked the lever, ejecting the hot spent shell up and away, and slamming another cold shell into the smoking hot breech. Again, he put the front sight on Penny's head, his finger caressing the smooth trigger. And yet, after several more seconds of deliberation, he lowered the hammer and sat down, hanging his legs over the edge. He gently laid his rifle aside, undid the top button of his coat, and pulled out a sack of Bull Durham from his shirt. He rolled a cigarette, licked it closed, struck a match against the hammer of his Winchester, and lit up. He flipped the spent match down at Penny.

Penny heard the flair of the match. Annoyed at the contemptuous gesture, he could no longer resist looking up at Tisdale, perched on the lip of the ravine, smoking a damned cigarette. Except for the cigarette, Tisdale looked like an avenging gargoyle from a drawing Penny had seen in a book.

"I'll not shoot you—not here, anyways," said Tisdale, as he looked down on Penny. He took another pull at the cigarette. "What's better than shootin' ya is spreading the word that you're a worthless coward. Wherever I go, whoever I meet, I'm gonna to make it my business to destroy you. You'll have pain and misery every day of your life. That's better than puttin' a bullet in your brain. When I'm through, you won't have a life anywheres out here. The story'll spread like a prairie fire. You'll be shunned—strays dogs won't even piss on you."

Tisdale grinned and drew at the cigarette again, then added, "You know, if'n I was you, I'd just stay up here, find a rock, crawl under it, and die, like a sick old dog. If'n I ever lay eyes on you again, Marcus Penny, and I mean anywheres, I will put lead into you with this here Winchester. I'll shoot you for the yellow pickle you are."

With that, he flipped the butt of his cigarette down at Penny. It missed. Caught by a breeze, it arched up before landing lightly on Pinas Creek, where it went out with a tssst!

Tisdale pushed himself up, using the butt of his rifle. With a final show of disgust, he kicked more rubble down on Penny. With spurs jingling, he sauntered back through the quakies to his horse. He shoved the rifle into its scabbard, caught up the rains, grabbed the saddle horn with both hands, and swung neatly into the saddle. Without a look back, he touched his Jingle Bobs to his horse and let it pick its way back through the stand of aspens, their leaves still trembling.

Penny still lay at the bottom of the ravine. The pain from his abrasive slide was nothing compared with the thought of having his cowardice spread like a plague, inoculating everyone against him and infecting all his family. It was shameful enough to know it of himself, but to have it made public was the absolute bitter end. He shook his head, trying to silence the thoughts. How had he come to this cruel end? He punched the ground with his fists. Rocks and pebbles tore and cut his knuckles and fingers.

He backed into the icy snow melt, hoping to snuff the scorching flames of shame.

Pinas Creek flowed and chortled, unperturbed down the mountain to the lake and beyond. The water stung his lacerated belly but soothed his parched throat as he drank. It cooled his face and stung his hands. For some time, on hands and knees, he stared vacantly into the bitter cold water, seeing his distorted reflection. Drops of cold water fell from his eyelashes, nose, and chin.

His mind went suddenly quiet, empty. He discovered the hundreds of brightly colored rocks and pebbles beneath the surface of the creek. How brilliant and gem-like they appeared. How different from the dull, dry rocks on the shoreline.

He began stumbling downstream, following the path of the creek. Like a drunk, he staggered and floundered among the bright, slippery rocks glistening and shimmering beneath the water. Though fouled by his muck-raking passage, and distorted by his reflection, he knew the gems were still there. He was now unmindful of the crisp, cold mountain air, and that he was drenched with nearly freezing water.

New growth at the stream's edge ensnared and entangled his legs. He yanked free, only to be caught again and again. He gave a wild, piercing sound that startled and frightened him.

He pulled the brush away from him. Silt from the bottom of the creek churned up, fouling the crystal water and obscuring the gems there. Sweat and steam poured from his body as he fought off the clinging growth at the stream's edge.

Spent at last, he dropped to his hands and knees into the muddied ice water. He noticed how quickly the muddied water cleared, and that the beauty of the rocks was not lost.

He stood and began running down the creek, feeling light. He stumbled on the slippery rocks, so he began searching for dry, solid rocks to leap from. He ran, jumping, from rock to rock. Where he could, he hurdled dead falls lying across his path, ducking under others as they came. He stumbled into the stream a number of times, but continued, undeterred. He fought off more large branches that whipped against him, slowly tearing the shirt from his body. All the welts, cuts, and bruises were testimony to his passage, his rebirth. He discovered, as he ran, that he was agile and well-coordinated, and that he enjoyed the rhythm and flow of dodging and twisting. He had no problem absorbing the pain from his fibrous tormentors. He saw them, more importantly, as his liberators. He could not remember when the transformation began to spread through him, inside to out. A sense of clarity and a lack of fear were staking their claims in him.

He was watching his body perform, detached from the exertion, the pain, and the cold.

Through the brush he could see where the creek emptied into Bear Lake.

He started to feel like he knew who he was and where he was.

Suddenly, up ahead, he saw a man on a horse, about to cross the creek. It was Tisdale!

A grin swept across Penny's face, and he timed his steps, leapt onto a dead aspen and sprang, skimming Tisdale from the saddle. The horse shied and leaped toward the opposite bank.

Tisdale's right boot hung in the stirrup as the horse bolted up the far bank. Tisdale's foot slipped out of his entangled boot and in he went.

Tisdale surfaced, blowing icy water from his mouth. He floundered back toward the bank, and it became clear he'd lost a boot. His wool coat was soaked and heavy with frigid water. He shook his head to clear the shock.

Penny rose from the icy snowmelt, shaking water from his battered head and face. With a rush, Penny pushed a wave of frigid water toward Tisdale.

"Jesus, it's you!" Tisdale stammered, throwing back his sodden coat, grasping for the .44-40 cross draw Colt that was no longer there. He threw a punch at Penny, but it was hampered by his waterlogged coat.

Penny slapped the fist aside with his right hand and drove two hard left hooks to Tisdale's ribs. The wet coat absorbed the power of the first punch, but the follow-up stunned Tisdale and brought a gasp from his open mouth along with a shower of saliva and creek water.

Tisdale staggered back from the force of the punches and pulled his knife, swinging it wildly at Penny.

But the blade passed, and Penny grabbed Tisdale's wrist with his left hand and dug two hard fast right hooks into Tisdale's body.

Tisdale's arms came down from the force of the punches and he dropped the knife.

Penny threw a hard punch that struck Tisdale between the eyes.

His head was driven back as beads of water sprayed from his hair, into the creek and onto the bank. His legs buckled, his eyes rolled up, and he pitched forward into the water. His waterlogged coat pulled him under while pockets of air here and there surfaced like dull, black blisters.

Penny grabbed a fist full of coat collar and dragged Tisdale, like so much wet laundry, onto the bank. He leaned against a boulder near the bank, his hands on his knees. He was weary and began to shiver.

Tisdale rolled onto his side, coughing up water. His left eye was already closing, blood running from a cut above it. His nose was bleeding. He tried to sit up, groaned, and then just lay still.

Penny stood, gathered Tisdale's Bowie knife, waded into the water, and found the Colt at the bottom of the creek. He watched Tisdale's hat calmly floating away toward the lake.

Tisdale rolled over, managed to get to all fours, and let his head hang. Blood dripped from his nose and eye, glazing the dry rocks on the bank.

Penny emptied his old boots of water, then stomped them on again. Gathering the reins of Tisdale's horse, he put the knife and the drenched Colt in Tisdale's saddlebag, then swung into the saddle to begin the trip up the mountain to retrieve his shot-up outfit.

"I think you busted my ribs," Tisdale slurred.

Penny drew up, turned in the saddle, and looked down at Tisdale. He watched him grimace as he shed his saturated coat—watched him gather his loose dry boot that had slipped from the stirrup, and watched as he limped to a boulder and remove the other boot and socks.

"At least leave me some dry tobacco. In my saddlebag." He pointed. "And my Colt!"

Penny retrieved the spare sack of tobacco, papers, and matches, and tossed them down.

"And my pistol!"

Penny was already moving across the creek and didn't bother to answer.

"How am I gonna get down this mountain and back to Del Norte?" Tisdale screamed after him.

"You can walk or wait," Penny yelled back. "Build a fire. I'll be back after I get my horse and any of my outfit that you didn't shoot full of holes. You didn't shoot my horse, did you Bob? …You will buy me a new outfit, Bob. If you don't, I'm going to bust you up good 'n' proper right in the middle of town, in front of cats, chickens, dogs, and anyone else looking for a little entertainment. And when I'm through punchin' your head, dogs will piss on you. Oh, and as far as you spreadin' a story about my cowardice, you'd best forget it, 'cause that Marcus Penny died along Pinas Creek. He's no longer with us, Bob. No-one or no-thing can ever bring him back, and fighting or dying against it is just fine by me. If that's what you still have in mind, have at it.

To be Continued

SIX PENNY

PART 1

I'M RUNNING FLAT OUT, FOR ALL I'M WORTH. NEVER HAVE I BEEN SO FRIGHTENED as I am right now. I'm glancing over my shoulder to see if I'm followed.

We'd paralleled this crack in the earth, this arroyo, for the last two days. It has been the only blemish on the otherwise pancake, flat plain. It is deep and dark as pitch. It's full of tumbleweed and sagebrush and other wind-blown debris. It is possibly my only chance of escape from the slaughter raging behind me. This reminds me of our foot races back home. The prize for winning this sprint is not money or a jug of store-bought whisky—the prize, if I win, is that I continue breathing and get to keep my hair.

My name is Six Penny. I am that number in a farming family of eleven counting our Mom and Pop.

In Missouri, where I grew up, we often had foot races to break up farming chores, chores that to my temperament had been and will always be complete boredom. Others find their whole world of wonder watching 'stuff' slowly grow.

Often while running I'd see myself running and running westward until I ran into the ocean—at land's end with many high adventures during the run.

I always ran wearing moccasins, tied high around my ankles, no shirt and cutoff pants. I looked strange, almost naked, but I ran free from clinging clutter and won more often than not. Farming is my clinging clutter!

My pa, Hardy Penny, knew from watching me that I wanted to be on my own, doing anything but watching our hard work destroyed by cantankerous weather and the voracious appetite of grasshoppers. Don't get me wrong, I did my share of the work, as did we all.

When I turned eighteen, Pa was wise enough to know that I longed to be elsewhere—that it was time for me to go.

Pa, a veteran of the War Between the States, carried scars and a bad hip from that "bloody hell." He agreed that it's time for me to find my own way. Maw, May Penny, was not so eager for me to go, nor are my two sisters, Nelvene and June. Ma'd lost three of her nine children, one at birth and two to a fever when the twins were less than a year old. My two younger brothers Thomas and James want me to stay. My older brother Seth wants only to work the farm with Pa and gives not a hoot if I leave or stay. Seth loves the soil and growing things. Watching things grow does not excite me, doesn't make me feel alive. That's one reason I liked the excitement of foot racing and wrestling, plus the fact that I am good at both.

Charles and Florence Davis, neighbors of ours, sold their farm and joined a small wagon train heading west. They said if I would help with the journey, I could go with them. I want to go. Pa grinned at me and said, "Go!"

Our wagon train is four or five days short of our destination, a small town called Pueblo. We want to be there when the snow melts. Pueblo is set nearly against the base of the Rocky Mountains. Our plan is to cross them as soon as possible. I want to see that big ocean on the other side. I wouldn't be runnin' there, but I would be walking most of the way.

I sleep under the Davis's wagon and helped with our daily chores during the drive. Pa'd given me one of our horses and an old Spencer rifle.

I had gotten up before the Davises and had a fire going for coffee and what little breakfast we were to have. I'm slicing bacon from a slab when all hell breaks loose. There's shooting, screaming, yelling, horses bolting, men shouting, mad confusion. Out of the pre-dawn came a warrior, not much older than myself.

He is swinging a hatchet shaped club at me and I catch his wrist on its way toward my head. My bacon slicer is in my right hand and the both of us go down with me on the bottom. His wrist is oily and slippery in my grasp. He impaled himself on my bacon slicer just beneath his ribcage. His weight drives it deep. His blood, warm and slick, covers my shirtsleeve and shirt front. I roll him off me and try to pull my knife free but cannot. I roll under the Davis's wagon as a warrior shoots Mr. Davis and backhands Mrs. Davis. She falls against the rear wagon wheel. Another Indian grabs my foot and is dragging me from under the wagon. I kick him in the chest with my free foot. He falls back onto our fire and rolls off of it, his hair on fire. I am up in a flash, jump the wagon tongue and lite out for the arroyo.

Madness! Pure madness! What stands out clearly to me as I sprint away from the smoke, dust, screaming, and blood is the contrast between the warrior and the farmer/tradesman, those with whom I traveled. For the first time in my life I feel blind fear. Running, I feel light as a feather and capable of tremendous feats of strength. I know from racing that such a burst of energy will burn out quickly.

At least one of the Indians sees me leave out of there running and hurdling and dodging sagebrush. Our eyes meet as he is taking Mr. Davis's scalp, and Mrs. Davis is cowering with the look of absolute terror and shock on her face. Blood from her head-cut against the wheel of their wagon is streaming down her face. Mr. Davis was a farmer. He had not fought in the War Between the States. He'd been killed rather effortlessly—his rifle still in the wagon.

I know from that warrior's glance, from whatever tribe, that he would be after me. There was no fear in his bloodied face; only a kind of wild frenzy that absorbed him and probably all his companions. To him, I must appear a trophy, or at least my hair did—an unarmed trophy—a tall trophy, running scared. I appear slender at nearly six feet two and weigh somewhere near a hundred and eighty pounds.

Before me is the arroyo. On my present course I will not be able to jump the chasm, as it is more than thirty feet across. I cannot see into its depths. It is still pre-dawn. Farther to my right I can jump across it, the gap is only maybe ten feet, an easy jump for one running for his life. On the other side I will have a better chance slipping into its dark depths or maybe outrun the devil I know he will follow me. I angle to my right then cut back sharply to my left and at the edge stretch out my stride and more than clear the crevasse. I land on my hands and knees in a cloud of dust. I find a fist-sized rock at hand, pick it up, and crouch behind a clump of sage. Sure enough, not two minutes behind me comes that older Indian who had killed the Davises. He is not skulking along either. He comes straight for the spot from which I'd jumped and without hesitation, rifle in hand, he leaps, as I had done, and that is when I throw that rock straight into the middle of his face which makes a sound similar to hittin' a pumpkin with a flat plank. His body, now limp in the air, hits the edge of the bank like one of Nelvene's well used rag dolls. His body kicks up a lot of dust, and he drops into the black depths of the arroyo. His rifle continues without him and lands a short distance from me. Dirt and debris rattles down after him. I crouch near the edge and squint down into the gloom and near-darkness. He is on his stomach and not moving. His head appears to have hit a small boulder at the end of his fall and is twisted at an unnatural angle. His face is mashed. If my rock hasn't killed him, the small boulder has.

I pick up the rifle; it is a Henry lever action rifle and it looks to be relatively new. I run my hand along the loading tube that houses and feeds the shells. I'd heard the tube could easily get dented and not feed shells properly when levered. It feels smooth and undamaged. From the position of the spring lever I guess it has four or five shells in the tube. A leather pouch hangs from the lever containing more shells. It is a handsome weapon. The stock is studded with brass or copper. I blow the dust from the action, lever the action part way, and stick a finger into the opening and feel a round pulled slightly from the breech. It is so dark I cannot see the shell but it is there. I pull the lever closed and make certain the hammer is on half cock.

I jump into the arroyo causing more dirt from the bank to partly cover his body. The floor of the trench is heavily covered with tumbleweed and other debris. I move back toward the stone killed warrior and take the knife he'd used to scalp the Davises with, and another small pouch of cartridges for the rifle and a beaded bag containing two scalps. The scalps I leave with him. They all belong together. To the victor go the spoils.

Not much will be left at the wagons. I can see smoke rising almost straight up in the quiet morning air. The sun is just beginning to show itself, waiting for no man, living or dead.

I shove the knife between my belt and pants at my back, hoping not to cut the belt. It is a big blade and sharp. Walking or running, holding the rifle in one hand and my pants up with the other 'cause I accidentally cut the belt, although a humorous image, could quickly become deadly serious. Still the image did not lack humor. The image dispels the frenzied fear I'd felt while running for my life. Death at their hands is now not so certain.

I move beneath overhanging sage near the body and lean back against the bank, under the overhang from which I'd jumped. Dirt trickles down to where I sit against the bank. Tilting my head back, I see another warrior standing and looking across the gap above me. He's wary and searching the prairie beyond for his companion but can see nothing. He disappears, then leaps the gorge. As he does, I pull the hammer to full cock on the Henry. I tilt the muzzle up toward the sagebrush over which he's jumped. After thirty or forty heartbeats, he slowly probes the darkness from the opposite bank. Then quickly he is gone. I don't shoot him. I am concerned others will come to the sound. If he is foolish enough to follow me into this gully, he will die. I watch and wait. Sweat runs down my face. There is no movement of air.

Did he see his comrade? I wonder. I did when I looked but I knew where the body was. Now it was partly obscured by crumbled earth from his fall.

All is still. I do not move. Will he come down after me? Does he know I'm in the arroyo? Had he seen my brogan prints? Is he looking for the rifle? This Henry is a fine weapon. Surly he'd not want to leave it behind. It's a prize worth any cost.

I ease down to the dead warrior and remove his moccasins. They are snug on my feet, but they'll do. With a piece of brush, I wipe my tracks, and pull tumble weeds over his body. I then tie my brogans together and sling them around my neck.

It is hot and still in the arroyo; the ledge I sit under will give shelter from directly above. The second warrior wouldn't know where I am and didn't care. I was sure he just wanted this Henry. If that is his plan, he will find it when he finds me.

I don't hear or see anything for a time. I remain motionless; only my eyes move along the edge of the arroyo above me. I watch for movement out of the corners of my eyes. My position is excellent. I can not be seen from above, yet I can see anyone coming down the bottom of the arroyo. I ease my body into a more comfortable position.

I'm thirsty. My mouth is as dry as the bottom of this crevasse. Beads of sweat cover the backs of my hands. There are no sounds from the wagon train. Are they all dead? Will more warriors come seeking my scalp? I can only wait. I am determined to be as ruthless and uncompromising as those who have slaughtered my companions.

Movement on the rim above me catches my attention. It's a third warrior that followed. I wonder if he wants the Henry also or my hair—probably both.

I poke the knife straight up into the new face. he blocks my thrust away. He raises his hand holding a war club and is about to club me when the edge of the bank he's kneeling on gives way and he tumbles to the bottom among the tumbleweed, sage, other debris, and me. Dirt rattles down after him, covering my hair and back. I am on him in a flash pinning him. He rams a knee in my back and heaves up with all of his strength, trying to buck me off. I struggle to keep a strong grip on his club hand. His skin is oily too. I am larger and stronger and finally thrust that big knife between his ribs, plunging it in several times and twisting the blade viciously each time. He has my wrist in his left hand but I have the leverage and the strength. He can't stop me. After seconds he ceases struggling and makes gurgling noises. I can feel the air leave his chest as he dies.

All is quiet. More blue smoke drifts upward. I pull the knife from his chest and wipe it free of blood on his lifeless body. I move away from him, further down the arroyo. I stop for a breather, my chest heaving with the exertion. He is the second person I've killed in just a short time. This is not the adventure I'd dreamed of.

From the bag of shells, I thumb more shells into the loading gate. I wait and watch for other pursuers. None come and I quickly move two hundred yards down that arroyo and find shelter up under another overhang. I pull a large tumbleweed in front of me and wait. There is no movement.

Time passes. My thirst grows. Pa told me of his sucking on a pebble or two when he was thirsty during the war. I try it. They only taste like dirt. I spit 'em out. The sun is up and I know I have to get out of this oven. No clouds drift above me. The yelling and noise from the train has stopped for quite a while. I decide to inch out of there. I feel they've left—I hope they are gone.

I come upon a place where I can easily crawl out of that cooker. I ease my head up very slowly and search my immediate area. I wait for a while then ease up, and while bent over, move away from the burning wagons, circling to the far side of the destroyed train. My destination is a small knoll about a hundred yards from the wagons. From that vantage point I will be able to see the arroyo where I'd been, as well as the burning wagons and bodies. Should anyone come after me, they will be an easy target.

The warriors have fired the wagons. Clumps of clothing lay scattered about, some smoldering and some not. Smoke from the fires is now blowing north over the arroyo. The smell of burning flesh is mingled with burning wood and canvas.

I hope some water remains in the barrels strapped to the wagons. I wait and watch for nearly an hour. There is no movement anywhere that I can see. I began moving down toward the wagons, Henry at the ready.

The clumps of clothes cast about are bodies. Everything has been pulled and dumped from the wagons and gone through. Chests and trunks of clothing, dishes, rocking chairs, and all manner of prized possessions of the recently departed are scattered about. Most of what had not been taken has been set afire or broken and scattered. Pots and pans have been crushed and ruined. I find no one alive, and not one dead warrior. My guess is that none of the warriors had been killed here—but I know where there are two dead ones.

I look for my possessions and find the slab of bacon I'd been slicing. It is under the skillet covered with dirt. I also find my hat, somewhat scorched and wet but wearable. I also find several bags of ground coffee overlooked by the savages, a bag of jerky, and one of pemmican—also two canteens and a pot that is not too damaged. All of the animals and weapons are gone. The wagons are mostly burned to the ground. I find a piece of unburned canvas.

To bury my companions would take more time than I dare spend here. I decide not to bury them as the Indians might return and I want to be miles away should they return for their missing friends in the arroyo.

I gather the spoils into a burlap sack I'd found under a piece of canvas. I could use the canvas as a blanket and shelter. I find a shirt that had survived and a barrel with some water. I drink my fill, fill the two canteens, then wash the dirt from the bacon and the grime and blood from my face, chest, and arms. In the bottom of the cask I find a cloth pouch with nine gold coins and loose silver scattered across the bottom. The silver had been used to keep the water drinkable. I roll the canvas with the burlap bag in the center, tie the ends with a piece of rope, and sling the whole package over my shoulder. With the Henry in hand I head for the distant mountains that Burt Finch, the wagon master, had said were the Rockies and the town called Pueblo. Burt said those mountains were four or five days distant. For those folks that lay dead behind me those mountains will never be closer. A short distance from the massacre, I turn to face the smoldering remains. I remove my hat and say a quick prayer for those I am leaving behind.

I turn to continue and there he is, waiting for me. He has found the rifle with me attached to it. I'd written him off. I'd assumed he had crossed the arroyo to rejoin the slaughter. Without hesitation or the blink of an eye, I lunge toward him punching the barrel of the Henry into his shoulder. It's a hard thrust and it lands right on the point where the collarbone and the shoulder bone meet. His arm must have gone numb. His Sharps drops from his hand. Why he didn't shoot me from ambush is beyond me. He pulls a long-bladed knife and lunges at me holding the cutting edge up and sweeping upward with it. I feel it bite into the tip of my chin and it casts blood up into my right eye and my hair. My scorched hat is still in my left hand and as he is preparing to swipe again at me. I slap at his face with my hat, and it draws blood from his left cheek and the bridge of his nose. He pauses momentarily, wondering how my hat had cut him. The razor blade my dad had attached to my hat brim years ago gave me a momentary advantage. I then jab the Henry again, only this time I hit him where I'm aiming, in the center of his chest where the ribs come together in the front. He goes down like a stone in water, writhing in excruciating pain, clutching his chest, and looking up at me. I pull the hammer back on that Henry and lay the muzzle just under his left eye. He looks at me across the front sight and I, back at him over the same. There is pain on his face but no fear. Blood is running down my neck soaking my fresh shirt. My whole jaw aches. I decide to show him no mercy. Killing him would be merciful. I ease the hammer down to half cock, check that the razor in my hat brim is still attached, put on my hat, pick up my canvas bundle and his Sharps. I hold my shirt sleeve against the cut on my chin and continue on my way west toward the Rockies.

Occasionally I look back at him. He has lost interest in me for now. Whatever he does, and for a long time, be it breathing, eating, walking, sitting, or trying to kill someone else, he will have to decide. Will the gain be worth the pain? Killing him would have been more merciful than he or his fellow warriors had shown some of my companions. Our pain will last for only a short while in the scheme of life.

I walk until I can scarcely see my next step. I find a concealed portion of that arroyo that is beginning to play out. I build a small fire—boil water from one of the canteens, toss in coffee and chew on some jerky while the coffee sets up. I let it set for a time, then pour water from the canteen to settle the grounds and sip strong, bent-pan coffee, and chew jerked buffalo. Every chew hurts my jaw something fierce. I leave the pemmican for later. When the coffee is finished, it is totally dark. I drink, then smother the fire. My eyes adjust to the darkness. I pick my way south of nature's gash. The sun, setting beyond the Rockies, casts a beautiful glow, silhouetting their peaks. I move a half-mile from the arroyo, find some boulders on a patch of high ground, and nestle down for the night. I use the canvas for a blanket and the bag with my meager provisions and boots for a pillow, but only after unloading the Henry, blowing and wiping any dust from the rounds and the rifle's action. I'd destroyed the warrior's Spenser by caving a lip of the arroyo over it. I work the action several times to make certain it's free from grit and clear. I don't care how many shells it contained. However many it held would be enough. I remember my Pa repeating what he'd heard during the end time of the war. Someone with the new lever gun said, "You can load it on Sunday and shoot it all week." I fed the shells back into the tube and levered a round to the breach, and set the hammer at half cock.

Just before dawn, I hear movement close by, stones rattling. I open my eyes, sit up, pull the Henry across my lap. The noise continues. It has to be an animal. There's coarse chewing and the pulling of brush with a yank. I look over the low boulder and see in the pre-dawn, a mule. It's Gem, Burt Finch's mule. The first thing the wagon master did every morning, after putting on his hat and boots, was to saddle Gem. Somehow that mule had survived and found me. I reach out and Gem snorts and shakes her head and shies back a bit.

"Come here old girl, it's all right, I promise not to eat you," I say with a grin.

I gather the reins at the bit and trace them to where they are looped and tangled over the offset saddle. I free them and right the blanket, the saddle, and saddle bags, then cinch up. I pour water from one of the canteens into my 'surprise' hat and hold it for the mule to drink, which it does noisily. I slap the hat against my leg, careful of the razor in the brim, tie my kit behind the cantle, and step up.

It will be dawn in a short while and I dearly want some coffee, but decide I can wait for daylight, and put more miles behind me. As we trot west toward the Rockies, I wonder how that Indian is making out having been hat-slapped and muzzle-poked. My chin is blood crusty and damned sore. His blade nicked my chin bone. Seems there is a hammer pounding in my head. He could have killed me from ambush. I could have finished him also. It ended in a sort of draw, both of us in pain, both having drawn blood. I feel no hate for him or what his tribe did. It all seems to have been a huge waste. All our blood is red—I need another clean shirt. Maybe in Pueblo.

To be Continued

SIX PENNY

PART 2

I found a small stream and a patch of grass. I washed some of the dried blood from my face and from my shirt. I was remembering our mother instructing us boys in keeping clean as possible after a day of hard sweaty work. She would have no 'stink-pots' sitting at her table eating with her girls present, or any woman person. She was the same and more so with June and Nelvene, my sisters. More than once she quietly suggested that Pa lighten the air a trifle.

They were a loving couple. I can still see Ma bathing Pa's wounds and scars with a vinegar and beeswax rub and massaging his pained areas from the war from hell.

For Pa's part, whatever Ma wanted or needed or desired he would provide, and woe to any resistance or complaints. It's true that he had debilitating injuries but when you looked into his eyes you knew if you valued being a member of the family you would do your share in that effort. Ma was the touchstone, the heart of our family. She saw to the entire family, with the help of each of us. All of this filled my mind as I reflected on my recent actions. I'd killed. I wondered how that act would measure up to Ma's sense of right and wrong or her sense of decorum? She believed in survival but with a degree of compassion. Pa would have said I should have killed that brave, not just walked away from him, as I had done. That mistake might, some day, down the path a ways, give me grief. I would be forced to finished that episode or die for my choice—maybe someone I will be close to will suffer that omission.

I looked at my distorted reflection in the stream. *I am alive and well off.* I had prospered from the death of others, my companions and the two I'd killed in that dark trench. Did I owe a debt for my gain? Who did I owe? I grimaced and shook my head. These thoughts were getting too serious for a simple farm boy. Droplets of water dripped from my eyelashes and face back into the stream headed elsewhere, now tainted with my blood.

I removed the saddle from Gem and brushed her with some dried brush. I looked thru Burt Finch's saddlebags. I found a brass monocular wrapped in a soft cloth, similar to the one Pa had from the war. There was a large bag of oats, a coarse brush for Gem, a pair of leather gloves, a spare shirt, and a .32 caliber rim fire Pepperbox gun wrapped in a piece of soft leather with a box of shells. There was a small pouch of silver dollars. I was getting rich and not having to weed a garden on hands and knees or plow a field for it. …or run a race as though my tail was on fire.

I saddled up and headed west again. Rinsing my face and chin had loosened the scab and it was bleeding again—dripping on Burt's shirt. My wet shirt was drying across the saddlebags. I was thankful for Burt's shirt even if it was tight across the shoulders and way short in the sleeves. I wondered how that warrior was making out. I hoped he was hurting as bad as me. My whole jaw ached 'cause his blade had nicked my chin bone.

I passed several head of buffalo. They looked me over and I looked them over. Dried buffalo jerky and pemmican crossed my mind, but I kept moving. It was then that I saw faint smoke on the horizon. A voice in me said to turn south and avoid it. The dreams of adventures in me said ride toward it. Maybe there is a young and beautiful girl in peril that I could save and my dreamed adventures would begin at last. So far, there'd been only fear, noise, and a lot of death.

Using Burt's monocular, I saw a wagon. Its canvas cover had burned away and the wood of its frame was smoldering here and there. Three bodies were scattered about. They looked exactly like the bodies in my destroyed wagon train. …Dead bodies seemed to lay flatter on the ground, drained of blood, breath, and life. The animals were gone. Their camp was next to a dense growth of brush and several trees. I saw movement at the edge of brush. Closer inspection showed it to be a horse's tail swishing flies.

I circled around south of the cluster of trees and brush and came up in front of that swishing tail. A brief look from behind a tree, maybe 100 yards away, showed two horses and two men. On the ground in front of them was a woman. She was holding a gun of some type. Both men held their guns pointed at her. Her dress was pulled above her knees. There was blood all over the dress. Using Burt's glass, I could see that an arrow was stuck through her right leg. Just above her knee. Her face was streaked with dirt and soot. I wondered how she had survived the killing.

I steadied the Henry against the tree, sighted on the hand holding the pistol of the furthest man. The one closer to me put his pistol in his waistband and picked up the one laid down by the woman.

I aimed a couple of inches above the gun hand and squeezed off the shot. I'd guessed right and hit the gun hand. The pistol went flying, the man spun around bending over holding his left hand to his chest, hopping up and down and screaming. He stomped his feet and looked at his hand. It looked as though fingers might be gone. His partner was looking toward me through the puff of black smoke from my shot.

He took a couple hasty shots at me with his pistol. They fell way short. I shot again at him and watched dirt fly near him. He was taking careful aim toward me as my second shot hit his foot. He jumped like a scalded cat and his shot went wild. They both sprinted to their horses. Three Fingers used hand and arm to mount up, his horse already moving. The foot-shot man ran for his mount like a man with one short leg. Through the glass I could see that I'd shot the heel from his boot, though not by design. They were making tracks, looking back expecting pursuit.

Had they killed the three dead near the wagon? The woman was crawling for the pistol I'd shot free. I'm sure she was in pain. How long had that piece of wood been in her leg? It had to come out and soon.

I remembered Pa telling me of gangrene and what it looked like and how it smelled and that it would kill—that it was not a painless death. He said that at times he could still smell it, mixed with gun smoke. I tied Gem to some brush where there was some edibles for her. She was going to need water soon.

The woman was watching me and holding that bloody pistol pointed at me. Her hand was shaking. She appeared tall for a woman. Her hair was brown. Her eyes were brown. Pain contorted her face. But there were no tears. I couldn't even guess at her age for the dirt and ash covering her face and dress. And the blood over both legs and the dress.

"See here," I said holding my palms toward her. "I mean you no harm. You're in a bad way and that arrow has to come out and soon cause your leg can fester and maybe have to be cut off if you get gangrene. My Pa told me about it from the war. After I get it out of you, I'll see to your husband and your family—if you're gonna shoot me, get on with it." I pulled my knife,

35

knelt next to her, and cut the shaft and point off up next to her leg. I didn't look at her face but it must have hurt like blue-blazes. I heard her intake of air as I whittled away on the shaft. Without warning I pulled that shaft from her leg. Blood flooded from both holes. There was no pulsing of the blood which would have been very serious according to Pa. Pulsing blood meant the heart was pumping blood out and death was probable. I looked at her face, she had passed out. I let it bleed a little, hoping it would flush out any debris still there if any, and any festering. I'd never been this close to a woman's bare legs before. Or a dress pulled up this far. I knew how babies were made ...you don't grow up on a farm with animals and not witness their mating. Thinking of the act between a man and a woman was not unpleasant. In fact it made my face red just thinking on it. I could almost feel Ma watching over my shoulder as I was going to patch the wounds with Burt's fairly clean shirt.

I cleaned around the wounds with water from the rain barrel and decided to leave further cleaning to her when she could do it in private. I bound the wounds with strips I'd cut from Burt's shirt. I hoped to stop the bleeding and wanted to keep dirt from the two holes. The bleeding seemed to stop after a bit. I pulled her dress down to cover what I had done.

I laid the three bodies together and went through the man's pockets. I found his watch and some coins. The woman had a cameo pin and a ring that I removed. The little one had a small wooden gun in his pocket. I laid these aside and dug a shallow grave and laid them to rest together.

It was nearing sundown by the time I'd finished. I then built a small fire near the woman who was still out. I rolled her onto her side and placed a spare canvas I found slung under the wagon bed in a sling used to keep firewood and dried dung found along the trail. I rolled her back onto the canvas to keep her off the dirt. In the bed of the wagon I found a blanket that I placed over her and some women's clothes which I thought might be hers and bundled them as a pillow and placed it under her head. I put the Merwin & Hulbert beside her. Having it near might give her comfort and satisfy her that I was not going to hurt her. I was going to have to clean the blood from her leg, but after a while and when she was awake. Her dress was sticky with it. I found several dresses I thought might also be hers. I remembered how Ma was always scrubbed clean, and the girls too. I'd have to help clean this woman up and help her get into a presentable dress, unless she could manage by herself. I noticed that whoever attacked these folks must have been in a hurry. The canvas burned but the wagon was only lightly charred. They'd taken only guns, horses, and what food they could find. The two I chased off may have chased the ones doing the killing and looting. Maybe that's how the raiders missed this woman.

I began boiling water for some broth. I added a generous scoop of pemmican from my bag of food. I also had several small wild onions which I'd found near the stream earlier which I peeled, chopped, and added to the broth. I removed the saddle and gave Gem water and moved her to a larger patch of greens. I put a couple handfuls of oats in my hat and held it for her to eat, careful of the razor on the brim.

"Am I going to lose my leg?"

I looked around and she appeared very pale. Her right hand was near the Merwin & Hulbert shooter. "I don't know. Time will tell, you need a real doctor. I patched both holes and the bleeding has stopped. What happened here and what's your name? You can call me Six."

"I'm Cheryl Bowman. What kind of name is Six?"

Well, here we go! I thought to myself. At least if I have to fight her over my name, I'll just kick her in the leg and win. No blood on this shirt! Then I remembered I wasn't wearing one. "Later about my name, okay?"

She looked at me with a slight frown blending with the pained face she was wearing. "Three of them came at us this morning. Ben my stepfather, my brother, and mother were killed very quickly. I was hit with a wayward arrow and don't believe I was seen. I crawled into this brush and didn't move, then I must have passed out for a short time. I watched them rummage through some things then set fire to the wagon. They took our two rifles, the horses, and left. They seemed in a hurry. I passed out again and came to when I was being pulled from the brush by those two. I had my .22 but they told me to drop it and if I didn't they were going to shoot me where it hurts then do some other things to me. That's when you chased them away. There are two fingers over there. How come you only shot the gun?"

"I've killed enough for a lifetime in the last four or five days. ...I've made some pemmican broth. Think you could take a little?"

"My leg really hurts but I could sip some. Where's your shirt?"

"It was fresh this morning and it's around your leg."

"Pa had several. Maybe you can find one. It's going to get cold tonight."

I spooned broth for her. Finally, her eyelids wanted to close, and she slept. I found a shirt and a jacket. They smelled of smoke. I briefly thought about the shirt, then put it on and tucked it in. Is wearing another man's shirt bad luck I wondered? Seems every time I put on someone else's shirt I proceed to bloody it up—with my blood!

My chin hurt and my entire jaw still ached. I hoped that warrior was hurting with every breath.

I wrapped up in my canvas blanket and kept adding wood to the fire but slept off and on. She'd slept most of the night and when she woke, I'd spooned more warm broth for her and put a cool damp cloth to her forehead and face. I checked her bandages early and cut up more shirt and dress cloth I found not burned. I also found a partial bottle of whisky with which I doused her wounds and wiped smeared blood away. She moaned. It was painful I know. There was discoloration but no redness—a sign of infection. I gave her a drink of the whisky for her pain. She did not like that one bit but swallowed it anyway. I also used some warm water to cleanse the grime from her face. She had wonderful, even features. So far, saving the beautiful girl from bad men was working according to my daydreams of adventure. I helped her change into another dress. I kept my eyes closed and helped where I could.

She sat in the saddle with a blanket wrapped around her. I was walking, leading Gem when we saw a wagon heading our way. They stopped and were concerned about my wife. My wife? "We're not married. I… I… stopped to help her. Her family was killed. She needs a doctor to see to her wounds. I am fearful of infection and worse. Her name is Cheryl. My name is Six Penny. Just call me Six. Penny'll do… it's a long story."

"I'm Mathew Tillman and this here is my wife Jody, our son, William. We call him Will. We're only about a half day from Pueblo. I think she, uh Cheryl, would be more comfortable in our wagon. We've heard there is a doctor there. There are other wagons there, preparing to cross the mountains or moving on to Denver.

I sat next to her for a moment in the wagon. She looked at me and smiled. I smiled back at her and handed her the revolver. The grip was pitted but its action worked fine. It was the first Merwin & Hulbert I'd ever seen. I don't know that it would give her any comfort, but she took it and placed it under the blanket out of sight. I patted her cheek as though she was a sister and climbed on to Gem from the wagon. When I patted her cheek, I was not feeling brotherly toward her. My ears and neck were not the only part of me feeling hot and bothered.

The store fronts were unpainted and rough cut. They were not false-front struc-tures. They were permanent stores. The street was rutted and well-traveled. There was much horse dung, and blue horseflies having a great time. Here and there imbedded in the ruts were the occasional can and tatters of papers.

The Tillman's were going to follow the tracks leading to an encampment a quarter mile north of town where other wagons were resting and preparing to cross the Rockies or go north to Denver. Children were playing near the wagons. There were fires about. Winter was gone but there was still a chill in the air. There were clouds and a brisk breeze blowing.

I shook Matt's hand and nodded at Jody. "Thank both of you for your help. I'll find the doctor and send him. When I find a place to stay, I'll come for a visit and move her into town. I'll pay the doctor. You don't have to worry about that. I have enough for that. Is there anything you need from the Mer-cantile, Jody?"

"No, but thanks, Penny. We've got all we need. Come any time you want. You are always welcome," said Jody. Matt nodded. I tipped my hat to Jody and walked Gem to the center of town. The Marshal's office was at its center. I tied up in front.

He wore a dark city coat and wool pants. A badge was pinned to the lapel of the coat. His hair was gray as were his eyes. His handlebar mustache was neatly trimmed and waxed. He was leaning against the door of his office look-ing Gem over, a frown on his face.

"Sheriff?"

"Sheriff Landers."

He nodded for me to follow him inside. The room was very warm due to the potbelly stove in the center of the room puttin' out serious heat. "What happened to the owner of that mule?" he said, both hands on his hips, holding his coat back exposing the pistol in his waistband. "I know that mule and its owner, Burt Finch. He's a good friend of mine. You'd best have a good reason you're ridin' Gem and Burt's not!"

"Five or six days back, by wagon, our wagon train was hit by some Indians. I don't know the tribe. Everyone was killed except me and Burt's mule. Charles and Florence Davis, I was traveling with, were killed and scalped. The mule and I teamed up and here we are.

"There is a young woman in the Tillman wagon, just pulled in. She's been arrow shot in the leg. A doctor needs to look at it. Her family were all killed also, in a different raid, maybe a day or so out."

"You are?"

"Six Penny. …It's a story for later …just call me Penny." Family and friends back home had no trouble calling me 'Six'. But out here among strangers … well I'd make it simple for 'em.

"Tell me where I can find the doctor. He needs to look at her wounds right away."

"Doctor Ari's across the street. His wife is his nurse. Don't leave town, Penny. I need more details than you've shared."

"I'm not leaving soon. There a place we can stay, the woman and me? No, we're not together. I just found her and need to make sure she is safe. …A stable where I can put up Burt's mule?"

"The Steiner Hotel up the street may have space for you. Stable's at the end of the street. When you get settled, come back. I need to pass details on to the Army garrison near Denver. They'll check out your stories."

"By any chance a couple of men come into town, one with shot off fingers and the other needin' his boot repaired?"

"Missing fingers and a bad boot? Doc Ari would know about missing fingers. The Mercantile next to the Doc's office would know about a boot repair. I've heard nothing. What happened to the fingers?"

"Cheryl Bowman, the young woman with the arrow wounds can tell you what happened."

"I'm askin' you."

"Bad Boot and Three Fingers were gonna do bad things to her—I sort of changed their minds. Five Fingers was holding a gun on her and I saved his life by only takin' two fingers." I watched his expression, there was no amusement there.

"How'd you survive that raid that killed my friend?"

"I sort of outran 'em at first, then jumped into the arroyo we'd been following. Several came after me."

"The hell you say. I ain't never heard of no white man outrunning an Indian. There's some who could run 100 miles in a day… course that was before they liberated their first horse. We have foot races here on occasion to break up the monotony. You run fast, Penny?"

"Depends on what's chasing me. …Ya, I'm fast." He didn't even smile at my attempt at humor.

"Well we'll see about that soon enough, if you're here long enough. And your stories check out. Don't leave town, Penny. Unless you check with me first."

Doc Ari was a short, white-haired man with spectacles. His wife was bandaging a man's arm. Their clinic was very clean and appeared organized. "My name is Penny. I came in a few minutes ago with a family. There is a young woman with them. She has arrow wounds in her leg. It happened several days ago. I pulled it an' patched it best I could. I appreciate your looking at her for me. I'll pay for whatever you can do for her. She's with the Tillman's. She can't walk very well. …Oh, and we're not married."

"I'll fetch her. We can keep her here for a day or so while we keep an eye on her. After that it's on you and her to find a place to stay."

"Jean Aberdeen, at the edge of town may have a room for her," said his wife. "Jean could use the money and company since her husband died a week ago.

"This is my wife, Ethel. We'll go have a look at her. What's her name?"

"Cheryl Bowman."

"When we get her back here and see to her injuries, I'll ask Jean if she is interested in a boarder. Having a person near might be good for both of them."

I took a $20.00 gold piece from my pocket and placed it on the desk.

"Doc, one more thing. I'm looking for a man with two fingers missing."

"He was here several days ago. I asked him how it happened. He said they were pulled off by a rope. Problem is I picked several small pieces of lead from the stumps. Pulled off looks different from shot off. You do the shooting?"

"Him and his friend were going to do some bad things to Miss Cheryl. Ask her about it. Is Three Fingers still in town?"

"Don't rightly know. Could be at the hotel—we have a lot of folks comin' through on their way to someplace else. You ought to check in with Sheriff Landers. He'll wanna know about what happened. He might know about a three-fingered hombre. I bandaged the hand pretty good. Hard to hide."

"I already told the sheriff everything. Thanks, Doc. I'll stop in later if I can. I guess I'm all Miss Cheryl has for the moment. I surely hope she doesn't get gangrene."

"We'll keep an eye on her till she's out of trouble. …You know about gangrene?"

"My Pa from the war told me about what he saw and smelled. I am just hopeful she's ok. I did the best I know how."

"Don't worry, we'll do all we can for her."

Cheryl was in a proper gown and a proper bed. She was clean. The second bed was empty. Sunlight coming through the window showed the room to be very orderly and clean. Standing there I could hear Ma pointing out that I probably smelled like a 'stink-pot,' one of her favorite phrases. My face felt red as though Ma was right here pointing at me to wash-up 'cause there was a very lovely young woman looking at me… and she was lovely with all of the dirt and soot gone. I removed my hat and was hesitant getting too close to her. I felt I was making a poor impression and embarrassing myself and my upbringing.

She smiled at me and held out a clean hand. I was unable to resist. She touched my dirty hand. I withdrew it quickly. "Forgive me, I need a bath and clean clothes."

"Don't worry about it, Mr. Penny. You saved me. From God knows what. Those two brutes were worse than any dirt and sweat from honorable activity."

I handed her the items I'd taken from her dead family. I'd wrapped them in a clean cloth. She opened it and tears came to her eyes.

"I'll be back later," I said as I backed out of the room.

"How does her leg look, Doc?"

"It's okay. I'm not concerned about gangrene, only about some minor infection, which we can treat easily enough. She's young and healthy and needs rest and good food. Whatever you did saved her from dire complications. You did good young man. She talked as though you are her hero. You saved her twice from Sunday. …Oh, by the way Mrs. Aberdeen seems agreeable to having a young woman as a boarder. I want to keep Miss Bowman today, then we'll move her tomorrow. I have crutches she can borrow. She'll need to get up and move around to help the healing process, contrary to popular medical beliefs. I saw it in the war. Gunshots sent back into battle seemed to heal just fine."

"Thanks Doc, to both of you. I need a bath, I'm beginning to smell like Burt Finch's mule. Hoping no one tries hookin' me to a wagon!"

Doc Ari smiled and nodded in agreement. "We knew Burt, he was a good man. Sorry he's gone. The barber, Neil Southern has a tub or two. The emporium can fix you up with clothes."

"You want a room with someone else, or by yourself?"

I slept with brothers my whole life—had enough of that!"

"You want second floor or ground floor and for how long?"

"Don't know how long. I'll be here three or four days for now and upstairs will do. I'm hungry. Restaurant?"

"In the bar. They serve nearly all day. The food's basic but not bad."

"You seen a man with a bandaged left hand?"

"Can't say as I have. He's family?"

"No not family, I have something that belongs to him."

"That'll be two bits a day and no eating in the room. Drinkin's okay."

I moved my things into the room and took Gem to the stable to board her down.

Both of them were sitting at a table against the far wall of the saloon. They were eating. They had not seen me up close and didn't recognize me. I walked to the table next to theirs. They both looked up at me. They were eating a thick stew and sopping it with homemade bread and churned butter. "Looks mighty good." From my shirt pocket I removed a small piece of cloth, unfolded it and dropped the remains of two fingers into Stubby's stew—now finger food. That's how 'finger food' came into being. Startled, he slid his chair back, its legs caught against a raised floor board and tipped backward, dumping him. His holster was empty, his pants were smeared with dried blood. He had an older percussion pistol in his waistband. His partner jumped up, jarring the table, spilling their coffee. He was reaching for his Remington but stopped while looking down the four barrels of Burt Finch's pepperbox pistol.

"I'll take the .22 you took from her when you threatened to despoil her as she lay there with an arrow through her leg. Take it from your pocket with two fingers—do me a favor and use more than two fingers," I said while watching both of them. "Any wrong move from either one of you and you're both dead. When she tells her story," I said loudly for the benefit of the other diners and the two men at the bar, "both of you will probably swing from the pulley at Steven's Stable. Was I you, I'd git out of town now! —no, not now—right now! If these folks don't fetch you, Sheriff Landers will, and you'll still swing for attempting to molest a helpless and injured young woman, and maybe even for the murder of her family. You do not want to be here when this town comes alive, lookin' for you, under every porch and flat rock."

"… Come Saturday we're havin' a foot race to Brace Creek and back, about 2 miles. You've won two races so far. This time I'm not so sure, Penny," said the Sheriff.

I was talking with Dr. Ari and Ethel, his wife, and Cheryl, on crutches, when the Sheriff said, "Runners toe the line!"

I turned to the line and noticed a newcomer already on the line, his back to me. It was an Indian. The Sheriff had placed a ringer in the race. I could not see his face, but he looked strong and very very brown. He was dressed similar to me. Moccasins and a breechcloth, where I was in moccasins, cutoff pants, and no shirt. There were several others with us. The Sheriff fired his pistol and we were off. I never did get a look at that Indian's face. All I saw of him were his heals and his back—he was gone! He was Smoke! Each time I attempted to catch him, he'd throw a glance over a shoulder, and speed up. I never did catch him. I crossed the finish line in second place. The crowd, the entire town, were collecting their winnings or paying off their lost bets! I looked for that Indian to congratulate him but could not find him. He was gone like smoke on a windy day. Sheriff Landers had a grin on his face and winning cash in hand. "You're fast, Penny, but not faster than an Indian. I told you so! …Oh by the way. A scout from the Army said they found both massacres. Your details checked out. They found two bodies in the ravine. You're cleared of any wrongdoing. I guess you can leave our fair town whenever you've a mind. I see Miss Bowman is up and around now."

"Well Sheriff, I hope you gave that lightning bolt something for making me look bad in front of Miss Bowman!"

"He got what he wanted. An' looks like you got the girl. An' I got what I wanted" and he shook the dollars in my face.

5 Weeks Later

I got down from Gem, walked to the edge of the stream, removed my hat, knelt and splashed cold water in my face, then drank. I began filling my canteens. Gem drank also. Sheriff Landers said I could keep Gem since Burt Finch had no known relatives. He gave me a paper sayin' as much. I wondered how Cheryl was getting along with the Tillman's on their way over La Veta Pass and into the San Luis Valley and Fort Garland. I was headed that way myself because of two men I believed to be cousins. I'd written a letter to my family telling them about all that had happened since I left. I mentioned about two Pennys as deputies in a Colorado town I was aimin' for.

Pa had fought for the Union, but his brother had worn the gray uniform. Pa almost never spoke of his brother, Charles Penny who, after the war, became a detective for the railroad in Kansas City, Kansas. That's all Pa knew of his brother.

I figured those two Pennys were cousins. On my way to the Pacific Ocean I wanted to meet these two blood relatives. I replaced my hat, stood, and waited for Gem to finish drinking. Looking across my saddle, I saw an Indian. He was armed with a rifle and a bow and quiver of arrows. His pony was drinking, same as Gem. I removed my Henry from the saddle horn, levered a shell, and walked toward Pa's prophecy come true—it was that hat-slapped, barrel-poked warrior from before. He'd showed up again, like a wounded bear with a long memory. I touched my chin that had met his knife. It had healed and my chin did not ache anymore. I'd forgotten all about him. He, with a clenched fist, tapped his chest twice where I'd punched him with this Henry. He had another rifle now. We walked toward each other. It would have been easier killing him before. Pa had warned that this could happen, and here it was.

Quick as a wink he shouldered his rifle and shot. I grimaced against the heavy bullet hitting me. But it did not strike me. I heard it strike behind me and a grunt because of it. I turned and saw 'Stubby' lying on his stomach, spread-eagled with a huge hole ripped open in his back. I looked to the Indian who apparently had saved me from being back shot. That's when I saw Stubby's partner drawing down on the Indian from behind. I shouldered my rifle and the Indian dropped to a knee as I shot Stubby's partner. The Indian looked around at the dead partner. He stood. We looked at each other. I levered another shell. He ejected the spent shell and inserted a fresh into the breach of his single shot Sharps Carbine.

We stood that way for two whole minutes, just waiting for a move. I had no hate for him. I had no desire to kill him. I felt we were even. We'd given each other pain. I released the hammer on my Henry to half cock. Held it hanging at my side and moved toward the tree line. He was moving also. We did not take our eyes from each other for a long time. I began building a small fire and put water on to boil in my bent pan. He was gathering small branches. I kept my Henry at hand. And Burt Finch's pepperbox within reach. We sat across the fire from each other. He was not as tall as me, but he looked very strong and fit. From a pouch I took a piece of jerked beef, then offered the open bag to him. Still looking from my face and the pepperbox in my lap, he took several pieces of beef. We spoke not a word. I poured coffee into the boiling water and stirred it with my knife. I walked to Stubby's partner and retrieved his Remington, Winchester, and cartridge belts. My nemesis was watching my every move, the whole time chewing that jerky. I handed him the weapons and cartridge belts. The Winchester was better than his single shot Sharps. The Remington revolver was a fine weapon. He took the weapons and grunted and nodded acceptance. I added lake water to my bent pan coffee, and we chewed and drank coffee, which he seemed to enjoy. Finally, I pointed to myself and said, "Six." He said "Six", then said "Quick Bear." I said, "Quick Bear." Minutes passed then he pointed at my scared chin. I smiled and pointed to his chest and cheek. He smiled back at me.

"You fast," he said. "Me more fast."

Then it dawned on me. "Me fast," I said, "…you more fast."

We'd left the two dead back shooters side by side after removing Stubby's weapons. We decided to keep their mounts.

We found the Tillman's wagon with Cheryl walking with their son Will. She was tall, healed, and very wonderful to look at. She gave me a dazzling smile, bright and warm. My face and ears felt like they were glowing even in the light of day. We hugged briefly. Quick Bear was easily accepted, and Will's eyes were as big as silver dollars. It was his first encounter with an Indian. We tied the two horses to the back of the wagon. We all were heading the same direction and joined up. Look out San Luis Valley, here we come.

The End

TURK 'PEACHES' THOMAS

BENJAMIN LORD WATCHES TURK THOMAS, A HUGE BRUTE OF A MAN, LEAD HIS limping pinto to his corral.

Benjamin, called Ben by his friends, knows Turk Thomas's violent reputation all too well. He's a giant of a man, a lumberjack, working his way to Oregon. Turk knows what he wants when he sees it, and he's big enough and vicious enough to take it. He don't care nothin' 'bout 'Hoyle' or the law—what law?!—there ain't no law this far out!

If you have something that Turk has seen with his own eyes and decides he wants, it's his and you're just holding it for him till he comes for it—and then, by golly, you'd best give it or he'll chop you into chips.

Turk is going to swap his lame pinto for the healthy sorrel he'd seen prancing around the corral. Ben pretends he doesn't want to swap the sorrel for the pinto.

"My pinto for yon sorrel."

"No, it ain't a fair swap."

"Pinto for sorrel!" Turk's eyes narrow.

"It ain't fair!"

Ben lets Thomas' face get a hardness to it and a bit red. His ham-sized hands bunch into fists. Ben's been studying Thomas while stroking his beard. He finally surrenders and nods okay. Thomas nods curtly, unsaddles the pinto, saddles the sorrel, attaches all of his personals, mounts, and trots away, not looking back.

While examining the pinto's tender 'starboard' front hoof, Ben smiles at the big man's nickname, 'Peaches', spoken only behind Turk's back.

Turk likes the sorrel's size and color. It stands more than 16 hands and is built powerful, like himself. For the first week, the sorrel does everything asked of it on the straight and level. Then Turk needs to cross the Bighorn River. Much to his consternation that horse balks at going down steep embankments. He turns around to go up the hill behind, to get a running start down to the river. The darned nag wouldn't go up the steep hill neither!

Disgusted and angry, Turk bites a knuckle and harbors unkind thoughts of Benjamin Lord. He dismounts, grabs hold of the reins, and tries to pull that stubborn animal to get it started down the embankment. The sorrel tosses its head and refuses to move. Turk leans his broad, muscular shoulders against its rump, mindful of the beast's kickers, and yet cannot move it. It just pivots in a circle. Strong as Turk is, he cannot budge that stubborn critter. Turk tries again to pull the sorrel down the embankment. Again, it tosses its head no and refuses to move. Turk pulls his spare ash ax handle from his bed roll, grabs the bridle at the bit, jerks its head down, and stares that critter in one eye and then the other, then points down the steep slope several times with the ax handle.

It's a no go!

He takes a step back with his right foot and clobbers that cantankerous beast between its ears hard enough to get its attention. Down Sorrel goes in a tangle of stirrups, saddlebags, bedroll, and grub sack, sending a cloud of Wyoming dust boiling. The crash mangles Turk's coffee pot, tin skillet, breaks the stock of his Winchester, and ruptures three cans of peaches. Peach juice dripping from his grub sack causes Turk to lick his lips, and for a moment, he's tempted to suck the juice from the sack. Instead, he harbors more unkind thoughts of Ben Lord.

Mule-brain lies there struggling to raise its head to get up but it cannot. Turk squats on his heels and rolls a smoke. He puts fire to it and fixes his attention on that jackass of a horse while blowing smoke in its face.

After a fist full of minutes, the horse finally staggers to all fours and shakes its head. Its front two legs buckling and staggering one way, the hindmost performing a separate totter and lurch. The saddle, bedroll, and food sack are askew. The food sack is still dripping peach juice. The rifle's stock is in the dirt.

Turk doesn't touch the reins or nothin'. He just remains hunkered, puffin' and blowin' smoke up at that sorrel and watchin' it with a cocked eye. That sorrel keeps a wild eye on Turk, while tossin' its head free of horse cobwebs and Bull Durham smoke, and getting all fours under control.

After a few final puffs, Turk stomps the finished butt into the dirt with his size 14 boot. He grabs the reins with a jerk, straightens all that's crooked, then swings into the saddle.

The sorrel and Turk proceed down the bank at a fast trot. They cross the Bighorn River and take the far, steep incline at a run. Not once does that sorrel hesitate. That sorrel goes everywhere it's pointed—and at a run! It don't care what's in front of it, it just runs over it or thru it—just like Turk. All the while, Turk's laughin' an' rakin' that sorrel with his 'jingle buck' spurs. He's slappin' with his hat, and shoutin' at the top of his voice.

Now, all who knew about that sorrel's proclivities have absolutely no doubt that no-one and no-thing ever says 'no' to Turk 'Peaches' Thomas.

Turk holds Louis by a twist of his shirt. He yanks Louis around like he's a loose-goosy rag doll, Louis's feet barely brushing the floor. Turk cuffs Louis once across the mouth and asks again, "Where's Ben Lord?! Where is the bastard?! He owes me." He smacks Louis again. He lifts Louis off his feet while shaking him to and fro. Louis is getting a headache and his face hurts something fierce. He can taste blood from a cut inside his mouth. His cheek is scuffed raw by Turk's callused hand. There is not much Louis can do to stop Turk from smackin' his face and shakin' him. Louis is only twelve years old and weighs maybe eighty pounds, even with his brogans on.

Charlie, Louis's seven-year-old baby brother, is frightened for his big brother. He bites Turk's hairy right forearm as hard as he can. Turk yelps and yanks his arm free. He grabs Charlie's face in his huge hand and flings him against a chair at the north wall of the cabin—where the head goes, the body will follow.

Charlie hits the chair and wall with a crash and lies in a tangle of broken chair debris. He does not move.

"Damned little snot-nosed kid! That hurt!" said Turk, shaking the sting from his arm. "I hope that broke the little puck's scrawny neck!"

Turk pulls Louis's face up close to his own. Louis glances up at the tiny gap between Turk's hairline and his eyebrow.

"Where's your pa at?"

Louis winces at Turk's breath and screws up his face. "I ain't-a-gonna tell ya." Then he looks toward Charlie. Charlie is not moving. Louis is not really frightened so much as he's angry 'cause of his baby brother.

Turk tippy-toes Louis back up against the table that is set for supper. Louis puts a hand back to brace against the tabletop. His hand comes upon his ma's wood-handled, two-pronged serving fork.

Louis, with all his strength, stabs that fork into Turk's neck just under his left ear. He stabs thrice more as hard and as fast as he can. He drives the long tines of the serving fork all the way to their crotch with each thrust.

Turk is stunned and shocked, then flings Louis from him as though he were an empty peach can, his eyes large with surprise. He pulls out the fork and drops it. Jets of blood shoot out from his neck. Blood is gushing down into his shirt. He can taste blood in his mouth. His throat is sore. It hurts to swallow. Suddenly Turk feels nauseous. He sits on a chair by the table, grabs the checkered tablecloth yanking it from the table, breaking dishes and scattering utensils. He wads the cloth against his neck and looks at Louis whose eyes are open wide with astonishment. Turk stands while holding that wad of cloth against his neck. His intent is to crush this little puck.

When Turk stands, he feels light headed. He drops back onto the chair. It groans against his immense weight.

Louis scrambles to his feet, giving wide berth to the brute and runs to his brother, Charlie, who is beginning to stir.

Turk remains seated for several minutes, trying to gather himself. He is not feeling well. His thinking is confused. His strength is draining away. Blood continues pulsing against and around the tablecloth. It's filling his mouth. He spits it out. The cloth is sticky and heavy. Turk knows he's in trouble. He's seen men bleed to death as their hearts pumped 'em dry. He's more than once caused someone to bleed out.

Turk stands and seems to totter and tilt toward the door. The sodden cloth slips from his hand and makes a wet sound as it smacks the floor. Jets of blood shower Louis and Charlie.

Louis draws a sleeve across his mouth, smearing away Turk's blood. He shivers in disgust.

Turk sways like a tall tree in a gale and crashes full length near the front door shaking the cabin's plank floor. His eyes slowly find the two boys huddled against the far wall. He feels grudging respect for the older one what forked him. He sees no fear in the boy's expression, only wariness. He rolls onto his back, swallows, and shudders again at the taste of his own blood. He turns his head to drain his mouth. He thinks to close his eyes, to catch his breath, to gather his strength, and then try again for the door. *Why would I leave? Where can I go?*

The cabin door bursts open, and there stands Ben Lord, eyes narrowed, nostrils flared, teeth bared, both hands gripping the ash axe handle that he pulled from Turk's bedroll. He's ready to swing and break bones with it. His wife, Nelvene, stands behind him, a horrified look on her face at the sight of her two bloodied sons against the far wall among pieces of a broken chair.

An ironic grin comes to Turk's bloody lips. *Boot Hill is the closest place I can go. It is atop a steep hill. Not to worry, 'cause Lord's sorrel can make the climb easy now—lots a luck drapin' me across the saddle.*

The End

THE CURSE

THE MORNING SUN CAST WARM LIGHT THROUGH A CLOUD FORMATION THAT SHOT streaks of light westward across the big sky, like the rays from a child's drawing of the sun, as its rays found openings in the cloud cover. It was dramatic and quite lovely and yet went unnoticed to the group of men gawking the pile of yellow-colored coins and artifacts heaped on a horse blanket.

All three of these men were armed. It was still cool morning and they were high up on the west slope of the Sangre de Cristo Mountain range in Colorado. They overlooked the Great Sand Dunes to the west and far below them.

They had come together to search for, find, and share equally a cache of old Spanish gold coins and or artifacts, purportedly left on these slopes by Spaniards. The treasure in gold was supposed to be guarded by an ancient curse added to and perpetuated by a local Indian tribe.

The ancient Conquistadors were far from Spain with no chance in hell of ever seeing their beloved country and families again. They were stuck in this wilderness among hostiles, constantly hungry and thirsty, and in the winter, cold… always cold, and in the summer… well, not so cold. Why had they held onto the gold, carried it whenever they moved on? It was beautiful; it was the link to their origins; it was a constant reminder why they'd come to this world in the first place; it was a reminder that they would die rich and poor at the same time; that they were destined to perish in this bleak, uncompromising and dangerous land. Because they were strong, hard men, they fought and struggled and survived until they couldn't any longer, and didn't. There would be no rescue. There was no way out. They had no idea where the ocean was. They'd left their comrades behind years before. They were finally killed off or died from various causes, but not before they'd buried their treasures. Gold had become a burden to carry and to defend—defend from whom? The locals had only one use for the bright metal and that was to wear it.

Each of the three compadres stood with his own thoughts while looking at all that gold. There was a fortune before them.

Chas Leslie, the tallest of the three, wore a dark gray suit coat over a matching woolen vest over a white shirt and a cravat. His long nose rested atop a handlebar mustache. His clothing was rumpled, however his boots were polished but coated with fine Colorado dust. His pants were dusty and stretched out at the knees. He'd propped his Winchester against one of the three large boulders under which he'd spotted part of a leather bag containing some of the gold. When he pulled on the portion he could reach the leather fell apart in his hand. He had to dig at arm's length to retrieve the gold. Chas suspected there were more bags buried deeper, but was unable to get to them. The other two of the threesome tried digging but came up with nothing.

Scott Davis was the second man in the party. He was heavy with a light-gray hat and the same kind of dark suit, white shirt with a false collar, and black string tie. He was rumpled also, and of the three smelled a long-time unwashed. His shoes were scuffed and his rifle was also propped against one of the boulders.

Major Whitcomb was number three. He wore a full white beard. The corner of his mouth and his beard was amber from tobacco stains due to the corncob pipe clinched perpetually between his teeth. He wore his faded campaign hat, white shirt, and was also rumpled from living out of doors for the week they'd been on the search. The major had a shotgun slung with a leather thong over the horn of his saddle and his pants were tucked into his cavalry boots that he wore in the civil conflict.

"Is that all of it?" said Whitcomb.

"We all dug around for more, and as for me, that's all of it. I say let's split it and get out of here and back to town. I've had enough."

"Ya, there's nothing but hardpan under where the bag was. I even tried to dig with my knife and there was nothing more. What do you say, Major?"

"I'm with you, boys. Whoever buried it probably planted more of it elsewhere. That's what I'd do… not puttin' all my goods under one rock."

They divided the coins evenly and the three gold rings then bid each other goodbye. The Major was headed to Ft. Garland. Scott Davis was going on to Alamosa and Chas Leslie was headed to Del Norte. They all mounted up and wound their way down to the sand dunes and split up.

The major waited for a half hour then took a circuitous route back to the three boulders. He threw a loop with his rope over the boulder and tried to pull that massive rock away from the other two. As he sat there, stroking his beard against the problem, another loop snaked out and encircled the boulder also. The Major looked up and smiled at Chas Leslie. Together they pulled with their mounts at the boulder. That several tons of rock moved a small amount with the effort of the two horses. As the two looked over the boulder and its position, they dug away at the lip of dirt restraining the boulder. Finally they mounted and again pulled at the boulder. It moved even more this time. They kept at it and all at once the boulder began to move, slowly at first and then with a violent rush. As it picked up speed it entangled the two ropes that were tied to the saddle horns of the two saddles. The rolling thunder felled both horses dragging horses and riders to their deaths.

Had the curse come true? Now there was more blood on the boulder-strewn slopes of the Sangre de Cristo (Blood of Christ) Mountains.

Scott Davis was awed by the spectacle from several hundred yards away. He removed the gold artifacts from his two horribly mangled partners, while being elated that now he would have it all. It filled his saddlebags. He dug for more sacks of gold. Scott lay in the ditch he'd dug to make room while he dug the hole deeper. He was excavating, where the first sack had been found. The weight of the two boulders that had rested against the one killer boulder slowly overwhelmed the lip of dirt restraining its movement. Scott heard and felt both boulders move then looked up in horror as both rolled on to him, crushing him to a pulpy paste and coming to rest nestled in the channel he'd dug. His dead, crushed hand held the remnants of another leather bag. His horse was a living treasure trove.

The curse was true. La maldición era verdadera.

The End

CULLEN GRAFTON

PART 1

MANY ARROWS ARE BEING SHOT AT ME. SOME I BAT AWAY, OTHERS SIMPLY MISS. I'VE been told that I have the gift of quickness. During a schoolyard fight, I caught Bucky Myers' right fist as he threw it at me. He looked startled, his eyes flared, he grit his teeth and threw his left, and I caught that in my right hand. I came down hard on his instep and hit him in the chest with my left fist while standing on his foot. His ankle was badly sprained. He was the schoolyard bully—but not for a while, and never again with me.

After school that day, Bucky's pa came looking for me, then quickly went away when he saw my pa, standing 6' 3" with his shirt off choppin' wood with a double-bladed ax. Pa was all muscle and all serious. He took a couple of steps toward Mr. Myers who was making tracks and raising dust. Two bullies in one day.

I'm not willing to test my gift against a rifle or pistol ball.

I'm leaning against a boulder in a cluster of large boulders. It's a good shooting platform. The attacking savages are very close now. From my vantage point, I'm hoping to shoot as many as I can, but I'm not having much luck with that. They are up, running zigzag, then down again behind cover. They're very quick. Then another, at a different location, makes his move, and by the time I fire, only to miss again, another darts closer. Their tactics are faultless. It's clear they've used them before. I see my eight-year-old daughter, Sue, being carried away draped across a pony. She looks at me, tears streaming down her cheeks. I consider shooting her rather than have her experience what's in store for her as a captive, but I can't do it. I truly believe that where there's life there is always a chance to survive. I don't believe they took her only to kill her. My heart aches for her. I am fearful for my whole family—my son, Charles; Amy, my lovely wife; and my sister, June, with dark red hair who was with Sue.

I fire at another and miss again. My plains rifle has a smooth bore and shoots one ball at a time. It's painfully slow to load but a bit faster than a rifled barrel. I've missed every shot; my shotgun would have served me better. June was to bring me our shotgun or use it to defend with. Both she and June were only two wagons away. Doggedly, I begin reloading, knowing that I'll be dead before I can shoot again and that all is lost. Several of us had lever guns, even pistols shooting the same caliber as the rifle, but most of us did not—and they are so very near now. I can almost hear their running feet whisper against the dried grasses and weeds as each sprints then ducks for cover.

Until now, our crossing had been uneventful. We'd been lulled into complacency by the monotonous, even tedious, routine of waking up, getting up, eating up, packing up, then advancing a few more miles.

Today at sunrise, all tedium was abruptly blown away. We were totally unprepared, even though we'd been warned repeatedly by the wagon master, Burt Lower, what we should expect every hour of every day.

They caught some of us with our pants down. We are outnumbered and outgunned. I know all of us are going to die. I can feel it. The grisly torture and death that the savages visit on their captives is widely known. I want to die shooting and clubbing them.

We are merchants and farmers, ten wagons of forty-eight people, several age ten and younger. We hoped to build a town together—a new life for all of us. We came upon this idea as a group, at day's' end. We were all invigorated at the prospect of a brand-new town and community. We began moving toward our dream with a new and exciting purpose. Several want to raise cattle, others to farm fresh new soil. Still others want to continue as merchants, carpenters, and blacksmiths. All our hopes and dreams are now about to be erased—in only half an hour of terrifying, bloody madness.

They set upon us at sunrise. The sun was directly in our eyes as they came. After their initial attack, most of us adjusted to meet them—they then came at us from all directions and in larger numbers...

Amidst the chaos and reloading, I hear Amy, my wife, scream. A savage with a vermilion- and black-painted face is holding Amy's head back with a fist full of her blond hair. His knife is against her throat. In Amy's hand is the Philadelphia Derringer I'd given her. Smoke curls from its barrel. The warrior is bleeding from his left ear. Her single shot had notched his ear—she'd missed the head shot. He grins at me, and calm as you please, slowly draws the knife across her lovely throat, ear to ear. Blood sprays out from the gaping wound as he shoves her to the ground on top of our son, also dead by his hand. Then he takes her hair and that of my son, Charles.

Before I can absorb the full horror of the sight, I am hit a vicious blow to the side of my head and knocked into the valley between these boulders. So much for the gift of quickness without the gift of sight from the back of my head. I fall to one side of the boulder, my rifle clatters to the other. The blow does not knock me out, but it badly dazes and disorients me. In desperation I slither, wiggle, snake, and worm my way among the tight base of the boulders, and by instinct, squeeze into an opening that is a lair of some animal. The entry drops down a few inches or so. It's a cavity beneath the boulders and further dug out by an animal's scratching and clawing. The closeness of the space causes me to panic; I feel smothered. I also fear one of the warriors will come after me. The shallow pit is dark and reeks of animal. I am alone in the dank darkness. It is cool, but I am sweating. Panic has me by the throat. I cannot crawl out of this terribly suffocating pit feet first. With great difficulty I turn around, my clothing catching on the rough jagged surface of the boulders pressing down on me. With my head finally at the cramped opening, the terrible pounding in my head is so great that I pass out. The fear of being suffocated in this tight space fades with the light.

How long I had lain beneath those boulders I don't know. I come to with my head still pounding. I touch above my ear and at the corner of my right eye. The area is badly swollen. The gash there is encrusted with filth. I'd lain with the wound in animal dirt. The dirt has at least stopped the bleeding, but I worry that I might get sick from it. My right eye is swollen shut. I feel the puffiness and tenderness around the eye socket. I notice all is quiet. No more gunshots. I try to lift my head, forgetting for a moment where I am. My hair keeps me from another bleeding cut as I crack my head on the jagged boulder hanging a few inches above me. The feeling of being smothered returns. This close space is squeezing the life out of me. The fear and panic of being buried, entombed here alive, becomes unbearable. I lay my head down again, my skull not feeling right. Darkness swallows me once more.

When I awake, I know that I have to get out of this overwhelming, suffocating place—hurt head or no, I have to get out of here—and now! I begin crawling, in near panic, to find my way through the boulder maze. In my wild crawling, I careen into several of the boulders, not helping my already damaged head. At last, an opening. I lie, gasping and sucking in fresh clean air in the open space again. The panic in my chest subsides, and I know that I would rather die twice over at the hands of those Indians than be closed in ever again.

It's dark. I can see nothing. I look to where the sky should be—there is only darkness. There is no sound beyond the roaring sound in my ears. I'm cold, thirsty, and hungry. It occurs to me that I might be deaf and blind, and if so, I'm as good as dead should those warriors return. I would hope for a quick death, but I know that will not be the case. I ease back into the track, feet first. Being able to sense open space, much of the panic from being closed in has left me. The terror of tight, smothering pressure confining me remains fresh. I just drift away again.

I know not how long I am out. I don't know if I was unconscious or just asleep. Over and over again, it seems a horse's hoof is kicking against the inside of my skull, trying to break free. It finally wakes me. I stand and lean against a boulder to steady myself. At least I am only half blind and there is a lot of space around me. What little I can focus on is whirling and spinning with white specks everywhere. I feel my stomach turn over and I become violently ill. I heave several times, but nothing much comes up. My legs are weak and unsupportive. I touch my head again. I smell of animal, the stench is in every breath.

I have my knife, a dirk, and my pouch of .50 caliber lead balls—just nothing to load them into and no powder. My hat is gone. I feel the lump on top of my head and remember Sue being taken away. She and I are probably the only survivors. There is no sound of any living being, just that waterfall sound in my head. I hope she is still alive. Amy and Charles are dead, lost to me forever, and probably June as well. June's fate has an icy grip on my heart. The gash in my head will heal. The terrible pain in my heart will not—maybe never. I am overwhelmed by the noise in my head, and with despair.

I stand supported against the boulder, my hands on my knees and my head hanging in total misery. Which is not good 'cause the pain in my head increases. Will I ever see my Sue again? Could I even find her? Can she even be alive? I know I'm in a bad way. My heart feels destroyed, crushed—my body is not far behind.

At least I'm not blind. I thank my lucky north star for that. The sky is heavy and grey with a light snow falling. The ground is littered with cold, dead bodies, all blanketed now with a gentle covering of dry snow. I can see only out of my left eye. My thirst and hunger are great. The smell of death mixed with animal from that tomb is strong, even in the low temperature. I now hear the flapping of wings and cawing sounds coming through the roaring in my ears. Carrion are fighting and feasting on the bloody remains of bodies, my wife and son among them. Sound has returned. I am not deaf. The image of birds pecking, tearing, and eating my family is terrible.

I find their bodies. I can identify them only by their clothing as I brush the snow from them. I try not to look at their faces that are chewed to pulp and torn and ravaged—so much for not looking at their faces. I begin scooping a shallow grave; the soil is not yet frozen. Tears and sobs come with each scoop of dirt. When the shallow grave is finished, I lay a piece of scorched canvas in it and drag them on top of it. I clasp their hands together, my heart aching. Will I dig again for June?

Part of me wants to join them in death. I kneel there, looking at them for the last time, hesitating, then the sight of Sue being stolen flashes again in my mind. I fold the remainder of the canvas over them and add the scooped dirt and a layer of rocks and small boulders on top of them.

It takes me a long time. I nearly pass out right there on their grave several times. I am trembling with exertion, with cold, and my stomach is gnawing at me. My tears and grief slowly transform into rage and anger against those who have destroyed all these fine folks. All of the hopes and dreams we'd recently shared are now just smoldering ash and smoke. The fire is long gone. Our bright, hopeful future is an empty black hole, as dead as these snow-covered bodies. My teeth and fists are clenched in rage. I want my daughter back, and I want revenge. Vengeance, it is said, is not part of the Christian faith. Well, I am going to be a complete nightmare and pure living hell when I find those responsible. The thief who stole my daughter? He will not be able to father a daughter or son of his own when I'm finished with him. He'll have to squat to pee. That will suit him better than killing outright.

I stand, facing the west as the shrouded sun dips behind the plains of clean white snow. I am dirty and exhausted. That horse's hoof is still banging away in my skull. My teeth are chattering from the cold. The snow has stopped. I wad snow into a ball and put it into my mouth. I am parched. I wrap up in another piece of seared canvas and fall asleep among the safety of my cold, cold boulders. Next I must find June, my lovely and wise sister.

Sometime during the night, I am awakened briefly by new sounds. I am too exhausted to search for the source. I don't care if the savages have returned. Maybe they will find me and free me from my agony. I sleep again.

It's still dark when I wake to the smell of wood smoke and coffee. It takes me a moment to remember where I am and what I am smelling. I get up feeling steadier than before. Smoke means fire. Coffee means someone is near, hopefully friends to help. But being cautious and with my dirk in hand, I follow the smoke and the smell of coffee. Two men are sitting at a small fire talking. I can't hear what's being said, two ruined wagons separate us. The sun is not up but there is a very faint glow in the east. The sky seems clear. I can see several stars, the Dipper and the North star. I creep closer, taking my time. With every step, my head feels as though it will explode, and I worry that it will not finish me. I'd rather be with my dead family—then I remember Sue, and I become angry again. I cannot abandon her. Death is not the answer I needed. The smell of rotting flesh is strong. The fragrance of coffee and the scent of cooking food is the scent of hope.

They're on canvas, covering their bedrolls against rain and snow. They're drinking coffee. There's a pot full of some kind of food and a coffee pot with steam rising from both. The smells are intoxicating. I'm now in the deep shadow beneath a wagon about ten yards away on my empty stomach, which is making noises that I fear will give me away. That's when I recognized Ben Johnson. He was one of the handlers to the Wagon Master. Ben is talking to the stranger.

"This here is our best one yet, Stu."

"Ya, they'd better not be late. I don't want to be caught here. This one's got me spooked. It's too big to go unnoticed for long. They'd better not be late, Ben," says Stu.

"They won't be, they're a hungry and greedy bunch. They'll be here in a couple of hours."

"We'll have to be choosy about what we take. You think Gray Eyes kept his word and took no prisoners?" says Stu.

"I don't trust no half-breed Indian, 'specially that one. I don't want to see that wild-eyed devil ever again. This here is my last job. I'm giving us five hours to get, then git. Sooner or later we're gonna get caught or seen. I got me enough put up. I wanna see Montana, an' not from high on a hangin' tree. I don't want no one to remember my face from here neither. What about our crew? The three of 'em won't wanna quit. They know us. They're the loose ends to this here string."

"I been thinkin' on that," says Stu. "When we git to Oregon with this load, we'll talk on the problem again. I got me an idea or two. Not a word in front of 'em, Ben."

"Okay… Look, Stu, I got me a date over yonder. She's under a heavy quilt—fancy that—it's almost like she was 'spectin' me to come a callin' an covered herself up for me. She still got her red hair! Her brother got hisself bashed in the head. I saw it."

"I've asked you not to tell me about that any of that, Ben. It ain't natural. Can't you wait a few days? You make me sick—there's plenty to poke that's alive, warm an' willin'. There ain't no female safe around you, alive or dead— you killed her then covered her? There's somethin' wrong with your up here, Ben," Stu said, pokin' his own head with a dirty finger.

"You've spoke low of me one time too many, Stu. My fancies're not your business an' after we finish this here one up in Oregon, you and me is quits." Ben stands, smooths his rumpled and stained clothing, and turns to his waiting poke.

From out of the darkness comes a terrible wail and scream that seem not of this world. The hairs on both their necks stand up. Charging head down into the faint campfire light comes a battered and bloodied madman.

I couldn't listen no more. Now I knew where my June was. And what Ben was about to do to her. I lost my mind. I screamed and rushed 'em, knife and leather pouch in hand. Ben, that snake, faced me, and I hit him with my shoulder. He slammed into the side of a wagon and bounced off. The wind knocked out of him, down he went, mouth open trying to suck in air. The one named Stu rushed up behind me with his knife poised to stab me in the back. He could have shot me, but probably didn't want any noise in case someone was about. I kicked back at him, catching him in the stomach. He tripped over Ben's hand-tooled saddle and fell into their small fire, throwing sparks into the air—thankfully missing the food pot and coffee, which I had the corner of my good eye on. He howled, arched up away from the hot fire, he yelped and rolled off of the burning embers. His jacket was on fire, so was his beard and his long hair, which was slicked down with some kind of animal fat. So much for wiping your hands in your hair and on your clothes after eatin'. He was on his knees frantically slapping to put out the grease fires. It burned nearly down to his scalp. His skin was burned red and would blister.

I turned and with my sack of .50 cal. balls hit Ben square in the forehead. His head slammed into the iron rim of the wagon wheel, making a sickening sound, and he bounced away as though kicked by a very mean mule—me! The wagon belonged to our blacksmith, Nathan Penny, and now all of his possessions were up for grabs—all of our possessions were up for grabs. Nathan's wife Molly and their son Zebulon were dead and scalped. The skin of Ben's head, meeting the iron rim, split to the bone and blood cascaded down his face, drenching his soiled wool jacket.

I pull a broken pitchfork from beneath the wagon and drive the tines through Stu's waist from his back as he is slapping his smoking and blistering head. The tines enter below his ribs and miss his spine. He is forced onto his stomach. The tines come through his belly and bury themselves in a flat board intended for the fire. He screams and attempts to stand, then falls on his butt and is propped up by the broken handle of the pitchfork at his back. He tries to pull the plank off of the tines but the pain and shock is such that he wails then passes out. Blood is flowin' pretty good from the tines and off the wood.

I retrieve their pistols and knives and toss them onto Stu's bedroll. Ben, on hands and knees, is crawling away from the fire toward the front of the wagon where their horses and mule are tethered. He glances back at Stu and me. I walk to the end of the wagon and find Nathan's small anvil. It weighs only eighty pounds. Nathan had moved it around with little effort. In my condition I stagger under its weight but carry it to where Ben is crawling. He is just turning over when I drop the anvil on his ankles. I hear bones break. Even if he can manage to move the anvil, he is not walking anywhere, ever again. Stu had come to and was whimpering and moaning. I watch him gather himself and attempt to stand up again. His legs give way and he falls on his butt again. He leans back, the broken end of the pitchfork still propping him up. He groans, reaching a hand out to me. I slapped it away and kicked dirty snow in his face.

Wearily I collapse onto Stu's bedroll, grab the pot handle with a rag near the fire, and open my mouth for a spoonful of the hot stew or whatever it was. I am so hungry I don't care what it is—it could be toasted grasshoppers, for all I care. It burns the hell out of my lips and mouth. I spit it out and blow on the next spoonful. The coffee is just as hot and nearly as thick as the stew. As

I eat, I consider what I'd done to these two. I try to sip the scalding coffee but set it aside to cool.

Looking at the two of them, I am astounded that I am capable of such violence. This was not part of my nature before all of this. Yet here I am, wanting to give them even more pain. I am not gonna kill them quickly, especially Ben, the killer of June. I will think up something special for him. I needed to know where Sue would be taken. I wondered how many other deaths they'd caused. How many children and babies and oldsters were these two responsible for killing?

While I consider all of it, that damned hoof continues trying to stomp its way out of my head. I finish the stew and lean back against Stu's saddle. The warm food, coffee, and the fire make me drowsy. I am exhausted. The exertion of the last few minutes has brought me to the end of my energy. I close my eye and doze.

I startle awake a few minutes later, as that grinning, black and red face again slits Amy's throat. I grab a Colt. Both men are still where I'd left them. I dare not go to sleep. The others, their crew, will be coming soon. I have to find June. I look at Ben, wondering what I could do to him to satisfy my ravenous anger.

I collect their rifles. They are the new, 1873 Winchester 44/40's, the same caliber as their Colts. If more of us had these new lever guns, we might have survived the massacre. Their horses and a pack mule are tied to the tongue of the Irwin wagon. I squat and drink the remains of the coffee from the blackened pot, then pack it with clean snow, and look over my handiwork. The pain in my head had faded some. I still cannot see out of my right eye.

I am going to make them hurt for as long as I hurt. I have no compassion for these two pieces of human waste. I am not going to make it easy for them. They are going to pay for what they've done. They are going to beg for death. I will not relent. I will send them to hell.

But only after they've told me where my daughter has been taken.

Ben and Stu set us up for slaughter. Their plan was to loot the wagons, and the bodies, and sell the haul in Portland or some other place, far away from here. Maybe to a distributor who could resell it to various merchants. Merchants unaware of the origin of the items.

Stu dies a short while later before I can give him more pain. He simply stops breathin' and bleedin'. Ben keeps trying to move that anvil off his legs but the pain is such that he keeps passing out, still on his side. I put one of Nathan's handsaws near him and suggest he cut himself free, and if he does, I'll let him walk away from all this. He doesn't even look at me but just lies there shivering and whimpering.

"Where's their camp? Where's their camp, Ben? Where'd they take my daughter?"

He barely looks at me and says nothing. I wonder how long it will take the wolves to finish him. I add more snow to the grounds in the pot and more wood to the fire. I then prepare for the remaining three of this crew. There are no more tears left in me. The pain in my head and heart give me no peace. Grief has made me angrier and determined to kill every one of these bastards.

My plan is simple: I'll kill two of them quickly, spring upon them and knife them and smash their skulls. I will keep one alive to answer the question.

I find June in our wagon, beneath our heavy quilts and covers. She'd been smothered. And by Ben, I'm guessin', 'cause she was not scalped. I place her in a shallow grave beside our wagon, wrapped in the quilt she'd stitched by her own hand. She'd been a wonderful sister, smart and wise, just like our mother.

They pulled their three freight wagons upwind of the massacre. They'd done this several times before. It was still daylight but now heavily overcast with more snow falling. They'd been driving nonstop against being stalled by the snowfall should it become a problem.

"I want to avoid the stench of rotting corpses as long as possible… and for the rest of my life," says PJ Evers, the oldest of the group.

"We'll only have a couple of days of it," says Santos. "But the stink will be in my nose, hair, and clothes for a whole damned week after we're finished!"

"When the wind changes, we'll just move our night camp. It's simple. At least we don't have to sleep in the snow. Just find a wagon still standin'—upwind."

"Yeah, yeah, Charlie, I don't mind lootin' the wagons but searching dead, chewed-on bodies ain't good for my head—there's gotta be haunts about with all these dead stinkers! This is my last time. I wanna go back to K.C. and live a quiet life. No dead bodies, no stink, no nothin'… Ya know if we get caught, we'll swing, after we get the shit kicked out of us!"

"Ben and Stu usually come out to meet us. Where are they?" says Evers.

"Stu's probably found a stash of cash money or maybe he's prying up wood for a gold stash in a wagon-bed. There are a lot of wagons. Ben's found himself a woman, and's working it off."

"Yeah! That's one sick bucko. This is my last job with him. I cain't do this no more with that crazy bastard. Maybe I'll just shoot him and not have to think about it anymore."

"Let's split up and look for 'em. If ya find them, give a holler—look for a fire or maybe some scratching noises of Stu diggin' thru stuff rummaging for gold, or maybe heavy breathing from Ben."

"You would have to say that, fart brain."

They all chuckle a little.

I'm waiting for them. I've decided to make this quick and clean, one by one as they spread out and move slowly through the jumble of wagons skirting the snowy lumps. Charlie Pintos is the first. I stab him in the throat—no warning, just up and do it, smooth. I was crouched beside a wagon wheel. He was so startled and shocked that a dead person could be standing with a knife at hand. It was too late to do anything except to die.

The second, short and squat Santos, I hit from behind with a hammer from Nathan Penny's blacksmith tools, crushing the man's skull.

The third sees the glow of the fire and gives a yell for the other two. He sees a shadowy figure walking toward him. It's not Stu, or even Ben. This one is too tall.

I grab the old man by the shirtfront and hit him hard in the middle of his face—twice. Each punch rocks the old man's head back as though it were on a spring. The second punch rocks his head back, and his body goes limp and falls forward, scattering blood and broken teeth into the deepening snow. I drag this one by a boot and tie him to Penny's rear wagon wheel, his arms stretched out and his neck held tight against the spokes. I then sit by the fire, sipping coffee. It's weak, but coffee nonetheless. I sit patiently, sippin' an waitin' for the old man to wake up from his little nap. I have one question for him—he'd better have the answer, by God.

It's a good half hour before the old man comes around. The snow has stopped, and the sky has cleared slightly. Faint shadows of the bodies creep westward toward where the live bodies were headed. Now only their shadows are reaching in that direction. Soon even the shadows will join the darkness.

"You broke my teeth!" His voice brings me back. It sounds strange with front teeth missing. "How can I eat without my teeth? Where's Charlie and Santos, Ben and Stu?

"They're not here anymore."

He sucked air in through his mouth. "Where'd they go?"

"To hell, I hope."

"They're all dead?"

"Yep, just like the folks you've killed.

"We …they never kilt no one! …Why'd you not kill me too?"

"What's your name?"

"Who I am don't matter none. You're gonna kill me anyway."

"I'm just trying to be civilized." I glance at the result of my "civilized" behavior and swallow. "Ok, I don't need a name."

"It's PJ Evers."

"I have a single question for you, PJ Evers."

"If I answer, then you'll kill me, right?"

"Maybe, maybe not …Depends."

"Ha! You expect me to believe that? My mouth hurts and my nose, I can't breathe through it. Can I have a drink?"

"You answer, I might not kill ya and you can have a drink. You can get your nose and teeth fixed. Then again maybe I'll fix you so's you have no need to eat or breathe no more. You and your friends killed my friends and family. Ben there," I say, pointing at him, "killed my sister and was goin' for her. He ain't goin' nowhere, ever again. My daughter was stolen. Where did they take her?"

"How should I know? I didn't do nothin'. All I know is Grey Eyes must've took her."

"Wrong answer. I wanna know where. I don't care who. I'll find out who when I get there." I put my coffee cup on a flat rock near the fire, walk over to Evers.

He looks up at me. "Stu or Ben do that to you? You look like hell."

I jerk and cut his coat off of him, rip open his shirt and cut it away from his body. I keep my dirk real sharp. I cut his belt and pull his pants down below his navel. All the while Evans is thrashing his body all around, but to no advantage. I place my knife just above his right hip bone and nick the skin. His eyes are wide as he watches my knife draw blood from his belly.

"Honest, mister, I don't know where your daughter might be took. All I know is what Stu said, that Grey Eyes was to kill everyone, except Ben, take the guns, livestock, fancies, and head south for the winter. He wasn't to take no prisoners."

I watch him say the words, and I choke on the images his words dredged up. I'd been helpless as that painted devil, that murderin' bastard, held my wife's head back and nearly cut her head off. He was grinning at me as he did it. He enjoyed it! When I find him, I'm gonna fix him, by God; I surely am gonna do him up proper.

"None of this would have happened were it not for the five of you. You have as much mercy coming as was given to everyone here."

"I didn't kill no one. I wasn't even here. Ya got no cause to murder me for what them red devils did to your family an' all." He looks over to where Stu was sitting up. "How can Stu be sitting up if he's dead?"

I walk over and kick Stu in the shoulder, and he rolls onto his side, the pitchfork handle and board plainly visible.

I walk back to Evers, who is staring at Stu, then Ben. He begins kicking his legs at me, so I stick the point of my dirk in his thigh and he stops. I lay the blade at the slit I made earlier and slide my knife around just under his belly button from his right hip to his left. Blood runs down into his crotch. He screams and screams and cries, then begs. The cut is just deep enough that his intestines squiggle out of his belly cavity, making a moist, slippery sound.

Evans's eyes are wide open with wonder, fright, and pain as he watches them wiggle out with authority, like they'd been trapped against their will. He'd been gutted.

"Ooooo!" he howls. "How'm I gonna get 'em back in?" He closes his eyes and lets out a wail that sends shivers up my spine. I am awed again by what I'd done to these five.

Truth is I feel not one blink of sorry or mercy—Still, I shiver.

"Ya can't leave me like this. What am I gonna do? The wolves will eat me alive. They'll pull all my guts loose and chew em! The vultures'll peck out my eyes while I'm alive. Please, ya can't leave me like this! Ain't right! Ya have to kill me, ya just have ta, mister!"

"Killin' all these folks," I said, wavin' my bloody blade all round, "was not right and you were party to it. So don't tell me what's not right. My life is finished! My daughter stolen! My wife is dead, my son, my sister, and I'm gonna get my daughter back an' probably die doin' it. An' I'm getting tired of sayin' it. You and these other poor excuses for human beings had chips in this here game—an' you lost—we've all lost! If I kill you, you're suffering' ends, but maybe not. I'm guessin' hell's waiting' for ya, but don't fret none, Mr. PJ Evers, you'll have plenty of friends there, 'cause I'll be sendin' a bunch more to keep ya company!"

I cut the horses free from pulling the three wagons and scatter them. I keep the three riding mounts that were tied to the back of the wagons. They're good horseflesh. I roll all of the rifles, pistols, and ammunition into canvas to use as trade for Sue or to kill anyone in my way. The horses I might use for a trade. I will ride Stu's gelding. One of the three mounts will be for Sue. The mule will carry the food and bedrolls. Ben's horse will carry all the weapons. I find my moneybox in my own wagon. I lay the two bodies beside Ben. I clean myself as best as I can. I carefully wash the animal mud from my head wound with hot water and wrap a cloth around my head, covering my blind eye. I change shirts, then pull on a buffalo poncho and hat from Penny's wagon. He has no use for them no more.

As I am about to leave, I look down on Evers. The horror in his voice finally gets to me. I draw Ben's Colt from my waistband and shoot him in the head. I didn't want Evers' screams an' wailin' fighting for room in my already over-crowded, horrifying memories and nightmares. Am I softening up, I wonder?

I am going to follow the tracks of the horse that carried Sue away, if I can find them. I'll begin where I last saw them.

All of the hungry critters can feast, now, in peace and quiet, save for fighting amongst themselves over the most tender choices. Ben, on the other hand, is still alive but unconscious. When he comes to, he'll discover that he is all alone—but not totally. He will see PJ Evers tied to the rear wheel of the blacksmith's wagon with his guts strung out, and Stu, dead on his side, with the two I'd killed layin' beside him—all his partners will keep him company on his last adventure. He will be terrified. Maybe he will find the small pocket pistol I found in Stu's saddlebags. I placed it near the anvil and saw.

Maybe he won't find it. Either way, he'll be fought over.

I can just hear him clicking away with that old empty gun.

Continued

CULLEN GRAFTON

PART 2

THE WARMTH OF THE DAY IS MELTING THE DUSTING OF SNOW. TRACKS OF THE unshod horse become clear on the hard ground beneath. I begin following a single set that is soon obscured by many. These other prints are of our attackers. After killing us and looting some of our possessions, my guess is that they are retreating to their main camp. Following the many to get to the one will be easy.

Full-on winter is fast approaching, and I am eager to catch up with the murdering brigands who stole my daughter and killed my family. My eye is still swollen shut and my strength has not fully returned. I must bide my time, temper my eagerness to catch them. I will know when it's time to save my daughter and avenge my family and friends.

I know little about the tribe I'm following, but according to gutless PJ Evers, they will be moving further south for a milder winter climate and easier hunting. I don't care what their tribe is called. I know firsthand what they are capable of. They will come to know that I'm the one person they should have followed beneath the boulders and finished. I have discovered that I am not a forgiving person.

They don't know that I'm alive and probably wouldn't care. As to my following them, one against maybe fifty or sixty … I've not yet formed a plan to get my daughter back and deal with the killer of my wife and son. I will know what to do when I come upon the bunch.

I've already taken care of the bastards who'd planned our destruction, Stu and Ben. They wanted to profit from having others slaughter us, so they could say their hands were clean from the killing before happening by to salvaged what was left to rust and rot.

Greed is an illness afflicting nearly every two-legged critter alive and is responsible for much pain and grief.

I'd surprised Stu's crew and killed them one by one—except the one who strangled my beautiful sister and hid her against mutilation by the savages so he could defile her dead body—I left him alive to experience the terror of various critters tearing at his throat, violently ripping it out of his neck while others beak and peck at his eyes and devour all his villainous parts.

I'd found June, my sister, in a nearby wagon under a quilt where Ben had concealed her against the butchering, scalp-hunting renegades. I'd buried her with Sue and Charles.

The second day, after washing my face in a very cold creek, I gently explore my cut head and ear. The swelling around my eye has gone down somewhat, and I am able to open it a bit. Light comes through, but what I see is not clear. Near noon, I make a small fire and eat a wedge of pemmican, a handful of jerked buffalo, and dried apples. I wash it all down with the strong coffee and sugar that I found in Ben's saddle bags. My strength is slow to return, along with my eyesight. But while not perfect, it is better. The hoof in my head must have got tired and quit stompin' or found another way out.

I'm moving slowly, examining the trail and all around for hang-behind scouts. There are none that I can see with my good eye. By the end of the day, even that eye is tired, and I am weary.

Just before noon on the fifth day, I hear a single gunshot off to the west. I ride into a line of scrub pine and boulders, dismount, and hope that my six animals remain silent. They are eating wild grasses.

I hear the clatter of trace chain and the rumbling sounds of wagons as they roll over uneven ground, and the blowing of animals pulling heavy loads. I remove my hat and peer between the branches of a stunted pine.

Two horsemen come thundering from the wash. They circle around, apparently looking for problems. One of the riders waves his hat in a circle above his head and the wagon noises become louder. Creaking and groaning, from the wide wash come two wagons. I'm stunned at the sight of the driver in the lead wagon. It's Stu…!

Stu's dead. I pitch-forked the murderin' rat—then it hits me, this is his look-alike brother, Stu's twin—they're a coupla' crooked peas from the same foul pod.

The two wagons appear loaded to the top and then some. The wheels are cutting deep ruts in the dirt. All eight horses are leaning into their collars. It takes nearly an hour for all of them to get out of sight after they turn north on my back trail. The two out-riders swinging out wide, scouting ahead. If they're going to meet the brother I forked, it isn't gonna be a happy family reunion! Who has this bunch slaughtered to fill up these wagons, I wonder. Maybe that was the gun shot I'd heard earlier.

It wasn't much of a fight, one shot.

I see buzzards circling high overhead. They don't wait around when food is near. I pull my string of stock and supplies up the deeply rutted wash and glance up a dry stream bed a few hundred yards from the entrance. Foliage over hangs its entrance. I nearly pass it by.

Sitting on a rock with a very big rifle across his lap is a youngster. In front of him is a dead animal, either a horse or a mule. Saddle bags and a burlap sack are next to the youngster's perch. The youngster does not look pleased and is not happy to see me either. As I approach, he pulls back the hammer of that single-shot cannon and points it toward me. If I'd had such a weapon during the fight, I might have saved Amy and Charles and killed the slug riding off with my daughter.

I poke my hat back and look him over. He's doin' the same at me. I'm at the edge of the narrow stream bed. My horse stretches his head and neck, wanting slack in the reins to nibble greens at the bank. I give him his head. The youngster is dressed in loose gray pants and a worn canvas jacket. A neckerchief holds the jacket's collar up against the chill of the day. A wide-brimmed hat covers his head, and he's wrapped a rag over the crown of the hat. It's tied under his chin, holding the brim down about his ears. I cannot guess his age. I've never been good at guessin' how old folks are. I know horse flesh better than human flesh. Out here, age is not as important as common sense, determination, and a handful of skills. A big gun helps too. Many youngsters are older than their years.

"That shot I heard was one of them shootin' your mule?"

"Not that it's any of your business, but yeah, Beulah found a speck of water to drink, left over from a recent rain. One of them no-account riders mistook her for an eatable critter, 'cause he was blind as my Aunt Ethel. He shot her. He then saw it was a mule and rode off in disgust. My thought was to go fix the jackass, when another rider passed by followed by two wagons, I think they was haulin' my family's possessions. I would've jumped them, but six to one is not in my favor. Now it's me and you, one-on-one, an' I got the bigger gun an' the drop on you. I can use it too."

"I believe you. I'm not lookin' for trouble with you. Seems you and me might have similar problems."

In a youthful voice he says, "I was just ponderin' what I'm gonna do about my problem, 'cause in this country, if you have no horse or mule, chances of surviving are slim—and then here you come, right on time, it looks like." He cocks his head and looks at me, then leans out a bit and looks at my string of animals munchin' again. "While I have the drop on you, maybe I'll just take one of them fine animals you have strung together. What do you say to that, Mister?"

"You're gonna have to kill me, and if you do, those buzzards …" I point up, and he looks up, following my finger. As he does, I draw Stu's Colt, "…are gonna have two bodies to peck and tear apart."

The boy looks back at me and at the end of the 44-40 Colt pointed at him.

"Before we shoot each other, maybe we should talk this over," I say. "Talkin' will be less painful. What are you doing in this stream bed, where are your folks, where are you heading?"

"I was followin' the tracks of those redskins," his eyes moving from my Colt to my eyes, "who massacred my ma and pa and the McCann family we were trailin' with. They killed all of them. I was huntin' far off when it happened. They were all dead when I got back with my four squirrels. I buried their bodies—took me near two days. Then I followed the pony tracks.

"I think those wagons were full of our belongings and supplies. They might have been in cahoots with them who killed my family… Ma and pa were good folks …" His eyes get a shine to them. He hesitates, swallows, and continues, "When it got dark yesterday, I camped here. Those damn looters must a watched me bury my folks then stole our things after I left. Our teams were gone, and our guns—all our stuff was strewn about. I had no way to carry it, so I left it all, right there on the ground, 'cept for a change of clothes.

After they killed Beulah, they didn't even bother to look for me. I just stayed hid and they passed on by—maybe they didn't know the mule was my ride. And if they did know, they figured I was just a no-account kid. I was over yonder, amongst the trees, tryin' to stoke up my fire when they killed her. Now you come by—you lookin' for more trouble? By the look of your face, you found some already, maybe you're looking for some more, Mister. I can't punch your face, but I sure can blow it clean away."

"My name is Cullen Grafton, what's yours?"

"What difference does it make... we ain't kin or partners or even friends."

"I know you're upset an' you got good cause to be, same as me. I wouldn't leave no one stranded out here. So, you're gonna ride one of these horses and try hard to get along with me. So, what do I call you? How about, Hey You."

"Call me Josie."

"Well, Josie, a few days back, the train I was with got hit by a passel of Indians. Maybe they were part of the same group who killed your folks and friends. Might be we should team up and set about making things right... Then there's the looters. I think I know where they're headed."

"Seems I don't have a choice. It's join up or walk myself outta here, after 'em. I may be young but don't get any ideas about bossin' me around. ... Where'd you get that string you're pullin' and how'd you come by that beatin' you took?

"It's a long story—maybe later."

"I ain't a grown man yet, but I can hold up my end. An' when we catch up with 'em, maybe I'll never get grown up neither."

He carefully eases down the hammer on that big rifle. I holster my Colt. He picks up his burlap and says, "I'll reheat my stew. You have any coffee on that mule, Cull?"

"... You have stew for two in that pot, Josie?"

"Well, Cull, you see if you've got coffee on that there mule and I'll see if my pot's got stew for two."

"Spoken like a true horse trader. You're old enough to drink coffee?"

"If I'm old enough to put meat in stew for two, I'm gonna drink coffee."

"I'll see what I can find on Levi—an' just you go right ahead an' call me Cull." *Seems I've been shortened to Cull... It does have a ring to it.* "Start up that fire, Josie, while I anchor these critters so as they don't drift off on us—'cause then we'd both be hoofin' it."

"That was mighty good squirrel stew. You shoot them squirrels with that 45-100?"

"This here is a 45-70." Josie affectionately pats the heavy octagon barrel. "An' there wouldn't be enough left for stew, accept maybe for claws 'n' tails, if I'd shot 'em with this chunk of lead." He holds up a finger-sized bullet. "I rocked 'em. I shot right beside the critters as they was yappin' at me. Pieces of rock flung by this bullet killed 'em."

"You must be a good shot to do that."

"I shoot okay for a kid. Only I don't like being called a kid."

"Okay, Josie, I get that… How's that coffee? Drink up, we've got a-plenty."

"You look terrible, like you was in a fight an' lost," Josie said.

"I was hit in the head. I believe that's what kept me alive and from bein' scalped like Amy an' Charles and all my new friends."

A sad, wistful expression comes over Josie's face. A silence settles over us. He is sittin' beside the fire with fire light showin' in his moist eyes. He is chokin' up again. His family killed and all. He's alone, sittin' with an old, busted-up stranger. He turns to the fire and pokes at it with a stick, sendin' up glowin' sparks.

I get up to check again that my stock is secure for the night, giving Josie some space to grieve. I also want to think on Stu's twin and his friends. They'd turned north. I felt it was to be a rendezvous with his brother, dead Stu, and our belongings. I decide right then that if I survive what's coming, I might just follow Twin-Stu to wherever he's goin'—then I'll fix his little pinto and send him for a proper reunite with his forked brother—in hell—with the rest of his pack rats. The best I can say for the bunch is that they didn't go cheap on their getaway mounts. That horse flesh was bread for speed and distance. Seems a body could almost tell thieves and buggers by their getaway transport.

A heavy loaded wagon might make sixteen to twenty miles per day. That is probably the best they could do, less if it snowed or a bunch of it was uphill. Traveling light, with two of these fine mounts, I could do sixty or eighty miles in a day. I heard tell of a group of Texas Rangers doin' a hundred miles, chasing someone. Indians used to run a hundred miles in a day taking messages and news—then came the horse from Spaniards after gold in South America.

I return to Josie with dried apples from Ben's saddle bags. There is shine smeared on his cheeks. I make no mention of it, just hand him some of the apples.

Josie asks me right off, "How come you just got beat up and not killed an' scalped?"

"In a bit. I just wanna enjoy these apple pieces. Any coffee left in that pot, or did you pour it all into that hollow leg you call a stomach?"

"I saved you some. Pass your tin cup, Tin Cup," he says, grinnin' at me.

"You call me Tin Cup just one more time, and you'll be 'Hey You, Kid' from now on. The name is Cullen or Cull, which I like just fine… My story is pretty much same as yours. They hit us five or six days ago. Killed everyone except me and my eight-year-old daughter, who they taken off with. That's nearly fifty of us they killed. The group of us decided to build us a town, to organize an' run it by our own selves… The town's gone forever, but I aim to get Sue back. I'm gonna catch up with those murderin' rascals and take flesh for flesh. We lost everything, and I aim to kill the chief, Gray Eyes—maybe I'll steal her back or die trying. He cut Amy's throat and grinned at me while he was doin' it. That's when I got slammed in the head …"

I picture it again and take another bite of apple and a sip of coffee to swallow down the lump that lodges in my throat. I follow with a deep breath. Josie is lookin' at me. I force a grin and finish that apple slice. "…I crawled into an animal roost beneath some boulders and passed out. When I came to, I found the looters about to take all our possessions in three wagons. I took care of 'em. And that's about it."

"Gray Eyes the chief?" said Josie.

"I think so. But he's the one who killed my family… How many loads you have for that squirrel gun?" I said, changin' the subject.

"I got four left—an' this ain't a squirrel gun, it's an all-round fetch 'em gun. My pa used it to kill buffalo. If you can't get that chief, it'll be a fetch 'em, squirrelly-chief gun. All I need is one of these." He holds up that big cartridge again. "That chief's gonna get the full load, plum dead center. An' I don't rightly care what happens to me after I fetch him an' three others just like him."

"Well, Josie, we'll see about all that. I'm gonna put my bedroll down. I'm wore out. Where's yours?"

"I'll sleep next to the fire. That way I can feed it and keep it going."

"I've got a spare roost you can use. I gathered it for Sue. It's gonna be cold. I'll be right back."

I put the bed roll where he wanted it, next to the fire. "I should'a made a bed roll," he says, "but I didn't even think about it. I just wanted away from all the blood and whittled-on bodies of my family. We'd better clean that cut to the side of your head. It's gonna fester. My ma said hot water and whisky would make it better. We'd best do it before sleep. A festering wound can kill you as sure as any gun or knife, it's kind of a poison, ma said—you got whisky?"

"I got a bottle. I'm not much of a drinker."

"Drinkin' the whisky ain't what ma had in mind, though pa took a nip on occasion, and so did ma. I seen her one time."

I watch as his eyes get a little teary again, talking about his family. I pretend not to notice. "I've got jerked buffalo and elk, hardtack, dried apples, a lot of pemmican, and some sugar for the coffee if you want—we'll be eatin' fine from here on."

He sorta grins over a shoulder at me then turns back to the fire and sends more sparks into the darkening sky through pine boughs. We share the same kind of pain and anger. Here he is, a youngster, trailing a tribe of Indians lookin' for some revenge, same as me, an' him not dry behind the ears, lookin' to take on the whole bunch, not carin' too much about himself. I just know he'll stand when the time comes.

Josie cleans up my cut head and is real gentle about it.

Two days later we come upon where that tribe had camped. They'd up and left. Their tracks tell they are headed further south. They don't seem to be moving very fast. I think they feel no one is coming after them. We are a couple of days behind and still moving cautious-like.

We stop while we can still see.

"We'll be comin' on them soon… maybe two days. That single shot can take care of business, but you might consider packing it on Ben's horse."

"Who's Ben? …You 'spectin' him? We surely can use the extra help, you got a spare rifle in that bundle?"

"Ben won't be here. He's dead… How'd you know guns were there?"

"See the outlines in the canvas? Not pots and pans or boots. You a gunsmith?"

"Just a collector," I say. "Would you consider swappin' 'fetch 'em for one bundled up there? … Help me take it down and unpack it."

We untie the ends and roll it open.

"Jeepers! Look at 'em, four Winchester rifles, six Colt guns, and look at all that ammunition. You plannin' on outfittin' an army? …You steal 'em, Tin Cu— I mean Cull?" Josie grins at me, a devilish twinkle in his eye.

"No, ya might say they was left to me by acquaintances who don't have no more need of 'em, kiddo."

"…You mean those folks are dead. Dead by these Indians? If that's true, how come they left these fine guns behind and those prime horses? That don't ring true."

"I took 'em from those who set the Indians on us. Enough of the questions, just pick the rifle and Colt you want and ammunition …they all feed on the same 44/40, except those two old pocket pistols. None are loaded.

"We need a plan when we come upon them. You'll know the chief when you see him. If I see the thief of my daughter, I'll let you know. Do me the favor—I don't wanna die before I get Sue away from 'em. I hope you're as good a shot as you talk. I'm guessing we'll come on 'em the next day or so. I think we should turn west and come at 'em from the west. Could be they'll have a scout or two watching their back trail a bit, considering what they've been doing. An' I noticed they dropped a few things along the way, fell off their travois... I just want Sue and Gray Eyes, he was grinning at me while he did the cuttin'. I'm gonna fix 'im if I can. I don't give a damn about the others in the tribe. You might keep anyone off my back that wants to even the odds in his favor."

"You are confident, I'll give you that. You can count on me. You thinkin' of swapping these fine guns for her, or are you just gonna jump him and take her?"

"Not swapping nothin'. One of the other mounts is for Sue. Nothing like good horse flesh between your knees when you gotta git out of town quick."

Josie gives a nod, then inspects each of the Winchesters and Colts. I just sit back against Stu's ornate saddle with a grin on my face sipping coffee and watchin'. It's the same as watchin' a kid in a sweet shop with some pennies in his pocket. He listens to the action of the rifles. He spins the cylinders, cocks and re-cocks the Colts tryin' to jiggle the cylinders for looseness while fully cocked.

"Grit!" he says, looking at me while rejecting a Colt. Swapping a cylinder from one revolver to another and re-cocking and listening all over again. "What are you grinning about?"

"Just enjoyin' your selection process. You look like you know what you're doin'."

"I do know what I'm doin'! Maybe I oughta look yours over for ya, TC," he says, grinnin' back at me.

I just shake my head and frown. I have to admit that I admire his gumption. At last he chooses the two he wants, loads them, and puts aside two hundred rounds of ammunition. We bundle the rest with that "fetch 'em" canon.

Josie starts a small fire. We're looking forward to pemmican with cooked wild potatoes, onions, and tasty greens we'd picked earlier in the day. Sugared coffee and dried apples after is always a treat. I look after our animals while Josie fixes the food. That kid—young man—can sure cook… He coulda cooked in a restaurant in our stillborn town.

It is very early. The morning light is just a promise on the eastern horizon as I walk Stu's gelding into the camp, pullin' a spare mount behind. Camp fires smolder as several dogs put up a ferocious ruckus, bringing a dozen warriors to their feet from beneath their robes. They are still setting up their winter camp. My Winchester is slung from the rawhide thong tied through the saddle ring on the rifle and slung from the horn of Stu's hand-tooled saddle. A Colt is in a saddle holster also hanging from the saddle horn. My dirk is in its scabbard on my hip.

Within a couple of minutes, the entire tribe is up and wanting to cut me down. I stand my ground showin' not a breath of the fear that I'm feeling right down to my boot heels. I hope the tradition holds whereby even an enemy coming into their village in peace is treated as a guest. The moment that 'guest' leaves, his possessions, his life, and his scalp are up for grabs. Several warriors make aggressive feints toward me. Three or four are admiring my horses even more than the Winchester. I ignore them and look for Sue. I spot her and nod toward her, signaling that I've come for her. She is restrained by one of the squaws and is surprised to see that I'm alive. Arrows and rifles are aimed at me. I hope Josie holds his water and does not discharge that 44-40 too soon. I'm counting on that to be a surprise.

Gray Eyes walks from among the crowd, holding his hand in a manner to stop his warriors from abusing the traditions of their tribe by killing the 'round eyes' enemy/guest. He appears supremely confident that he owns the situation. I point toward Sue. "My daughter. You stole her from me. I have come for her."

Gray Eyes smiles, looks to the one I called Sue. "You trade for little one?"

"I no trade. I take."

"You no take. Small one belong me. I win in war. Make good strong, brave squaw. You go now. My braves take you hair. Take you spirit. Eat you heart. Drink you blood. Little one stay. You squaw brave. Shoot ear," he touches the scabbing over his left ear and grins. "I give quick death. You watch. I see."

"We war," I say. Hot, loud anger is rising in my chest. It's so loud inside my head that it's deafening to me. Momentarily I fear that hoof may return.

Pointing, I say, "You win, you keep all." I wave to the two horses. "I win, I take you hair, my daughter—I know you fear me!"

"I no fear everything!" he says, swinging an arm wide.

Several of the braves step forward, willing to kill me now or fight me in his stead. Gray Eyes stops the movement. He looks me over, sees my bruised eye and still swollen head. He nods, turns, and waves his people back to give room. Then he says something which I do not understand, and a young brave comes to me with a lance that he thrusts into the ground before me. It is the same warrior who rode away with my Sue. I know Josie is watching. I point to his face, make a gripping motion and pull air, his soul, toward me. His eyes widen briefly. He understands and grins at me with a nod.

I look at Gray Eyes. He holds a long lance in his right hand. The bruising around my right eye is still there but the swelling is nearly gone. What I see is sharp and clear.

Gray Eyes speaks to the same brave now beside him and nods. I watch him. He holds the lance in two hands and shakes it, testing its balance and flex. I yank my spear out from where it has been thrust. The tip has come off, it's still in the ground! The shaft has only its blunt end, split where the stone tip was to have been cinched. Only a couple of rawhide strands still cling to the end. There are a few whoops from the watching tribe. Just as I look again at the chief, he has drawn his arm back and hurls his lance at me with great force and speed. I sweep my shaft, twisting my body out of line with his spear and deflect it away from me, striking it just inches behind its tip. I can even see the individual knaps forming the cutting edges of the tip. The blow to my head has not taken away the gift. I follow the spear on its flight into the onlookers, where it buries itself in the stomach of a young woman standing there. Surprise erupts from the tribe. Gray Eyes runs past me to the woman, great concern on his face and then anger. With his head back, he howls a scream to the heavens that sends chills down my back. He spins toward me, his shoulders hunched forward, his knife held in a tight grip. He takes three large steps toward me, intending to cut me into a dozen pieces. I swing that flexible toothless shaft with great whipping force, catching him on the ear Amy notched. He lands on his belly in the dirt at my feet. His ear is mashed. He rolls onto his back, his knife hand held high in defense. I swing the shaft at his knife hand and miss. I lose control of the shaft and it spins out of the encampment toward where Josie is waiting and watching behind a fallen tree and several large boulders.

Grey Eyes sweeps with his leg and knocks mine out from under me. I land on my side on several fist-sized rocks. I pull my dirk and roll away from him. He gets up, slowly measuring me. I'm up and we circle each other. My ribs complaining, probably bruised. He lunges at me and I jump back and thrust at his face; he dodges me and cuts my arm. I suddenly realize that he has more experience at this kind of fighting. He cuts me again. He's grinning at me. He's gonna whittle me down with small cuts. He's a better knife fighter. It's as though his crushed ear is not a bother. He feigns high then comes in low, aiming for my belly. I block his arm and swipe my blade across his chest. It is a thin cut, but he comes at me again, high then low, and cuts my right thigh. I back up and he keeps pressing me. I back into the warriors watching. There is a savage blow against my swollen and damaged head. I see dots before my eyes and it feels as though my head has exploded. I glance to the person who hit me. It's the same one who rode off with Sue. He reaches toward me, grabs air, my soul, as I did to him, and pulls it to him. He understands. He's not the only one in the know.

I drop to the ground, on hands and knees, the pain in my head is nearly blinding, however I do see Gray Eyes' moccasins as he stands over me. He grabs my hair wanting to pull my head back to slit my throat as he'd done to Amy. I stab my blade into his right foot all the way into the dirt beneath. He releases my hair and sits down heavily. I roll away, viscously twisting my blade, attempting break the small bones in his foot, destroying it. I stumble to my feet, swaying unsteadily as the ground rolls under me. Gray Eyes gets up and hobbles toward me, his ruined foot slowing him. I stumble to meet him halfway, deflecting his knife arm away with my bloodied right arm while spinning to my left and sending my left elbow back into his face. It is a short blow but powerful due to me twisting my body and putting all my weight into it. He lands, legs and arms outstretched. He might be knocked out. I don't wait. In a stumbling fall I'm on him, driving my blade into his eye to the hilt. I cannot pull my blade from his head. My hand is wet with my blood and I don't have the strength there anymore. The many small cuts were meant to bleed me dry. His plan was to toy with me, giving small cuts then ending it at his leisure once he's shown his domination. I would have been a goner, and Sue as well, if this had continued. Once again, getting hit in the head has saved me, sort of.

Bleeding from cuts and my head throbbing, I hear a bullet striking flesh and bone, then again and again as the report of Josie's rifle rolls across the tribe that is scattering for cover. I glance to the thief of Sue. He is on his knees clutching the center of his chest, blood running off his elbows. He then falls face first into the dirt. There is much gunfire. Sue helps me to my feet and pulls me toward our horses. I help her into the saddle and slap the horse's rump while pulling the slip knot, freeing her mount from mine. If I die now, at least Josie and I got her away from them. I swing under my horse's neck and grab the saddle horn as it bolts into a full gallop. I put both feet to the fast-moving ground and the momentum swings me into the saddle. The reins I'd tied together are draped over the saddle horn. I lean forward and hug its neck as it speeds like a thrown spear. Sue is two or three lengths ahead of me. Her mount's head is stretched out, its mane streaming in wind. Sue is leaning into the wind, riding as though she were born to it.

They'll be after us when they get to their horses. There is more firing from Josie's 44-40.

I hear bullets seeking Sue and me through the dust we're raising. We race west and catch up with Josie who is not standing around. He's twisting in the saddle firing behind. I try to free my Colt but decide to just hold on. Our string of horses and mule are moving with the same urgency; we all keep ahead of our pursuers. After miles, we slow to a distance-eating gallop, then a quick walk. I have to hand it to Stu and his four misguided and dead companions— they came by excellent riding stock, bread for distance.

None of this is over till I'm looking at Stu-two over forked-Stu's Colt.

I look to our back trail. They are nearly out of sight. Seems they've stopped chasing; their horses' heads are probably hanging. I feel we can go all day with the occasional stop for water.

I look at Sue, then at Josie. Both are smiling with relief. Josie's hat has blown off of his head and hangs down his back, held on by the chin strap. All of that long sun-streaked hair seems better suited to a young woman than a boy.

—Now, I consider myself very observant... Boy, that's a myth! I now have two females to look after. I'm gonna need help... but then again... a second look at Josie and remembering his—her—skills... maybe not so much!

Continued

81

CULLEN GRAFTON

PART 3

I'M AT THE END OF THE BAR IN A SMALL SETTLEMENT NEAR SAN FRANCISCO. IT'S A Friday night. All are drinking. There are a few cowhands and farm hands from local ranches and farms. There are many lumberjacks, a few taking a break from cuttin' tall, heavy timber into slabs, chips, and sawdust. Many others are on their way to Oregon and the Seattle area and the rich timber lands there.

The man I am lookin' for is at the other end of the bar, talking with the man I had recognized as one of the out-riders—the hat-waver at the mouth of the ravine where I'd first set eyes on Stu-two and found a youngster named Josie. I also saw this individual in San Francisco selling two wagons loaded with salvaged items from wagon trains headed west. Some of the goods he was selling I recognized as belonging to a blacksmith from our wagon train. Massacred by the late Chief Gray Eyes and his tribe.

I ask the bartender the name of the man at the end of the bar.

"Sam Brodie's his name. An' he don't like no one askin' after him, 'less it be for business."

"No, the one he's whispering to."

"Oh, that be Wilbur McGregor—they are two dangerous men. You'd best move along, stranger, 'less as I said, you got business," he says, setting my beer in front of me.

"What kind of business?" I say, but he is already moving to the other end of the bar. His back is to me, but I think he's saying something to Brodie and McGregor, while pouring them drinks from a labeled bottle.

Stu-Two, is what I've been callin' him. He's the twin brother of the con-triver of the clever destruction of the wagon train, by a band of rogue Indians. Leaving him free to claim salvage rights. And absolving him of all murders.

The out-rider, Brodie, spots me at the end of the bar and gives me a double look. His expression turns sour. His drooping and stained handlebar moustache frames his sour mouth. He then whispers in Stu-two—McGregor's—ear. His eyes search down the line of revelers along the bar then finds me at the end. He becomes another 'sour puss,' lookin' at me.

The bar is elbow-to-elbow for the entire length. The air is filled with smoke, animation, and loud conversation and laughter. Friendly folks getting along. Here and there, a 'woman of the line' is the center of a conversation. There is an intermittent stream of couples climbing to the second story by the stairs along the far wall. A sign on the far wall above the stairs reads "Her golden gateway, smooth as silk, lies just ahead."

Some men folk, and I'm one of them, about to get down to business, doin' a certain thing, roll up their shirt sleeves, spit in their hands for grip, and jump right in to get 'er done. I watch Stu-two hitch his pants up, adjust his belt, and with his right hand sweep his hat back off his head. The hat lay by its chin strap against his back, and then, from his shirt collar at his back, quick as a strikin' rattler, throws an ivory-handled knife at me. I know in that instant that he'd done this before and practiced the move often.

Not more knives! I'm sick o' the damn things!

In a single rotation of the thrown knife I see that the ivory grip is worn smooth and yellow from much handling, with fine cracks stained dark. The three brass rivets holding the grips to the thick full tang are worn shiny. The blade is smooth and free of any rust. Its cutting edge is chipped in two places and a small portion of one of the grips is broken off. It is about ten inches of deadly beauty with a needle tip like my old knife. I simply bat it away from me. It narrowly misses the barkeep who flinches and drops to his knees. He just gave me up to those two snakes. The blade embeds itself in the wooden frame of the big bar mirror. It has drawn blood however, from the heel of my left hand. There is a gasp from those at the bar, then they all move way back.

"I ain't never seen nothin' like it. He just swatted that blade like it was a floating feather. He didn't duck, or flinch, not one little bit. How'd he do that?" says a voice from the crowd.

Sam Brodie strides halfway down the now-empty bar, accidentally upsetting one of the spittoons on the floor. He frowns momentarily at the mess splashing on his fancy boots and pant legs. He stops, not eight feet from me; spits at the next spittoon, misses, and draws his Colt from his slim-Jim holster, cocking it as it comes out of its resting place, saying in that same instant, "Bat this away, you son of a bitch!" He thrusts the Colt toward my head, pulling the trigger.

4 weeks earlier, at the end of the chase

We pull up to give our horses water and a short breather. I pull a spyglass from a saddlebag and hand it to Josie. He opens it, peers through it, then gives it a puzzled look. "Other end," I say. She turns it around and looks again to where our pursuers should be. Scanning left and right she shrugs her shoulders. *Geez, I'm still thinking she is a he—loss of blood. I don't feel well.*

"Don't see the whole bunch of 'em. I do see two comin' on. Those two are ridin' a couple of fine lookin' horses—thoroughbreds, or Arabian stock. They're two, three miles back and loping right along, eatin' distance."

"Josie, pull Ben's horse in and grab your .45-70 squirrel gun." We had roped all of our futures together, so they wouldn't scatter. I wanted a horse ranch if I survived this. "Think you can hit the closest rider with that .45-70 while missin' the horse?"

"I think it's a mare."

"If we can catch her, she'll make a good addition to the horse ranch I want to put together, when all this is done." There, I've put it out there. "We've some good breeding stock, assuming we can keep our scalps and our horses. Don't even think about rockin' him. Just dead center... If you can hit the other one, good, if not, burn him some, to change his direction."

Josie rests that buffalo gun on her bundled coat on a boulder, waits until the distance is right, takes aim and lets fly. I squint at the two Indians. One is swept from the back of the mare as though he'd rode into a heavy tree limb and forgot to duck. His horse shies some, gallops a short distance, then stops running, probably feeling the load no longer on her back.

I look at Josie. *With all that hair framing her face, he's a very handsome young woman. I like him better as a young woman. I gotta get off this horse and stop the bleeding. Nothing seems right.*

Josie drops the trigger-guard/lever, opening the breach that cocks the hammer at the same time, pulling and throwing the smoking empty cartridge from the breach. She thumbs in another big cartridge, pulls the lever closed—sights and fires. Sue is watching through the glass. "You hit the second warrior," she says, "but he's holding on. That horse is changing direction and really moving now, spooked by your shot." She continues, "The horse just veered away from a large group of boulders in its path but the rider just continued on, into those big rocks. It was not a smooth landing for him. I think he landed head-on. The horse is still running back the way it came, Pa. You wanna look?" she says, holding the glass toward me.

"No. Help me down, Sue. Good shootin', Josie. I need water and I need to wrap these cuts, they're still bleeding. I'm feeling weak as a colt. Gray Eyes nearly had me. That hoof is pounding in my head again. Josie looks at me and, shaking her head, "You surely did step in front of that chief's big knife. I was gonna fetch 'im when you stabbed him in the foot and then finished him with an elbow and that pointy knife o' yours, right in his eye. The one you pointed out was comin' for you when I took 'im down, hard."

Sue helps me down from the saddle.

"Josie, you kept the rest of them off me. I owe you my life and Sue's. You are not a kid. You're as brave and as smart as any man I know—and even more so as a young woman, though you had me completely fooled—a mighty fine young woman at that. It's gonna take me a while to get used to you not being a boy, person. My brain's not workin' like it should."

Josie's looking at the first Indian's horse. "It's now trotting toward us. Maybe sensing our string."

"Both Indians are still down. I winged the one on the rocks. He's draped over one of 'em and not moving. His mount is still headed back to wherever it came from—the tribe, probably."

Sue helps me take off my shirt. Josie cuts strips from it where there is no blood. She and Sue bind the cuts on my arms. She wads a piece of shirt, places it over the pant leg and cut, binding it with a longer shirt piece. The leg wound is the deepest and the one bleeding the most. She cinches it tight. Sue pulls my spare shirt from my saddle bag. The shirt I'd taken from Nathan Penny, our blacksmith. I'm chilled to the bone. With shirt and poncho on, I'll live.

We take turns drinking from our canteens and decide what we should do next, all the while keeping an eye on our back trail and that rock-draped warrior.

"That mare is closer now. It's eating grass here and there. "I hope it seeks the company of our string," says Josie. "That far range of hills and mountains to the west looks kind of familiar. I think I was here two years ago. Pa and I rode out here hunting and visiting Uncle James and thought we might move here. It's getting mighty crowded in Kansas. I remember that range from the hunt. When you're out hunting, you have to know how to get back to home. Knowing what the way back looks like, complete with outstanding landmarks to help you get home. I think we are several days from my Uncle's farm, near Carson City. That means we are still in Nevada. That's where we were headed when set upon by those rascals. Uncle James is gonna be outraged when he learns Pa, his brother, and Ma are gone. Uncle James and Pa were the only two of the family still alive. The war took two other brothers. Both were killed at the 'Bull Run' fight. They might have shot each other there, for all we know— one was blue and the other gray."

"Let's keep moving. Josie, you use that glass and keep a watch if we're being followed. That tribe might just be restin' then come on again. We—you hurt 'em bad during the fight as that Chief was bestin' me… damn, I hate knives for fightin'. I wonder who it was who took that spear in her belly that set the chief's war-bonnet on fire."

"We'd best keep movin' and keep a look-out for a defendable campsite," she says.

"I'm all in," I say, "but I can pull a trigger if I have to."

Josie hangs back a mile or so to see that we weren't followed. And as best she can tell we are free of 'em. The mare is following our string. It's a fine look-ing, long-legged mare. Somewhere, a person is missing this fine horse. More than likely, if they are still alive, and I've heard of it happening, they could be missing their own hair more than the mare.

One evening we're fixing our supper when an old man shows up, a mountain man, dressed in decorated, soiled, and well-used leathers, pulling a mule loaded with bundles of who knows what. "Hello the fire!" He looked to be a hundred years old. He came on in and we shared our paltry meal with him. He added two rabbits to the mix. They were shot with a bow 'n' arrow. He said that we were two, maybe three days from Carson City, an up-and-coming "me-tropolis".

He said that he liked the high and lonesome of the Rockies, that settlements were too crowded, too noisy, and smelled bad. He said that he had never seen so many horse flies in one place. He told of a massacre he come across. Very bad. He shook his head in disgust. Several of his stories were of this country when a body could go days, weeks, and even months and not see another white man. Many of the tribes, back then, were friendly. He lived with several tribes. He learned about survival from them. They admired and were fascinated by his rifle and pistols. His name was Randy Goodman, originally from Tennessee. He and his mystery bundle were gone before we were up the next day.

By now I'm feeling stronger, from sleep and because Josie killed a deer. She and Sue found coral mushroom, potatoes, onions, and other greens—local edible vegetation. We're low on coffee, the dried apples and sugar are gone, the pemmican also. We feast on several meals of venison and greens and stay put so I can rest.

We three finally arrive at Josie's uncle's farm. And they are happy to see Josie, and angry and bitter over her family's death at the hands of those Indians.

I decide to rest for two more days. James' wife, Sally, along with Josie, clean my wounds and properly rebandage them. I don't tell anyone what I am planning. I ask Josie's Uncle James for directions to San Francisco where I believe Stu-two is headed to sell what he'd taken from us. James says he'd never been to Frisco but that I could inquire about the best route in Carson City when I was of a mind to pursue the lot.

Very early on the fourth day, I saddle the best of our horses and decide to take a second horse to carry my bedroll and meager supplies. Also, swapping rides will let me make better time.

I look at Sue sleeping with Josie, wanting to say goodbye but not wanting them to try to talk me out of what I've planned. For the past two days Josie has dressed as a young woman. In a dress, she is very feminine and wonderful to look at.

I'm still not recovered from Amy and Charles being murdered. It's best that I follow the murderous crew and finish avengin' our slaughter. I am hoping to catch up with them and follow them to their destination. When I am satisfied, if I survive, I will establish a horse ranch near to Carson City and my new friends, Josie's Uncle James Davis and his family. I'll be nearby for Sue to see Josie and James' son Samuel and daughter Gladys, who is about Sue's age. I hope to see Josie often. She is always on my mind and in the most pleasant manner.

I ride into Carson City. It's the largest town I've seen in quite a while. I locate a general store, selling clothes, some weapons, ammunition, and canned food. I buy coffee that is ground for me, sugar, some more pemmican, jerked elk, a slab of bacon, and dried apples that I have developed a taste for. I discover canned peaches and hardtack. I also get a pot for coffee and a pan for cooking. I buy two shirts and a heavy coat against the weather and another knife to replace the one that I left in Gray Eye's gray eye. Gloves finish my personals. I place all the food and shirts in two gunnysacks. I ask about the way to San Francisco. I'm told to follow the tracks 'cause there are a-plenty, and keep heading west and I can't miss it. It is a three or four-day trip. "You step in the ocean before the town, you're off course north or south."

I pull on one of the new wool shirts against the cold, then the fleece-lined jacket. I divide the other items between the gunnysacks and rope everything on the old second saddle on my second horse along with my roost, my bedroll. Bundled now against the cold gray sky I follow the tracks west of Carson City. The tracks are readable beneath the light dusting of snow during the previous night.

The second day out I'm still following tracks and now come upon two deep wagon ruts as they join in with other tracks headed west. I wonder about them. They are cut deep suggesting heavy loads. They appear recently made, possibly two days ahead of me. I hear a distant gunshot, a hunter probably. I continue on.

I'm halfway across an elongated park when from the bordering timber to my right I see two mounted riders, coming straight toward me, riding hard. Their horses' hoofs throw clods of snow and mud out behind them. Their rifles are shouldered, and they commence firing at me. I'm riding with my rifle across my lap and so it's up, pull the hammer back, point and fire. I hit the rider on my left. It was a snapshot. They both veer off and make a run for timber on the other side of the park. The rider not hit sends two more bullets toward me as they disappear into the timber.

Both shots miss me but hit my second horse, carrying my food and other items. I send three quick rounds after them where they entered the wood.

My second mount is hit twice in the same foreleg. He is in a great deal of pain and pumping blood with each heartbeat. I look into its eyes and pat his neck and mane and whisper in his ear that I am sorry that he is injured and in pain and hope that he will forgive me for destroying him. Then I put a bullet in his head to end his suffering. I find that both shots to his leg broke the leg into two separate sections.

Right then I decide to follow the two into the woods, that anyone attempting to take my life, or damage any of my horses, I will follow and end them.

Ever since I left Carson City, I've had the feeling that I'm being followed. I double back several times but there is no one.

I enter the forest, going after the two who missed killing me but destroyed a damn fine horse. Why were they after me? Were they just wanting my goods and horses? Or was there some other motivation? When I find the two rascals, there will be no mercy. They will answer my questions, or just like Ben and Stu and the rest of those scum-suckin' pigs, I will take them apart piece by piece.

No one from now on gets away with trying to kill me. I'm angry beyond reason. I trail them by their marks in the snow still on the ground in shaded areas. As I enter the woods, I hear two gunshots. They sound near. I hold up, listen… and hear nothing more. I dismount and with my rifle in hand, slowly limp—the wound in my leg is not healing as it should—in the direction of the shots and the tracks leading my horse. I come upon a third set of hoof prints, intermingling with the two I'm following. It's dark in this pine forest. It is late afternoon and the sun is sinking fast. The winter days are short.

I find both bodies in the snow. They seem to be stripped of any identifying papers. Both have been shot in the head, murdered, with a small caliber gun. I mount up. Everything personal has been taken, along with their horses. Who were they? Were they killed so they could not talk? The tracks fade in the closing darkness into another small park, free from snow accumulation. I stop and wait for a time, dismount again then walk another short distance in that park. It is now too dark to continue. I move slowly into the wood, walking deeper into the forest. I am wondering about the strange footprints in the snow around the bodies. One track was not exactly a boot print. The other track was as a kind of bear claw. "Who or what the hell made those tracks?" I know they'd been made by a human. Still they give me goosebumps. There was something not quite human about them.

I cold–camp beneath a recently downed Douglas fir. As much as I want hot food and coffee, I build no fire. That third person could be near, waiting. I think back over the past days trying to remember just who this third cutthroat might be. There has been no one standing out. And this one has been in front of me, not behind. Lying there in my bedroll, my horse taken care of, my thoughts turn to Josie. Even though she was dressed as a boy, she is a young woman and a very wonderful woman—strong, fearless, level-headed, tender, possessing all of the qualities required of anyone capable of surviving and even prospering in this new land. The past cannot be changed. The future, on the other hand, has possibilities that are limitless, boundless. Those who have come before and perished will never be forgotten by those who knew them, but time has a way of erasing all of our tracks and deeds.

I was up before the sun. I cut north through several parks until I came upon those same wagon tracks. I'd lost time but made up the distance by quick walking and occasionally galloping. I came upon both wagons at day's end. I made camp away from them in a secluded wood where I was able to build a small fire. There was plenty of grass for my mount and I fed him a hatful of oats and curried him down. I ate pemmican, had coffee with sugar and a can of peaches. Sleep came quickly.

I discreetly followed the wagons. One was driven by Stu-two. The other driven by a man I'd seen at the ravine, where they came from killing Josie's family.

There were other single mounted travelers, like myself, with the same destination in mind. I stayed near the end of the bunch. There were two men riding
in the wagons with their horses tied to the back of the wagons. I recognized
them from their exiting of the ravine where I'd met Josie, and learned of her
family's murder, many days ago. The fifth man that morning at the ravine is
missing from these four. Where could he be? Was he the irritation I felt at being
followed? Was he still behind me? Was he responsible for the two who attacked
me? These questions were very bothersome and kept me alert and tired. What
was that gunshot shortly after leaving Carson City?

In San Francisco, the wagons proceeded to a group of raw buildings and a
jetty, at the end of which were two schooners. As we entered the town of
rough, occasionally unpainted store fronts, single travelers like myself broke off
and went their separate ways. I hung back, dismounted, and watched the contents of each wagon be loaded, selectively, onto the two schooners. I was close
enough to recognize the blacksmith's anvil, especially the one I'd used to crush
Ben in place as the main course for the wolves. Also the special metal bending
forms Nathan had made and attached to the anvils. There were wheel rims
and some of the other items used by Nathan Penny who'd been the blacksmith
with our massacred wagon train.

The wagons were emptied, one by one. When all was finished and the
sale of the ill got goods was complete, Stu-two entered one of the buildings
and emerged with an envelope and a handshake from the purchaser of the
delivered goods. I then noticed that the two men and their horses were not now
with the two wagons.

An older man stopped beside me. "You lookin' to sign on to one of them
schooners?"

"I was thinking on it. Especially if one is headed south. I've had 'bout
enough of cold weather."

"My thinkin' too but them two beauties are full up near ever' trip."

"What kind of merchandise do they handle?" I asked.

"Just anything they can get their hands on. Some of it salvaged from failed
wagon trains comin' West from East. Some folks just leave off items to lighten
their load 'cause their animals pulling the wagons are near wore out. Now
that's a business I'd like to get on board with. Mister Samuelson buys goods

from whoever is selling. He don't ask no questions. Just pays, ships, and profits. The larger of the two beauties, the one on the left, usually heads south down Baja. The one on the right stops at Portland, Seattle, Vancouver, and along the Canadian and Alaskan coast selling their goods to the various settlements and ports along the coast both English and Russian, avoiding hard winter ports. Nice talkin' at you," he said. "Luck with finding work. I'm sure you'll make out just fine."

"Likewise, mister," I said.

I rode down to the jetty just as Mister Samuelson sent the two skippers back to their ships to set sail.

"Mister Samuelson," I said.

He turned to face me, holding a sheath of papers in hand. "You lookin' for work, I have nothin' for you."

"Not lookin'. The items you just bought were taken from our wagon train after my wife, son, and friends were murdered."

"Do you have any proof that what you say is the truth?"

"I am the proof, the only one who survived. I overheard the two instigators talking about what they'd done. They set those Indians on us."

"I don't know who you are talking about." He poked a thumb in their direction. "They said that they came upon two massacres and just salvaged what the Indians didn't take."

"You just loaded our possessions onto your schooners. Who were those two men who sold you our possessions? What are their names?"

You're a growed man, you want to know who they are, go ask 'em your own self."

"Where are they staying?"

"Who knows? I have no idea. I buy merchandise and resell it where there's a need. I don't keep track of my suppliers. If what you are saying is true, you need to talk to the law. I'm not saying another word. Now I've two ships to send off with the tide."

I mounted up and looked after the two wagons as they turned onto a different street several blocks away. I followed at a distance. They have never seen me before and cannot connect me to Josie's dead family and friends nor to the killing of his twin brother. All of that gives me a slight advantage.

They pulled into a large livery, talked to the young wrangler there. They then pulled both wagons in line with two others, took their saddlebags and rifles, and walked to a bar/restaurant/hotel, "The Three Pigs and a Poke."

The moustache with Stu-two looked at me just sitting there on my horse. His glance lingered on me a little too long.

The youngster stabled my horse.

"Who were those two men with the wagons?"

He just shrugged and shook his head while forking hay, and scooped grain for my horse. The young man returned to un-hitch the teams from the wagons and turn them loose into the corral with other horses.

I followed after the two. They entered the attached hotel. I entered the tavern and found a spot at the end of the bar, so I could see the rest of the room. It was hot, smoky, and noisy. After several minutes Stu-two and his partner entered the bar from the hotel. They took a place at the other end of the bar. Several already there moved over to make room for them.

The heavy-set bartender finally gets to me. "I want a beer, if it's cold."

"Our beer is always cold, even in the summer."

"Tell me, who is that man at the end of the bar? He just stepped up."

Josie enters the bar.

The burley logger looked down at me, bein' a thin youngster who'd just stepped into the saloon named 'Three Pigs and a Poke'. He was probably wondering what business a youth, such as myself, could have in a saloon. I felt the eyes of the tree-tamer lingering on the short barreled .41 caliber Colt Thunderer revolver stuck in my waist belt and the Winchester rifle in the crook of my arm. I was wearin' my slouch hat, brown oversized shirt, and pants. He looked at my smooth face, with no facial hair, then said, "There's gonna be a killin'. An' this ain't no place for a young-in. You'd best go on home, boy."

"Who's killin' who?" I said.

"The gent at the left end of the bar ain't long for this here world. That's Wilbur McGregor at the other end. For some reason, McGregor's twin brother ain't here yet. Them two brothers are always together. The other gent there is Sam Brodie. The McGregors, Brodie, and his two hands will make quick work of it. You'll see. Don't think your ma and pa would want you to see this. Was I you, I'd back on outta here and go on home before the cobra strikes."

"I see the two at the end of the bar. Where are the other two?"

"They're right there in front of us at yon' table," he whispered, nodding at the two. "I'm stayin' right here outa the line of fire. I ain't gonna say it again. You'd best be gone, boy."

I saw the two at the table move away from each other, one a lefty, t'other a righty. They drew their guns and held them under the table. Sam Brodie gave a quick glance toward the two. He saw that they were alert and ready to step up.

I recognized the leftie directly in front of me, wearin' a checkered shirt, an' wearin' that same faded and chewed-on bowler hat. It is the dumbest "Billy-cock" hat I ever saw, coverin' the hairy wart he probably calls his head. He'd shot Beula, my mule, then rode off wantin' no part of eatin' a damn mule he mistook for a deer in the early morning. Just one more damned fool with a gun, shootin' before lookin'.

The barman said something that I couldn't hear and several at the bar began to step back from it. The laughter, banterin', and conversation slowly quieted as those at the bar began to step away like so many dominoes in a row. The tension in the room became thicker than lard in December. A couple on the stairs stopped to watch the floor show about to begin. The stained, flat pine plank countertop was empty of elbows, except for drink glasses and burn marks from cigarettes.

The man with the ugly hairy wart for a head looked at his bald partner and they both eased the hammers of their guns back and made ready to stand and deliver.

I saw that Cull was focused on Stu-two and Brodie and was not aware of these two flaky flankers. I shook my head in disbelief. Cull had come all this way, alone, to avenge his family and friends and my family. The one thing I admired about Cull is that he was not afraid to tackle any problem, head on. But he often underestimates the problem. I'm mostly a hunter and used to observing and weighin' each situation. As I get older, I become quicker at picking the most advantageous moment when and where to make my play. Where Cull's a farmer type and just puts a shoulder to what needs to be moved and moves it, as in Stu-two and his partner... totally unaware of 'Hankie and Pankie', the flankers.

I cannot believe my eyes. That mustached fool marches down, draws to shoot Cull in the face. I don't remember drawing my Thunderer and shooting at that same instant that Brodie shoots at Cull. His shot is deflected by passing through the web flesh between Cull's thumb and forefinger of his right hand. The bullet then takes a bite out of Cull's right ear. My shot entered Sam Brodie's left temple just behind his left eye. A hole from the bullet appeared in the bar mirror with jagged cracks radiating from it, and sticky flesh matter, bone fragments, and blood spatter against that mirror, and slowly slides down onto the bottles of whisky beneath the mirror. His body upends another spittoon dousing his head in its revolting contents.

The bowler hat and his partner look behind them into the unblinking eye of my Colt with smoke curling from its short barrel. "Lay 'em on the floor, boys. Ease those hammers down first. You even hesitate, you're both dead meat, an' I never miss—not one single time."

They both comply and place their hands on the table. "You, you fool," I say to the 'wart', "you killed my mule. I grew up with her. This scar will be a reminder." I then rake the front sight of my Colt across his forehead tearing his skin and causing blood to flow into his eyes. His bowler lands on the floor and I stomp it flat.

"Hold on there miss, we're deputies. We'll take care of these two now. Go see to your friend. He needs the Doc. He's bleeding pretty good. Why he's not dead is beyond me. The knife should have finished him and the bullet to the head for certain. I never seen nothin' like it."

I glance to McGregor and see that the sheriff has him at gunpoint.

"Who in the devil are you?" says the lumberjack. "You shot Brodie in the head while holding that Winchester! You were quick getting that revolver out and puttin' that bullet in his head an' all from a squirt kid! Err, sorry, from a youngster, an' I'll be, a young woman. That do beat all."

The hosteler has hitched a team to my family's wagon. A light cold rain is falling. It could turn into snow. I am adjusting supplies, making room for the two bedrolls side by side.

I'd followed Cull from Carson City. I paralleled Cull's course, and nearing San Francisco, blended in with the single travelers to Frisco and the two heavy wagons. He was focused on the wagons and the brigands driving them and didn't see me in the herd.

I was facing toward the front of my wagon when I heard a clamor at the tailgate. There appeared a weasel of a man, and by the smell, unwashed for a long time. Many took a bath once or twice a year. Here was one of them. He held a small caliber gun on me. It had an octagon barrel. I guessed it to be a .32 caliber old timer.

"You and me is gonna take a ride out of this town. Get up there and drive them horses or I'm gonna shoot you right here."

"That would not be wise. You know what these town folks do to women killers? Who are you? I've never seen you before."

"You can ask that madman who I am. He knows. The bastard left me for coyote food with an anvil on my feet and this here gun with only caps and no powder and ball for defending myself against being eaten alive."

"So, you were part of the murderin' thieves who killed his family and friends and then killed my entire family."

"We kilt no one. It was them Indians what did it. We were just pickin' the spoils left by those red savages—salvagin' ain't agin' no law."

"How'd you get free from that anvil?"

"An old coot mountain man set me free and fixed my feet that weren't broke. Just twisted some. I helped him take what he wanted from several wagons. Then he was gone. One minute he was there and the next—like smoke, he was gone!"

"Wilbur McGregor drove this wagon here. I proved to the sheriff that this wagon is mine and belonged to my family. McGregor, his twin brother, and their crew are in jail. And after Cull gives a sworn statement, there is a good chance they will spend years behind bars. Now you can join them. I'm guessin' there's a good chance all of you will swing for what you've been doin'."

"Not a chance, girlie. You're gonna drive us out of this foul smellin' outhouse, then I'm gonna have me some fun with you."

"Here's news for you. You're the stink-pot. You want to live, you'd best leave and right now."

Josie saved me once more. I almost batted that bullet away. At least I deflected it some and only lost part of an ear. Out of the corner of my eye I saw her draw and fire an instant after Brodie sent that lead ball at my head. I swatted at the ball and tilted my head. I moved instinctively but not quick enough. I had no idea Josie was that quick with a Colt.

She was the one following me the whole while. There's much about Josie I look forward to discovering. I am glad Brodie was not aiming at my heart, otherwise I'd be dead right now.

I see that her Pa's wagon is hitched and ready to go. It's dark out, but through the drawn front canvas, drawn against wind and rain, I see the glow of a lantern. A light rain is falling. It's gonna turn to snow. My head is bandaged holding the ear tight against further bleeding, though some is seeping through. My hat, too small for my bandaged head, sits on top but keeps the rain from soaking everything. I hear voices coming from inside the wagon. I peer through the drawn canvas and much to my lightly laudanum-dosed brain's surprise I'm nearly knocked off my feet 'cause I'm looking at the rat, Ben! I'd left the bastard for coyote food for killing Amy and Charles and my sister June, who he was going to have sex with her dead body. And he's still breathin' an' walkin'? Then I remembered the two dead dry gulchers and that old trapper mentioning a massacre, and then there was the mystery bundle on his mule. Could that bundle be some plunder from our train? Could he have saved Ben? We'll never know the how of it.

The rat's standing against the tailgate. I walk to the lead horse, grab his halter, and with my good hand yank and pull with all my strength and weight. The horses all move forward a step sending Ben staggering back against the tailgate and he is sent flippin' head-first into a putrid puddle on the ground beneath the tailgate. I walk quickly to the rear of the wagon. He is trying to get up from the dung- and horse-piss–infused puddle, his head facing toward the wagon. I step on his neck, forcing his head back into the puddle. His arms and legs flail wildly, splashing horse poo everywhere, including on me. I'm sure he is inhaling and swallowing from the puddle. From behind me— "Here-here, we'll have none of that, step off him, right now. I won't have this activity in my town." The Sheriff runs up and pulls me from Ben's neck.

"He murdered my sister and was going to sex her body. He deserves to eat shit and drown in this pool. He was partners with Stewart McGregor, the twin brother of Wilbur McGregor. The massacre of our train carried out by Gray Eyes was planned by two brothers and this piece of dung. Josie and I tracked them murderin' savages and killed the chief out of vengeance. Not just for my family and friends but for Josie's Ma and Pa also."

"If what you say is true, and I believe you, he'll suffer the same fate as the three we have in custody. They'll all spend years in prison, or more likely, they'll all hang. Justice tends to be quick in this town with our judge who is determined to take a large bite of crime goin' on by setting examples."

"There is a fifth man I can't account for. I wonder where he is?" I said.

Josie said, "There was a shooting just outside Carson City. It was the fifth man. I remembered him from the ravine. He was followin' you, same as me. I confronted him, he drew and I killed him."

"How did you convince the sheriff that this wagon belonged to your family?" I asked Josie.

"I told him where I had carved my initials in one of the spokes when Pa was building it. He said I could have done that any time and said it was not proof the wagon belonged to my family. I told him of my Pa's secret box, that it is part of the water barrel platform at the rear of the wagon. He found it, pushed and pulled nails and pegs. It opened it up and he withdrew Pa's gold, silver, and cash money Pa'd stashed for our trip to Nevada and the farmland we located two years before. The Sheriff also found two tin-types, one of Ma and me in front of our wagon before we set off for Nevada and the other of Pa and me. …Maybe you wanna take a partner in building that horse ranch of your dreams. Pa's money and yours could get us up and running right now. What do you say, Cull? Uncle James has a parcel right near him that he says would be perfect as a horse ranch. There is a creek and good pasture land. He staked a claim on it for Pa. It is a 150-acre parcel.

"I …I, well I don't know what to say."

"I just put up supplies for us for our trip back to Nevada. It would be warmer if we slept together, but I know it is too soon, so as you can see there's a fold-down platform on that side. We used it as our table in bad weather. I can sleep there and you here in the middle of the floor. Or we can stay at the hotel till spring. In separate rooms or one room. I found a boarding house that will take us. But only if we are married. They'll have no shenanigans—"wickedness" was the word she used. It's gonna be awhile before you are all healed and capable of any wickedness or anything else. What did Doc do for that bad cut to your leg?"

"He cleaned it and stitched it closed. He said no running or riding until it is healed, or I could lose the leg. He showed me how to cut out the stitches when the time comes. Or he will do it if I'm still here."

"You're gonna need me around to keep you out of trouble."

"I didn't know you had feelings for me. When did that happen? And what sort of feelings do you have for me when you are a boy person? As a young woman you are wonderful. As a boy person, I'm not real certain how I feel—which am I likely to I bump into of a night? Whoa… why'd you pull that knife?! I hate knives. Just put it down. …What I just said about you as a boy person was an attempt at humor."

"I'm not gonna cut you. The Sheriff said this is yours because McGregor tossed it to you. It has the same needle point as the one you gave to the Chief. As for your little attempt at humor…"

"…Ouch! You could have punched my good arm. And who just punched me, Josie, boy person or Josie, young-woman person?!"

"There's one way to find out…"

Continued

CULLEN GRAFTON

PART 4

The Cave

I WAS TRYING TO RUN BUT WAS ONLY STAGGERING DOWN THE SHALLOW, DRIED UP creek bed that was full of smooth rocks and dried sticks. I was not moving very fast. I have never been more frightened in all my life. Frightened, not for myself but for my best friend whom I had draped across my shoulder and my cousin, Stephen Grafton I'd left behind. I was reluctant to leave him but I knew that I had to get Josie away to safety. She was a very capable young woman but was unconscious and I was frightened for her.

Stephen Grafton came upon a small branch, a park, that was pristine. He'd spent some time in the valley several years earlier when he just wandering. Experiencing the wild beauty of the West as many had done in the early days of the 1850s and 60s. Some like Stephen loved this new land and accepted its often harsh terms. Many prospered in the experience. Understanding, patience, and the application of force, when it was necessary, were the keys to survival. Stephen had been a trapper, hunter, and on occasion an Indian fighter. He was an excellent judge of character. He was now desirous of building a small ranch for himself, maybe find a woman, marry and raise a family. Just as a woman's body and internals eventually caused her to yearn for a child, so Stephen finally accepted that he needed companionship, a family, others to care for besides himself. He felt the need to leave clear sign of his passage on this great land and mark his journey.

Stephen shoved us into a bunch of shrubs that grew next to the sod hut he lived in on the edge of the seasonably dry creek bed as the Hennessey riders came down the wash at a run, shooting at everything. Stephen had stepped back into his shelter with the rifle he always carried with him.

"Go to the cave", he shouted. "I'll be along soon as I handle this."

"But Stephen, there are too many of them!" I counted four.

"Get!" he shouted. "Don't argue, Cull. Just get yourself and Josie to the cave! I can handle this. I'll be along shortly. Get her to safety. She could be hurt bad from the fall when her horse was shot."

I turned to see the men storming the tack shed. Stephen was firing at them. Two of them went down hard. Stephen was very good with that .45/70 Winchester buffalo gun. I heard horses screaming and a lot of dust hung in the blue-green evening air. There were more shots. I felt a blow to my waist above my hip. I fell again with Josie into some low brush at the creek bed's edge. Racing horses and shouting men filled the night air.

As I stood up, a heavy slap across my left shoulder knocked me sprawling again next to Josie into the brush. I got up, holding my side. The gnarly brush tore at my shirt. I pulled her into sitting up, then up across my good shoulder, and started down that creek bed. A rider less horse flew past me down the gulley. There was a dark stain on its neck that glistened in the brilliant moonlight, its reins trailing in the dust. I didn't want to leave, but Stephen had good judgement. I hoped that he could take care of himself. There were only two left.

The Hennesseys were a mean bunch. Old man Hennessey said he owned all of the valleys that networked off of the south fork. All the way from Baxter Ville up Wolf Creek Pass. The parks branched off the South Fork Rio Grande and wound their way between the surrounding peaks. They were beautiful flat parks with much grass and water—ideal for grazing cattle or sheep.

Old man Hennessey was called Palo Duro. It was Spanish for hard stick. He'd spent most of his youth near the Mexican border, mixed up in shady deals raiding and robbing back and forth across the border. He was a tall wiry old man, with a heavily wrinkled face that looked to have worn out two bodies. He was an unforgiving person and had raised his two sons with a heavy hand swinging a belt or a 'Birch.' One son left home very early and was said to be a gambler along the Mississippi. His name was Del Hennessey. Bret Hennessey was the youngest, an unpredictable youth—driven by violent rages that had left two men dead in the past year. One he had shot to pieces in a saloon quarrel. The other he had clubbed to death with his rifle barrel in an argument over a spot at the hitching rail. There was no formal law in remote places. In larger communities, citizens often became the law and would hang anyone for just a suspicion of skullduggery, some often innocent. Palo, as the old man was called, was the only one who could keep Bret Hennessey in line. It was done by fear. As Bret became older, his hatred of his father grew to enormous size and would one day override his fear of his father. On that day, Palo would die, assuming Bret stayed alive till then.

I don't know how long I had been running but it seemed a long time. My Levi's were full of dirt and my shirt was in tatters. I'd stumbled to my knees many times. It was harder getting to my feet each time. I was near the end of my strength. Josie was still out. The bullet burn across my left shoulder was throbbing and burning like fury. I knew there was a hole through my side, just above the hip bone. Draped over my right shoulder was my best friend, who had saved my life more than once. She was becoming more than just a best friend as time passed between us.

My name is Cullen Grafton. I am strong and have a furious will to survive, as do most. I do not easily let go of whatever I get a holt of. I finally paused in the arroyo, listening to the near sound of rapid water. The South Fork was near. I could no longer hear shouting and shooting. It was quiet. I moved over near a large boulder, carefully laid Josie in the grass at the creek bed's edge. I moved her hair from her face and felt for a pulse in her neck. I found it and listened for her breathing. It was not labored. There was no blood on her except her head. She was still unconscious. I sat down in the boulder's shadow and laid my head back. When I closed my eyes I wanted to go to sleep. I knew I'd lost a lot of blood and was near the end of my endurance.

I tore two patches from my ruined shirt, gingerly poked them against the holes in my side, and tied the ragged remains of my shirt around my waist to hold the patches in place. I was sweating heavily and light mist from my body drifted up around me in the crisp, clear, high mountain air. There was a nasty cut on Josie's head, It had stopped bleeding. I'd leaped from my horse as I saw Josie thrown from hers when it was shot from under her.

The moon was full and everything was lit like daylight. If the Hennesseys caught us in this arroyo we would be finished. I knew that I had to get us to the cave, and quickly. My strength was ebbing.

The sound of rough water told me that it was close. Once across, it was only yards to the cave and shelter.

I was lucky it was late spring, but still, the narrowing of the channel caused high, fast, treacherous water. Thinking about it made me conscious of my thirst. I could drink there. Have to get going.

I pushed myself up, reached to pull Josie across my shoulder again—and there he was—sitting on his horse not eight feet away. He had his rifle pointed at me. He held it in one hand. He was grinning. I could see his teeth in the moonlight. His hat was pushed back on his head and he was enjoying what he saw. "Grafton," he said. "I shot you twice and now I'm going to crush your head like an egg. I'm gonna enjoy the sound of it!"

Ken Waller was a rider with the Hennessey crew. He had a reputation for being mean and dangerous. I'd seen him around Baxter Ville the time or two we'd been there. He treated nearly everyone with contempt. I was wounded, unarmed, and appeared to be easy prey. He sat for another moment, then neatly flipped his carbine in the air, caught it by its short barrel—that he was a strong man was not in question. He dug his spurs into his mount, and down the bank they charged. His mount floundered as it met the bottom of the wash moving too fast. I'd waited for the last moment and with my quick anticipation—that I was known for—threw myself in front, grabbing the reins near the bit and with all of my weight jerked the floundering horse's head down and around. The horse's head followed me, and as Pa used to say, 'where the head goes the body will follow,' and so its knees folded and it came to a momentary stop, nearly lay on its side, on me, in the gravel, and Waller continued on without his horse. He landed in a tangle of legs, arms, dried sticks, and smooth river rocks, his rifle landing apart from him. His mount righted itself and bolted up the far bank past Waller. He came up quickly, staggering some. I was already moving toward him as he came off the ground. His hand came up with his pistol. My hand closed over the barrel and cylinder, blocking the cocked hammer. The flesh between my thumb and finger, scarred by a bullet in the showdown with the Stuart McGregor crew, was stabbed by the firing pen on the hammer as he pulled the trigger. I twisted the gun away while at the same time drawing and thrusting my knife up under his chin, through his mouth and tongue into his brain. He rose on toes as if trying to get away from it but it was past that. He hung there suspended for a moment on the knife point, on tippy-toes His eyes looking down at me. Blood emptied out of the wound and gushed down my arm. I jerked my knife free, not wanting to leave it in his skull as I'd done to Chief Grey Eyes. Down he went. His face looked startled. He lay in a heap. I'd killed before. Doing so was not a highlight of my life but it was another defining moment for me. I still had his pistol in my hand. I pulled the hammer back out of my hand and shoved it into my waistband. His horse had shied up the far bank, snorting and trotting away into a stand of aspen. Physically I was at the brink of the abyss. I slowly pulled Josie across my shoulder, staggering under her weight, and made for the sound of rushing water and the cave beyond.

I looked behind and around. I was still alone except for that pile of clothes once known as Ken Waller in the bottom of the dry wash. I thought of Stephen and was worried. I staggered off down the creek bed to the edge of white water.

Across this madness and up several yards was the cave, behind more brush and several boulders. I found a sturdy branch that I pulled free from between several rocks at the river's edge. I started to cross. I was too tired to be frightened.

The cold shock of it woke me up a bit. I drank a little, scooping water with one hand, holding the thick limb with my right arm draped across Josie's legs. I felt its cold energy moving through me. I forced myself to move. I tightened my grip on Josie and used the branch downstream, bracing against the rush of water and to steady me and my load, to keep from being swept away. I began crossing the madness of the swirling water. It sucked at my legs like a giant wet wrestler trying to pull me down. It ebbed and flowed, buffeted, battered, and pulled on me, making me flounder like a drunk. I went down to my knees a couple of times, found strength on the bottom, and came up, steaming and blowing like an old whale. A loud inhuman growl startled me until I realized it came from my own throat. I fought off the wet grappler, and at last, ever so slowly, staggered up the bank.

I lay Josie against a boulder. She was only a little wet. I held her head as she laid over on her side. I placed one of her hands between her head and the rocks.

I went to my knees, then lay there gasping for breath, dripping, half naked in the night air—nearly gone. The sheltered warmth of the cave and its cache of items lay only yards away. It may as well have been miles. Numbness closed in. The rocks and pebbles under my cheek turned into dot patterns as I stared blankly at them. A drop of water moved gracefully, pausing until its weight gave in to gravity and it dropped, 'splink,' onto a dry rock and was absorbed. I surrendered and followed the next drop and was absorbed into the numbing, ringing darkness that enfolded me in its cold wet arms and carried me away.

"When I came to," said Josie, "I found Cull lying on his stomach. I was afraid he was dead. A tattered corner of his shirt was held by his belt but strung out toward the water. There was an ugly, raw graze wound across his shoulder blade. I found two bullet holes in his waist. One a round hole the other the exit wound, a bit more ragged. I could hear him breathing. All of the wounds were free of dirt. A little blood was oozing from both holes. My pant legs were wet but the rest of me dry. He must have carried me across. I don't know how he got me here, wounded as he was."

"How did you get him into the cave," said Stephen through gritted teeth, while tying the rag—once Cull's shirt—over the bullet wound in his leg. "He weighs near two hundred pounds 'an you're, what, a hundred ten even as wet as you are?"

"I found a rope, a piece of canvas, and a blanket in the cave. I pinch-tied a smooth rock at a corner the canvas then rolled him onto the canvas, covered him with the blanket, then pulled on the rope over and over again inch by inch into the cave. It seemed to take forever. All the while there was a roaring in my head. I got a fire going. Cull's lips were blue. I feared he was going to die right there. I stripped him of his wet boots and clothes, then crawled under the blanket with him. He needed my warmth. He finally stopped shivering and I knew that he'd be OK. That's when you crawled into the cave... He's still out."

"...Who's still out? ...Josie, you OK?" said Cullen, now awake.

"I'm good Cull. You took good care of me. You've been out for quite a while."

"I need to get back to Stephen. There were too many of 'em!"

"There weren't enough of 'em to need the two of us... I see you handled Ken Waller. Someday you'll have to tell me how it happened. He was the only one that concerned me."

"You're here, Stephen! Thank heaven. You've been shot! ...I can't rightly recall what happened with Waller. All I remember is that I had to get Josie to the cave and then get back to you. We're in the cave, right?"

"We're all here. Safe and sound... until Palo Hennessey figures what has happened and comes a-lookin'."

"How'd you get me all the way here and across that killer water," said Josie.

"I don't remember anything except being chased by fear..."

"What do you remember?" she said.

"I remember you weighing a ton. You're gonna have to lose some weight, woman!"

"You hold it right there Mr. Cull. I weigh next to nothing compared to you. You were passed out. On that canvas you looked frozen stiff... it took me forever to pull you into this cave. Talk about weighing a ton! Then I had to lay on your cold wet body to get some warmth into it or you'd of died as an ice cycle."

"Where are my pants and my boots? ...You laid on top of me...? Now why can't I remember that of all things?"

"Well, I don't know about you couz, but if a woman like Josie ever was on top of me, I'd remember that even if I was more'n'half dead."

"...Don't you dare go there about my weight, Cullen Grafton! You know what I can do with my Colt!"

"Now hold on, the both of you. You're sounding like an old married couple, which you ain't... are you? ...You two just livin' in sin?" Stephen said with a grin.

"We aren't, not yet... and never will be if he follows that fool's trail he's on right now."

"OK, OK," Stephen said. "Let's eat some pemmican and have some coffee, from that tin box against the back wall. Then we have to get to Del Norte and face the Hennesseys. Better to take it to 'em than wait for 'em to get organize and bring it to us with his whole crew. I have two horses corralled at my soddi. One of you will have to ride double, whoever is the bluest can hang on to the other."

That's the sheriff's office but that ain't the sheriff. It's a youngster wearing a badge, thought Stephen as the trio enter Del Norte. What in hell is goin' on? A snot-nose squirt wearin' a badge—where is Sheriff Teal? This ain't right!

Deputy Sheriff Marcus Penny watched the three enter his town—temporarily his town—till Sheriff Teal returns from down on the South Fork.

The body found there, might have been a local killing dumped in the South Fork, hoping it would float down toward Alamosa and be their problem. ...Apparently a boot was caught between a couple of rocks, relocation did not happen.

The man in the lead was a stranger to him. His pant leg was showing blood. The second horse carried two—a youngster with a larger man with a bloody shirt and pant leg. Holding on to the youngster. They stopped at Doc Paulson's place, slowly dismounted, and limped in. I'll give 'em a couple of minutes then I'll get answers.

"Mornin', Doc. Looks like you've got some payin' customers. ...Been kinda quiet lately," said Deputy Penny.

"Deputy, if you're feelin' poorly, you'll have to wait. There are three ahead of you and gunshot ...Any word from Sheriff Teal? When'll he be back?"

"When he's thru investigatin'. Later today, I'm thinkin'.'"

"There's been a bit of trouble, deputy.

"Looks like the three of you've had an argument," said Penny.

"Deputy, just call me Stephen. We was paid a visit by Ken Waller and three of his partners. It was not a friendly visit. All four of 'em are dead out near my place, but not before they took a toll on us as you can see."

"Ken Waller, dead? Palo Hennessey won't be happy about that. Ken was his foreman, and a tough hard man. Palo seemed to care as much about Ken as his own son. How'd he die?"

"This here is my cousin Cullen Grafton and this young woman is Josie. Both from Nevadee. Cull took care of Wheeler. You'll have to get the story from him."

Cull gave a double take of the young deputy. "Your name is Penny?" said Cull.

"That's correct."

"I'm the sole survivor of a wagon train massacre by a tribe of Indians, west of here. Set up by a man I knew as Ben, didn't know his last name, and a man named Stewart McGregor and several of his crew. We had a blacksmith and his family with us. They were all killed during the raid. His name was Nathan Penny."

"...his wife's name Molly and their son named Zebulon?"

"The same."

"...Nathan was my uncle. This is terrible news. Tye, my brother, is gonna be some upset, and our pa. I'll get a letter off to Pa. I don't believe that Spit Ville has a telegraph. Tye should be here any day now."

"I'm very sorry about your uncle. He was a fine man and helpful when there was a need. I do not believe that they suffered greatly. My own wife and son were murdered. My daughter was taken but Josie, here, and I got her back and some payback."

"Pa, Tye and me will want to find this McGregor and whoever else and poison 'em with a lot of hot lead."

"You folks look me up and Sheriff Teal before you leave our fair town. Keep an eye out for the Hennesseys. The longer you are here, the more trouble we're gonna have. We have to protect our citizens—don't know how the Sheriff will want to handle this. The Hennesseys hang out at the Gold Dust Saloon. Tell me more about Nathan before you leave. I'll write my pa and let him know about his brother. I'll help find those responsible."

"That's not necessary, Deputy. We took care of it," said Josie. "Those rats killed my parents in a different slaughter. God knows how many other good people they murdered—all so they could steal and resell their possessions—they'll kill no one else—you have our word on it."

Cullen Grafton Part 5
The Gold Dust Saloon

"I haven't seen Waller. You seen him, Dusty?" said Palo.

"No boss, not since yesterdee. He was with them three hombres down from Jackson Hole, they was drinkin'. Ken said he'd have good news when they got back from a ride they was gonna take."

"Git back? Git back from where? ...I know... they went to get rid of that damn squatter up from Baxter Ville. I told him to wait on movin' that fiddle-footed squatter, off o' that park. I hear he's got a relative with him and a young woman. Ken'd better not be hurtin' no woman. I'll kill any two-footed critter, 'cept a woman. Any one of my men kill any woman and I'll hang 'em on the spot, and be damned quick about it. You keep that in mind, Dusty. Out here, woman is prize. ...I want you, Roy, Boil, and two others to fork your bronks out there and bring me back what you find. ...You find Waller alive, tell 'im to get his tail back here, an' quick ...Off with you now."

Through the batwing doors burst Chad Larkin, passed by Dusty on his way out. "Boss! Boss! I just saw that feller from the park you want to move out of there. He just rode into town with them other two. They're all bloodied up. Even the woman has a bloody bandage on her head. That Grafton fellow has a bloody leg and the other gent a bloody shirt and pant legs all the way to his knee. They're all at Doc Paulson's. That young fool deputy followed 'em into the Doc's."

"The Sheriff back yet?"

"Haven't seen him, Boss."

Don't you go getting uppity with that deputy—you hear me? You seen what he did to Tisdale. He'll walk all over you if you press him. He can't do nothin' serious without sheriff Teal. Go sit by the Doc's office and see if you can hear anything. Keep your eyes and ears open, an' your mouth shut. Now get!"

"Yeah, boss."

Palo looks to a nearby table where four rough looking men are talking. One of them he recognizes as Bob Tisdale. His face has purple blotches and scabs from having been in a fight, apparently with the new deputy sheriff, Marcus Penny. Tisdale is known as a tough man and it's a wonder there ain't no mark on the deputy. Apparently there is more to Penny beyond his youth. Palo nods to Berry Webber, sitting beside him. "Berry, see if you can find out about the three sitting with Tisdale. Buy 'em a beer, talk to 'em. I might want to hire them if push comes to shove with Grafton. If Grafton took care of Ken and two of his friends, Grafton might not be so easy to move off my land or get rid of. The larger determined force usually wins the day and that's gonna be us!"

Palo gazes into his beer and wonders where his oldest son, Del Hennessey might be. His last information was that Del was wanted for murder in Mississippi. Palo was worried about Bret, his youngest, who was becoming more of a problem. His thoughts were interrupted by Chad Larkin as he entered swiftly through the swinging doors. "Boss, that woman just passed out right there in the Doc's office. Somethin' about her head wound. They're preparing to come here, to seek you out. They are well armed. And some upset. Even the young woman has a pistol. They're gonna come here, lookin' for you. Those are not happy faces. What did Waller get us involved with and where are the boys? I seen 'em ride out of town."

"They've gone to find Waller and his Jackson Hole friends."

"Both of the men are wounded but not enough to slow 'em down. They'll be here in a couple o' minutes. I think they want your hide. That deputy is tagging along. There's only two of them an' three of us and only one stranger at the bar, never seen him before."

Tye did not see his brother Marcus as he entered town. He puts Summer (Smoke) Mellon up in the hotel and goes to the saloon, a good place to pick up local news. While looking for Marcus, he recognizes Tisdale, who looks to have been kicked by a couple of mules, both named Marcus Penny. He's not surprised because growing up with Marcus he'd had his share of brotherly 'scuffles' and nearly lost all of them even though he was older, stronger, and more experienced. Sitting next to Tisdale is the man he's been hoping to find, Farney Gibbon. Tye keeps his sombrero on and tilted low as he sips his beer. He also sees the two who tried to force him to buy them drinks, the Bowler-hat and his partner Chucky, both sitting with Farney. They appeared as ornery as ever.

Through the batwing doors walk two men, in bloody clothes. Following them is Marcus his brother wearing a lawman's badge. Things keep getting more interesting, he thinks. Marcus walks to the opposite end of the bar, and leans against it, not noticing his brother Tye at the other end.

Marcus is watching the two bloodied men as they approach a wrinkled old man, at a table near Tisdale's. The old man's face is deeply furrowed; it looks to have been ran over by several heavily loaded wagons crisscrossing over it. Tension springs to life. Marcus pushes away from the bar.

Tye senses movement a little to his right. A quick glance reveals a young woman dressed in men's clothes. She'd entered through the back door. At her waist is a Colt Thunderer pistol behind her belt. Her head is bandaged.

The focus of Tisdale' and Mr. Wrinkles is on the two bloodied men.

"The next time, Palo, have guts enough to ride with the murdering crew you sent to move me from the land I have filed on with the capitol.

This paper from them," Stephen says, waving the document at the old man, "says that I own that park and the park west of there. ...Pick up your dead and keep off my land! When Sheriff Teal returns I'm filing charges of attempted murder. Deputy Penny here has confirmed that what I've said is true."

"That land is mine you're a damn squatter. I claimed all of my land before there was a capital—before you were out of diapers. ...I did not send Ken Waller to move you. He did that on his own. If I'd planned it, you and your friends would not be standing—you'd be dead 'cept for that woman, wherever she is."

At Tisdale's table, Bowler-hat nudges Farney and nods toward Tye Penny at the bar. "That's the fella you said knows where the gold is buried. I knowed that hat because he cut me with it." Farney looks and recognizes Tye Penny under the sombrero. He knows where my gold is 'cause he buried it his own self, Farney thinks to himself. Then whispers, "Do not kill him."

Palo stands, knocking his chair over, and putting a hand to his Colt.

"That woman is right here!" Josie said, stepping from the end of the bar, hand on the bird's-head grip of her Colt Thunderer, wondering which of the two images of the old man she should shoot. The noise in her head is making her feel ill, like she needs to go to sleep for a while.

Cullen Grafton Part 6
Tye Penny Six weeks earlier

Somewhere on the west slope of the Sangre De Cristo mountains, above the The Great Sand Dunes and east of Del Norte. Tye Penny, on his way to join up with his brother Marcus, stops for the night on a small bench tucked against the mountain's slope. He finds a slab of rock—a reflective surface for his fire—leaning against a cluster of boulders. The slab appears to have been moved to one side for some reason. He is curious and pushes it aside, discovering a cave with a very small opening.

More to come

JULES

Twenty minutes of repressed horror.

JULES KNELT QUIETLY AGAINST THE WALL IN THE FAST-FADING LIGHT. HE HAD GENtly pushed the spindly hall table out of the way and was looking at a circuit box located a few inches off the floor. There was a pleasant, knowing smile on his face. He wore coveralls and a fleece watch cap. Very thin leather gloves covered the long, tapered, artistic fingers of a musician. Running shoes covered his feet. His appearance was so plain as to be nearly invisible. His persona was unmemorable, unimposing, boring, unexciting, bland, even insipid—but as a thief, by his peers, he was known as 'The Shadow's shadow.'

The beautiful old farmhouse was over a hundred and fifty years old and had been in the Eastman family the whole time. It was constructed of massive, native stone, covered with multicolored lichen. Many very strong arms had done the work. A sculptor's eye and a painter's heart had guided those arms and their fingers.

The ground-floor rooms had been built off of a long main hallway that traversed the depth of the house. The hall was wide and spacious, with twelve-foot ceilings. The ceiling and upper walls were finished eggshell white providing a wonderful contrast to the half-height wall panels in oak and cherry. Oak, old and waxy, framed the windows and entryway. Heavy oaken stairs led to the second and third floors. Opposite the stairway were two 'pocket' doors, opening into a cavernous and comfortable living room. Past the stairs were three swinging doors. The door on the right led to the dining room. The door on the left entranced the den. And at the end of the hall was the kitchen door. The kitchen extended across the width of the house, with entry doors into the den at one end and the dining room at the other end.

The swing mechanisms of these heavy doors were well-balanced, oiled, and moved in complete silence. Much attention and expense had been paid to maintaining and upgrading the details of the old family estate. The grounds were looked after and maintained by a groundskeeper and an assistant. The interior was attended to by a male housekeeper and his wife. The pair had the weekend off as the Eastman's were in Europe.

Mr. Eastman operated a very successful, third-generation printing business. Mrs. Eastman loved diamond jewelry. Both had assembled the collection over many years. It contained old and valuable pieces. Both delighted in their large collection. They also possessed a fondness for cats... and other nocturnals.

Jules read about the Formers and their "Museum quality" Jewelry collection and their beautiful estate in a local Sunday newspaper. Most of the collection was kept in safe deposit vaults. Many pieces were on loan to museums. Jules was sure that a few trinkets were kept around the house, to be worn, and Jules only wanted a few of them.

Jules hooked a gloved finger into the ring of the fuse box door, illuminated by a narrow-beamed penlight clenched between his teeth, and pulled the door open. He considered the fuses in the faceplate. He suspected this was a dummy electric box. He had noticed the unusual location of the box in the photograph of the couple in the Sunday paper. He grabbed two of the fuses and pulled vigorously. The entire panel slid out. No wires were attached. Carefully laying it aside, he reached into the large cavity, felt around, and pulled out a metal cash box. Then it happened. He heard gates close over the front door and similar noises coming from windows throughout the house. After a full minute of this, all was again quiet. Perspiration dampened his face. A very deep claustrophobic feeling of being trapped and smothered flooded through him. He panicked internally. With effort he let go of the feeling. His every sense was alert.

He reached back into the cavity where the cash box had been and felt around. The floor of the opening depressed ever so slightly. A pressure switch had opened when he had removed the cash box. This triggered a relay operating gates that closed off all exits. He turned off his penlight.

He remained still. He was sure an alarm had been transmitted to a security office or the police department. He estimated he had ten minutes before the police or security officers arrived... maybe less. It was a very large house though, and there would be many hiding places. Jules was good at improvising.

He remained against the wall in the enclosing darkness. He took a moment to admire the cleverness of the trap, but still there was a point in his stomach, just below the surface, that fought against blind panic. Jules pursued his avocation without malice toward his victims. He knew the risks. All other forms of crime were abhorrent to him. He was very careful about what he stole and from whom.

It was at this point that he heard, drifting down from upstairs, the sound of a noisy door being opened very slowly. That door was not well maintained. If designed to create panic, it worked—angst sent a wave of goose bumps up his neck and into his scalp. All was quiet for a short period. With relief, he ruled out attack dogs. He quickly opened the cash box, withdrew a small, heavy sack, and pushed it into a pocket of his coveralls. Jules replaced the cash box, reset the fuse plate, hoping the switch would be reset and gratings opened—fat chance! He straightened the table and moved back down the main hall into the kitchen, leaving its hall door open. Steel gates had closed across his entry window. He checked the other windows and the back door. All were tightly sealed. He was trapped!

He put his back to the wall near the door and slid down into a squat. He vacantly watched the second hand slowly move across the tritium-lit watch face on his wrist. He was so flummoxed he forgot his extinguished penlight was still clenched in his mouth. He put it in a pocket.

He stood up and walked to the door that led from the kitchen, down into the basement. He opened it. It was very dark down there. The thought of going to the basement unsettled him. Once down there, he felt he would be trapped, unable to move around. He was not familiar with the floor plan of the basement. The strong and familiar odor of cats drifted to him from the blackness. He did not like cats and they always seemed to sense his dislike. He had bad memories of cats from his childhood.

He knew instinctively that he must keep to open places or at least to familiar ground where movement was possible. He took a gamble and flipped the light switch on the wall leading down into the basement. No lights! Why keep intruders in the dark? Indeed, why not?

Now he heard creaking from the hall stairs. Leaving the basement door ajar he opened the kitchen-to-hall door a crack and looked down the darkening hall toward the staircase and the front door. Something was coming down the stairs. The fact that it was not dogs gave little comfort because whatever was coming down was big. He had climbed to the second-floor landing upon entering the house, checking for lights to make sure no one was awake up there.

Those stairs had made no noise under his weight. All had been silent and dark. Whatever was coming down was very heavy.

Silently he pushed into the dining room from the kitchen. The dining room was a very large room filled with a long, heavy, walnut dining table and chairs. There were enough chairs for twenty guests and the chairs lined three walls. Across one wall was a bank of doors that opened onto the back deck. Steel accordion gates were drawn across the doors. There was no chance of escaping here either. The door exiting to the hall was directly across from the study. The third door opposite the kitchen door lead to the living room.

He moved back to the kitchen/hall doorway. Sounds were still coming down the hall stairs. It, whatever It was, seemed in no hurry. It was taking one step at a time. Jules had been certain the house was empty!

Yet here he was, trapped with something or someone coming after him. Why was It taking so long to get down the stairs? Its lack of hurry annoyed and frightened him. Daylight was completely gone now. Darkness would not be to his advantage. He stood in the doorway looking toward the stairway, waiting...

A very large, dark hulk eased around the banister and moved into the hallway. Details were impossible, but it was incredibly large, well over six feet and weighing at least three hundred pounds. It seemed to fill the hallway. It was not sluggish in its movements. Had it not been for its great weight, its presence would have been discovered too late. Its stillness and light movements gave it a supernatural air. It projected an air of raw, massive power and sensitivity. The thing seemed to be probing the darkness. Jules felt it searching for him at the end of the hall. Jules stood absolutely still, only a sliver of his face and one eye exposed from the doorway.

Jules could hear blood pulsing in his ears. He felt his face flush. He was breathing through his mouth, fearing that breath inhaled through narrow nasal passages might be heard—he wanted to be away from this place! He began to hope the police would arrive and deliver him from what was becoming a living nightmare. He had a hunch, however, that they would not be coming to his rescue anytime soon.

The neckless hulk turned slightly, probing each part of the hall, searching for the invader. It turned back again toward Jules. Jules's eyes opened wide as he experienced the subtle contact. They both moved simultaneously. It moved more quickly, now toward Jules. Jules sped for the door leading from the dining room to the living room. He blew through this door into the spacious living room. The door closed behind him. He hurdled a low coffee table, then a couch, and drew up at the doorway between the living room and the hallway. His heart was racing with the exertion, excitement, and fear. The 'pocket' doors were retracted into the walls.

Directly out in the hall was the entryway for the front door and the stairs, down which that thing had come.

Jules peered down the hall. The hall was empty. Jules was in his middle thirties. He was slender and wiry… built like a runner. He was agile and well-coordinated, quick, and very alert. He had moved very fast. And for its size, It had moved incredibly fast too. Jules concentrated on the dining room door through which he had just come.

Jules was perspiring. He wondered how long he could keep ahead of it. Going upstairs only flickered across his mind. Again, an unfamiliar floor plan restrained him. He was afraid of being trapped. Deep inside, he hoped that the Calvary in blue would arrive in time to save him. A part of him rejected this fantasy. His fantasy mind was being forced to shut down. Strangely, he was beginning to experience a faint sense of elation and excitement in this night-mare turned real. How long could he keep going 'round and 'round without making a mistake or running out of gas? The night was just beginning. Should he survive the night, how could he possibly survive at daybreak?

Jules half felt, half saw movement at the dining room door, and he moved quickly down the hall and into the den, across from the dining room. His mind was instantly filled with absurd scenes of the pathetically frail, comedic hero being chased from door to door, around and about, by an enraged behemoth, as in the early silent films. Part of him was laughing hysterically at the absurdity of it, and partly crying, because in the end he would lose. He was also thrilled by this mortal challenge.

The den was dark and smelled strongly of furniture polish and leather. Jules groped around its perimeter, having forgotten about his penlight, trying to locate the entrance to the kitchen. He found it. It was locked! He faced back toward the door he had just entered. He felt it beginning to open. His hand found the latch and turned it. He squeezed through and into the kitchen. As he sped past the still-opened basement door, he threw it open with force, so it hit the wall with a bang. At the same time, he slid beneath the kitchen table. Under the table he crouched, not moving, not breathing, not thinking… not being at all, just being a shadow's shadow. This stillness or quietude was so developed in Jules that had the Eastmans walked down their hallway earlier, while he was at the fuse box, he might have gone unnoticed.

In the gloom, from under the table, back against the wall of the kitchen, he saw heavy legs appear not ten feet from him, in front of the opening to the basement. The basement door was still moving slightly from being slammed against the wall.

It put It's hands on the door frame, ducked, and leaned down into the darkness of the basement, trying to confirm that Jules had gone down.

No part of Jules moved except the pulsing of his heart. There were no sounds except the rush of blood past his ears and the faint white noise there. He found that he was holding his breath. He opened his mouth wide and exhaled slowly and silently, fearful that the sound of his breath would reach sensitive ears… if there were ears connected to that, thing. He inhaled deeply and remained silent and still. It moved to the dining room door, hesitated, then moved back to the basement opening and stood there for a moment.

Very slowly, It eased down into that black hole. Once It was swallowed by the blackness of the basement, Jules slipped from under the table in one fluid movement and flew once again through the door leading into the dining room. Out of the corner of his eye he saw a thick appendage reaching out from the total blackness of the basement. He had nearly waited too long to make his move.

Once in the dining room, he slid across the dining tabletop and burst through into the living room again. As he passed into the living room, he dove beneath the low coffee table and lay there on his stomach, his heart racing and hammering against his ribs. The penlight came out of his breast pocket and rolled across the floor toward the hallway door. The door through which he had just come opened a moment later. It entered smoothly and moved to the hallway opening. It hesitated, standing in the doorway, as Jules had done on the first round, looking and listening, trying to sense which way Jules had gone. It nudged the penlight that was at the door. It picked up the light.

Jules did not move. He did not think. He closed his eyes. He knew truly that he could not keep this up. How many times could he go around and not get caught? Then he thought of the basement. Maybe there was a hiding space there or a way to be lost among the cats. It was a chance. The basement might be the place to make a stand. At least it would be pitch black down there. A handicap for both of them? The presence of the cats might add to the confusion of that thing's radar. Even in the morning there would be darkness there. He might even find a weapon of some sort that could be used against that, that, whatever that is. The thought of making a stand made Jules feel better. He was up against the wall now and he felt elation at the idea of finishing this thing off, one way or another. Jules peeked at the shape in the doorway. It was just standing and listening. Jules had to get to the basement. Finally, maybe feeling the tension also, It moved into the hallway and its darker-than-dark cloaked shape disappeared.

Jules crawled soundlessly from under the table back into the dining room. Still on hands and knees, he skirted the table and made for the kitchen door. He was glad for the silence of the swinging doors. He pulled it in toward him and peered into the kitchen. It was empty... as far as he could see. The hair on his neck stood up. He took his chance and eased into the kitchen, the door moving air as it closed behind him. He moved, still on hands and knees, to the basement opening.

Jules sat on the jamb with his legs extending into the blackness of the basement. Something brushed against his legs. Jules tensed and shivered. He instinctively put a hand across his mouth to stifle a wild scream wanting out. Across his lap crawled a white cat, then another and another. They purred as they entered the kitchen, calm and comfortable as could be. Jules's heart began beating again. He drew in a lungful of cat air. He felt weightless. He sat for another moment, then inched down into the black hole of the basement. The stairs were not carpeted. They went straight down and were free from clutter.

Jules sat on the bottom steps waiting for his eyes to adjust to the darkness, but they did not. There was a cluster of three red lights across from him. Jules crawled over to them. He was certain they were circuit lights for the electrical gadgetry that had trapped him. He'd been a fool not to secure his penlight. Beneath the lights he found a small table which gave him an idea. He carried the table back to the stairs. He placed the table on its side about midway up the steps, a little surprise for his pursuer.

He returned to the three lights. As he was following the wall, he tripped over several boxes that he could not see. Heedless now of making noises, he moved on and found a second set of stairs leading up. He mentally crossed his fingers and moved up the stairs. Part way up he smelled fresh air flowing down to him. Simultaneously he heard heavy movement coming down the other stairs. Then there was the sound of It stepping on or through the table-surprise he had placed on the steps, followed by a moment of silence during which the enormous being hung suspended and then crashed down the stars with a deafening sound that seemed to shake the entire basement, maybe the whole house!

At the top of the cellar's exit stairs, Jules found a locked double door. He quickly ran his hands over the surface of the door. At the bottom of the door was an opening covered by a hinged flap. The opening was nearly fourteen inches square, perfect for allowing the cats to come and go.

In only a moment or two, Jules had his arm, head, and the rest of his thin body through the opening and at last stood outside the house in the quiet, fresh, beautiful night air.

He looked around, nearly unable to believe his good fortune. He was out! It had all happened so fast, about twenty minutes of near-blind panic. He stood there, inhaling freedom!

A noise at the cat entrance brought him back. A thick arm reached out from the small opening, groped around, clutched at—and caught only—the night air.

Jules watched for a moment, amused yet respectful. He reached into his pocket and withdrew the bag he had taken from the cash box. He tested the weight of the bag in his gloved hand, frowned slightly, then holding the bag by its string tie, lowered the bag to the huge groping hand. It caught the bag, held it for a moment, and then quickly pulled back into the basement. Both deserved a reward for the chase—Jules his freedom and that thing, the swag.

Jules grinned and began running toward the front part of the property and the line of trees that blocked the house from the street. He experienced enormous elation and energy. The fresh night air felt wonderful against his sweat-dampened skin and blew through his black hair—somewhere during his trek he'd lost his cap. He felt he could run forever. He was light, free, and alive! He looked back to the spot where he had emerged from the basement door. He scanned the huge, shuttered estate. A shudder ran through him. All was quiet, quite still, and still dark.

The End

AN EPIPHANY

Holy-Ground

SHE IS LYING BENEATH THE SOFT WHITE SHEET. HER NAME IS MARCI. I'VE KNOWN her for a short time, though it seems to me that I have known her for lifetimes. It's the same for her. We talked for hours over coffee in the café near my home.

Of the women I've known, Marci is without doubt the most beautiful of all, and not just physically. Her short walnut-colored hair, nearly black, contains strands of red and gold highlights. Her olive-toned skin is smooth and clear. Her eyes are as dark as her hair, her lips are full, and her cheekbones and chin are distinctive and even. The slight gap between her two front teeth, while noticeable, lends a sensual and open quality to her face.

I am in awe of this stunning creature; this intelligent, sensitive yet incredibly strong person, lying beside me, sleeping, while my sperm swims toward the possible fulfillment of all our mutual destinies, by penetrating and fertilizing an egg within her, as I have penetrated her body with my own.

It also comes to mind, and from where, I know not, the realization that there exists within her, a subtle, yet powerful and unique attribute not found in any male within our species, or the male of any species.

Within the body of this woman, the physical items—egg and then sperm deposited by this male—come together, and in that collision, another individual might join the 'free-will party' on this planet.

In that occupied chamber, warm, fertile vault, a spirit, a soul or two, comes from a realm beyond our sight, beyond our physical reach and measure, even beyond nearly everyone's conscious awareness—to animate this possible new person. This then is how I have come to see a woman and her body as holy ground. A spirit, a soul moves all our bodies. At conception it joins with the fetus in the female's body. When a body is old or damaged beyond repair, the animating force, the soul, leaves as the body dies, taking with it everything, I mean everything that individual experienced during its lifetime—the good, the bad, and the ugly. In the case of infant death nothing much at all is written.

The term soulmate comes to mind. If soulmates exist, this relationship is surely that—our recognition was mutually instantaneous. It occurred more quickly than a millisecond and we'd not met until that thunderous moment a few hours ago.

I believe one catalyst to this epiphany is finding one's soulmate. Short of finding that mate, the sexual act is the way we continue our species, and so it is with all lifeforms. In the proper setting, our bodies are wonderful playgrounds, even as the knowledge of the holy ground is obscured—all of these facts remain. Violating this sacred area for any reason is not recommended because at some point, this lifetime or in the next, balance will be reestablished.

What defines a soulmate? It is my belief that it is, at the soul's level, two individuals that have been involved together over several lifetimes and thus the instantaneous recognition, "old souls," beyond and before any current physical meeting.

Every part of her body that I caressed with fingertips and lips caused her to tremble in ecstasy. I explored her and found as much excitement and satisfaction in her reaction to my ministrations as I did climaxing with her.

We were spent. She has drifted off and sleeps as I, not far behind, marvel at the beat of her heart pulsing in her neck, the slow steady rising and falling of her breathing. The ecstasy of the copulative act, the release, the never-ending desire for this act regardless of age.

It is in this moment of satiated quietude, where all of my mental, internal noise has ceased, allowing insight to become clear, that this woman's body is indeed holy ground. Not just Marci's body, but every woman's body is holy ground, even though not every woman is conscious of this singularity. I find it difficult to understand how so few of us have experienced and embraced this epiphany. The thought also comes to mind that this realization could not be made clear to me, until multiple components of my neural wiring, including my heart, have become quiet enough to recognize this monumental pip of truth I now possess, among the countless numbers of pips, throughout the universe yet to be known.

Many believe and understand that the human body is created, in all of its magical complexities, by the force known by many names. I believe that force is not necessarily an individual, but maybe some formless, nebulous body of omniscient, omnipotent, and creative power not necessarily bound by or confined in a physical form, but then again, at times, maybe She is. If She has physical form, She has to be on this physical planet or some other planet. We see God as a likeness of ourselves because it is easier to relate to that igniter of ultimate creative and divine power present in each atom of our own physical bodies. And so—Michelangelo depicted God as a wise, bearded human on the Sistine Chapel ceiling, reaching across time and space to impart life and divine potential to mortal man, in "The Creation of Adam." Does that mean Michelangelo got it wrong—that in order for Adam to be created, that the creator could have been depicted a woman, wise and fertile, creating Adam? Such an image would give credence to both sexes. Is not a female equally possessed of wisdom more capable of Creation than a male, but then, what is the one without the other?

Procreation is accompanied by a taste of ecstasy. Maybe that same emotional release accompanies each of us after the moment of death—the surrender of all earthly concerns, our rebirth from our physical state back to spirit. Who can say it is not so? Might not a taste of ecstasy, surround the entire process, from beginning to end?

She adjusts her sleeping position and one smooth, tanned leg slides from beneath the sheet. It is magnificent, delightfully tapered, and so lovely, I cannot resist. I trail a light, loving touch from her knee up to where her thigh disappears beneath the sheet. She opens her sleepy eyes and smiles her beautiful smile at me. Her black eyes, languid with sleep, recognize me. Her wonderful chestnut hair is streaked across her forehead. She reaches and guides me back into her. I am powerless to resist and would not, if I could. We have been created for each other, just for this lifetime.

Of course, everything we possess during this lifetime is ours temporarily. I know that this is only my half of the story. Her half, just as relative, just as pertinent, just as powerful as mine, is far above my understanding. Maybe this woman already, in some way, understands her honored place, and my discovering it is why she is here and, with her help, this is just one more pip in my enlightenment.

The End

SYLVIA AND TRILLYA

SYLVIA SERVED THE LAST CUSTOMER IN THE BAR. SHE PLACED HIS BEER IN FRONT OF him. His eyes were not on hers. He was looking at her breasts and continued looking as she picked up his two dollars and turned away. She felt his eyes on her ass as she walked back to the bar and Bill. A quick glance sees him swallowing a mouthful of beer then staring at the beer in the heavy glass stein.

He'd come in alone near closing time.

"Drink up, friend. The bar's closed in five," said Bill Goodman, owner of the bar.

He swallowed the remainder of the beer and asked, "Mind if I hit the head?"

"Okay, but make it quick."

Most customers just wanted to have a drink with their friends, enjoy her friendly smile and some friendly banter, then be on their way. But there were always a few who made her skin crawl slightly. But that was bar work for you. No point in getting offended.

In spite of the last customer, she considered how lucky she'd been to land this job. Today was the end of her first week at The Bitter Root. She'd swapped shifts with Mitzi tonight. Now she was pooped and just wanted to put her feet up and spend some quiet time with her 15-year-old daughter, Trillya, and sleep in on Sunday.

Bill was the new owner, a generous and considerate boss. He collected some of the tips for the two women who worked separate times and gave the gratuities to each at the bar's closing or their end of shift.

George Blake, full time bartender and bouncer, known locally as the 'trash hauler,' and Larry Sims, 20% owner, left the bar 20 minutes earlier. George Blake came with the bar and was part of the sales agreement. Larry Sims was

Bill's best friend. He'd retired from the Army having served 22 years in service of the country. He and Bill had seen combat together and become fast friends. Larry was like the older brother Bill never had. Larry received a portion of the profits and could handle every operation of the bar. To Bill's mind, the bar was becoming a family affair.

Sylvia considered all of this as she counted her tips. She was pleased. It was a small but supportive and pleasant group she worked with. "Thank you," she said to Bill, and dropped the cash and change into her shoulder bag. She took her coat from the coat rack by the door that led to the kitchen and office.

Bill stepped from behind the bar and walked Sylvia to the door. "See you Monday at eleven."

She nodded. "Good night."

He smiled, nodded, and closed the door after her and switched the neon sign from green open to red closed.

The last customer exited the restroom. Bill locked the door after him, emptied the register, placed the money in a bank deposit bag, and put the bag in the office safe. He would do the deposit slip in the morning. He returned to doing a partial clean up. He still favored his left hip; there was pain and stiffness. He'd adopted a limp. He recalled the shooting and shook his head. As an Army Ranger, he'd been in combat many times and suffered not the smallest scratch. But back home in his second career as a police officer with the local police force, a drunk, robbing a convenience store, had tossed a shot at him without even aiming. It was a fluke 'hail Mary' that had hit Bill and damaged his hip. As Bill was falling, he'd scored a head shot on the assailant. He'd always been a good shot, but the head shot had been a fluke also.

When he was released from the hospital, he'd declined a temporary desk job at the precinct. He'd had enough of struggling against bad people as a major line of work. However, his future entrepreneurship would have its moments.

He'd saved much of his pay while in the Army and as a police officer, and he had a comfortable sum inherited from his parents.

Bill had known the previous owner of the bar. He'd died of a heart attack, and his wife wanted out from under the bar; wanted it sold and quickly.

She was appreciative of the local police officers. Their quick response over the years, breaking up fights and brawls, had added to her husband's longevity. She was grateful that she could sell it to a veteran and former police officer who wanted to work the bar and promised not to change its name or its 'trash hauler.'

Sylvia headed for her Honda Civic. She placed her bag and jacket on the hood to dig her keys from the front pocket of her jacket and was about to unlock the door when she heard steps crunching gravel behind her. She glanced back and frowned, her short black hair brushing her shoulders. The solitary beer-drinking boob-ogler was walking toward her. He was about six feet tall and a little on the heavy side. His hair was dark. His arms were covered with thicker, dark hair. He wore tan cargo pants and a green, short-sleeved shirt. He had a grin on his face. The grin was not kindly.

He stopped several feet from her.

"Whatever you need," she said, "I'm sure Bill can help you if you have a problem."

"No, there's no problem here. I just wanna talk to you for a minute," he said, looking her over. "I'm new in town and don't know anyone. I was hopin' we could get to know each other. My name's Jerry."

"Look, ah, Jerry, it's been a long day. I'm tired and talked out. Besides, I don't socialize after hours with Bill's customers." She turned and stuck the key in the door lock hoping that was the end of the conversation.

It wasn't. "Now that's not being very neighborly. You work in a bar. You must like men."

"What I like," she said while unlocking the door, "is putting food on the table for my daughter and a roof over our heads." She started to turn to face him down but didn't make it. He reached out with both hands and grabbed her by the back of the neck and forced his body against hers against the side of the Honda, pinning her there and choking her. She struggled to breathe. She could feel his erection pressed against her butt. She tried to scream but the only sound that came out of her mouth was a hoarse squawk.

There were no other automobiles in the lot. Bill lived above the bar in one of the two apartments. He would be in the small kitchen at the rear of the bar straightening up for Monday. She tried to push away from the Honda but could not. She tried to move her legs but she had no leverage. He was choking her and pressing against her. She was running out of air and beginning to see spots before her eyes. Her lungs seemed on fire.

He stopped choking her and spun her around and leaned his weight against her, bending her back against the contour of the Honda. She still had no leverage. His breath smelled sour and of beer.

"Hold still, bitch, and stop fightin'! You're gonna enjoy this same as me. Just relax and stop fightin' me!" He slapped her across the mouth, cutting her lips against her teeth. She was stunned for a moment. He began choking her again into submission. She was floundering, slapping the Honda, trying to catch her purse. Her lungs were screaming for air.

In a strangled voice, she croaked, "Stop, you're killing me!"

He relaxed his grip on her throat. "Try to scream again and I'll squeeze your neck till your head explodes, and then I'll fuck you till you wake up and decide to enjoy it."

"You guys are all the same," she said with great difficulty, hoping for time and distraction, praying that someone might come by. "It's all about your gettin' off."

He eased off choking her. She rubbed her throat and took some deep breaths. She tried to inch closer to her bag. He watched her closely for any crap she might pull. He kept her against the car. You're not goin' anywhere," he said.

He was still pressed tight against her. His breath was foul and his body odor was strong.

"You don't think we like fucking, too?" she said. "Why ruin a good thing? Let's get to know each other a little so we can both enjoy it. Women need warming up, a little space. Time to anticipate, to consider everything leading up to the main deal—with a real man giving us what we need in the worst way." She was talking quickly and trying to suck in as much air as possible. "I spent most of the day wantin' someone like you to give it to me real good."

He smiled to himself; he knew he'd been right about her. He watched her face and saw what he wanted to see. A beautiful, full-breasted, hot woman who wanted to fuck too. He pulled her face to his and kissed her, sticking his tongue into her mouth. Out of reflex, she bit down on his tongue, hard. He drew back, anger darkening his face, and excitement too.

"Not here!" she said, putting a hand against his chest. I have to work here! I don't want anyone happening by to see what we're doing. You have a car?"

"No."

"We can use mine, only not here, a few blocks from here. Okay?"

"You screwing with me, poon?"

"No! You haven't been listening with your ears."

She could feel that he was ready now. He didn't want conversation, all he wanted was to be inside her, and now. He forced her back against the car and with both hands, in one motion, pulled her dress up, grabbed her panties, and yanked them down below her knees, his fingernails scratching her hips and thighs. He had her by the throat again. With his left hand, he smacked her again, catching the corner of her eye and sending blood down her cheek and onto her blouse.

He was too strong for her. She was still being bent backwards against the Honda. Her flailing arms had no effect. Her knees buckled, but he held her up against the Honda. With his left foot, he forced her panties down around her ankles, scratching her shins with his shoes. She still had no leverage and now her panties bound her legs. With his right hand, he unzipped his fly, loosed his belt and the top button of his pants that dropped to his ankles. He pulled his boxers over and down from his erection.

Now she was frantic, floundering, struggling against him for all her worth. He grabbed her breast with his right hand and continued choking her with his left even as he attempted to kiss her again. She turned her head away. This infuriated him. She had said the things he wanted to hear. "Every word from your mouth is bullshit!" He squeezed her throat tighter.

In a strangled voice, "Stop choking me! I want it as badly as you. Let's both enjoy it. Choking me is not the way!" He released her throat.

"You still fucking with me!"

"No, I'm not! I want to fuck, but not if you're going to choke me to death. Do you have a condom?"

"See, that's what I mean. I don't need no fuckin' condom!"

"You don't know what shit I've been into. And where have you been? I have one here in my bag." She had managed to inch closer to her bag.

He began choking her again to shut her up. He didn't need no protection.

Her right hand finally found her purse and the Spyderco knife clipped to an outside pocket. She pulled it from the pocket and thumbed it open quickly. He was kissing at her mouth again while choking her.

She was again struggling to breathe. She was on the verge of passing out. She knew that if she went down, it was all over. Her lips felt numb. He forced a knee between her legs and her left shoe came off and her foot came free of her panties. He pushed her further up and back against the Honda, pulling her dress to her waist and shoving his erection up against her. With a desperate swipe of her knife over the top of his arm and the hand that was squeezing her breast, she sliced the lobe from his left ear. The blade opened his neck under his jaw, slicing through his Adam's apple and deeply opening the muscle of his right shoulder.

He staggered back from her, like a man in leg irons. His pants binding his ankles. His erection was framed by the bottom halves of his green shirt like an actor peeking between stage curtains at the end of a bad play, wondering where the audience had gone. He had a hand to his throat. His eyes were wide with shock. He shook his head as though he couldn't believe what she'd done. She'd lied! He felt confused. She worked in a damned bar, after all! Did he deserve this? He knew he was in trouble.

She pushed away from the Honda, taking in gulps of air, and with her bare foot, kicked him hard between the legs and all of him went down. Blood was already jetting from his throat. She pulled her panties up and, with one shoe off, ran for the front door of the bar. He reached a hand out to her as she passed him. She swatted it away with the knife.

With the bloodied knife still clutched in her fist, she hammered wildly on the door.

A half minute later, Bill flung open the door. Taking one look at her and the knife, he pulled his .38 from the holster at the small of his back and ran, limping toward the thrashing heap on the ground by her Honda.

Sylvia, trembling with adrenalin and still trying to suck air through her raw throat, dropped her purse on the ground by the door. Her trembling hands found her cell phone and pushed the emergency speed dial number.

The police sergeant, Ron Determan from Bill's former precinct, arrived with an ambulance in tow. Bill explained what he thought had occurred as a female EMT wiped away blood and examined the bruises on Sylvia's neck and face. Sylvia's lips and cheeks were scuffed and swelling where she had been smacked. She had difficulty swallowing. A butterfly bandage closed the small cut at the corner of her eye. The EMT's partner was trying to save the life of her attacker: Jerry Underhill, according to his ID.

"We need to get you to the emergency room," said Determen.

She refused at first, then changed her mind when she was told her attacker had bled to death.

"We have to photograph and formally document your injuries. And his," he said nodding toward her dead assailant. "We need to establish the attempted rape and your defense against it since there are no witnesses." He placed the knife in an evidence bag and sealed it.

Bill followed the ambulance to the hospital.

The medical lab found male secretions on her inner thigh where the attacker had pushed his erection against her. Sylvia was examined. There had been no penetration. Evidence was collected by a female police officer with a nurse present, and her bruises, scratched hips, thighs, and shins photographed, and all legal documents completed.

No charges were brought against her.

Mr. Underhill, her attacker, had a previous assault charge in an adjacent town. The charge had been dropped.

Bill walked into the examination room. Sylvia was dressed and ready to leave. She was standing next to the examination table with her head and shoulders slouched in exhaustion and despair. She looked up when he came in. He held out his arms and they hugged. Now this is a fighter, not a passive, willing victim, he thought, and Larry would be proud of her, and George also. This could cement my family.

"Sit in the wheelchair. The nurse will wheel you to the entrance. I'll drive you home. Tomorrow we'll get your Honda to you and see that your daughter gets to school if she's up to it."

She and her 15-year-old daughter, Trillya, were house sitting.

Trillya was as tall as her mother, with the same black hair, cut to shoulder length. Trillya's eyes were the most unusual hazel Bill had ever seen. She was young and still showing pre-teen plumpness on her face. He knew that she'd be a beauty someday, just like her mother. Trillya was nearly in tears when she saw her mother and the bruises and bandages and her swollen face. They hugged, and the young girl tried to choke back a sob but could not for long. Then the tears came and she sobbed and cried for her mother. "I'll tell you what happened but not right now. Please, I'm ok. I'm just a little sore—you think I look bad, you should see the other guy." She forced a grin.

The two ladies were still hugging as Bill mouthed "tomorrow." Sylvia nodded. Bill quietly closed the door.

George parked her Honda under the awning. Bill pulled in behind the Honda. He and George would return to the bar.

She smiled a shy smile at George and mouthed thank you while covering her badly bruised throat. George looked at her swollen face and bandages with a concerned expression and a curled lip and a tight angry jaw.

Bill said, "I know you have to move from here in a few days. Have you found a place yet?" Sylvia shook her head. Her throat was very sore. Trillya was holding on to her mom again, on the verge of tears.

"The owners are returning from North Dakota for the winter," she said with difficulty.

"You know, I own the bar, in fact the whole damn building. There are two apartments above the bar. I'm living in the smaller apartment. The larger one is being used for storage. We can move those things to the basement, and you and Trillya can move in, if you want. You'll be close to work, and still have your privacy and freedom to come and go. Trillya will be close to school. It's just five blocks away. Easy walking distance. On bad weather days one of us can give her a lift. Think about it, Sylvia. You've had a rough time. I'm comfortable in my apartment. The bar is paying for itself. Take a couple of days off. Mitzi can work for you, and George, Larry, and I will fill in. We can move the storage items out and you and Trillya in."

"I have to pay rent. I won't live there for free. How much will you charge us?" she said with difficulty.

"Just pay the utilities, that's all I ask. No strings attached. I promise. It'll be good for me to have a couple of beautiful neighbors—just think about it. You have four more days here. We can move the stored things in a couple of hours. Both of you can clean it up, and I'll have everything fixed that's broken, though I think everything's working."

Continued

Alaska and the Oil Pipeline

Simon Underhill, a big man, unshaven with dark hair and a broken nose and various scars in his eyebrows, pushed open the foreman's door without knocking. Lou McCall, engrossed in the numbers on his computer screen, looked up at the huge man dressed in quilted orange coveralls and an orange watch cap pulled to cover his ears.

"You ever consider knocking before busting in?"

"Never dawned on me, Lou. Never thought you was that busy unless it was belting down shots of Wild Turkey."

Lou's blood-shot eyes narrowed. He wanted to say something smart and cutting but thought better of it. Looking at the pale scarred face framed in orange with a day's stubble looking down at him, I'd be no match, he thought. He looked down at his keyboard. "What d' you want, Underhill?"

The big orange man looked on the pitiful foreman with bloodshot eyes, fiery cheeks, and bulbous red nose crisscrossed with fine blue veins. Most of the damage not from Alaskan winters but from years of guzzling Wild Turkey.

Lou considered firing the big man, but he was the fastest and most accurate welder on the job and could not afford to lose him.

"I have vacation time coming, Lou, and I want two weeks starting tomorrow. I've got family business to take care of."

"That little brother of yours in trouble again? I need two weeks' notice not to be short-handed—you know that."

"This is an emergency. Some whore in Arizona murdered my little brother, three weeks ago. The authorities just tracked me down."

"Sorry to hear that," Lou mumbled, not really feeling anything.

"I need to settle it. Clancy can take up the slack. I've got my plane ticket. OK this or I'll go to work for the competition just after I kick your fat drunken ass. Oh, and you refuse this, you'd best give yourself two weeks' notice 'cause that's how long you'll be in the hospital learnin' to walk and eat again." He turned and walked out of the office, slamming the door and rattling its frosted window.

A large man pushes through the batwing doors of The Bitter Root, walks to the bar and an empty stool.

"What'll it be?" asks Larry Sims, tending bar and wiping the counter.

"A draft."

Larry nods and draws the beer. "Two bucks."

The big man looks around. He notices several photographs, framed and on the counter below the bar mirror. The photos are of the bartender and another man in their BDU uniforms with their rifles held across their chests.

The new customer looks Larry over then says, "You the owner?"

"Partner—why do you ask?"

"No reason, really. It's a nice bar is all."

Larry nods and smiles. "It's still two bucks for the beer."

The big man puts a fiver on the bar. He looks around before taking a sip of his beer. *So, this is where my little brother was murdered. She the whore who killed him?* He looks toward the young blond woman delivering drinks to a nearby table. He notices that she is very fit. Her calf muscles are well defined, her thighs look strong, and her ass…! She's hot. He thinks, *Hey! You the whore that cut my brother?! I got the same and better for you, bitch, and we're gonna have some fun before I fix your cunt!*

His eyes flare with the fury of his thoughts. He takes another sip of cold beer and lets its coolness soothe his throat. He considers its frosty amber depths and takes a deep breath. There will be time enough later, he thought. And he relishes what he has in store for the whore.

Another man enters, and as he passes the big man, he looks twice. "Simon?"

The big man looks around at the newcomer, his angry thoughts submerge. He nods. "Hey, Steve. It's been a while. How've ya been?

"It's from one extreme to another," says Steve. "I'm still acclimating to the damned summers down here." He grins and reaches out a hand. "Look, Simon, I'm meeting a friend. Let's catch up before I leave." They finish shaking hands and he moves off toward the other end of the bar.

Larry follows Steve and takes his order and overhears part of the conversation.

"Hi Charlie, you feeling better? We missed you at work today. Hey, you see that fellow I just spoke with?" he says, pointing with a thumb. That's Simon Underhill. It was his brother who was killed here a little while back."

"Oh, really?" Charlie leans back and glances down the bar to the big man staring into his beer.

"Yeah, we worked together in Alaska for two years. He's a welder and a tough S.O.B. Him and I got along okay though."

Larry walks back toward the big man.

The whole bar staff had been alerted that Jerry Underhill has an older brother and there might be a problem down the road.

Forewarned is being forearmed, Larry thinks to himself. He gets the attention of another big man, talking with a lovely woman, a regular customer. The two men look at each other and Larry gives a quick tilt of his head toward the beer gazer.

"Haven't seen you in here before. You hear about the dumb-ass rapist killed here a month ago?" Larry asks the big man gazing into his beer. "He sure got what was coming to him. As far as I'm concerned, every damned rapist, child molester, and terrorist oughta be shot on the spot or have their throats cut from ear to ear, just like that dumbass, Jerry Underhill. What do you think about that, Mr. Underhill? You a rapist too? Or are you just looking for revenge?"

Simon Underhill slowly looks from his beer, his anger moving in him like a magnitude 7 earthquake. He gnashes his teeth, his nostrils fair, his face turns red with fury, his lips thin against his teeth. He is about ready to explode and he doesn't give a shit who gets in the way, he'd take on any one of them or all of them. The more the merrier!

"Your brother," Larry continued, "tried to rape one of the women who works here. He got what he had coming. What're you here for? You lookin' for payback? You've come right on time, friend. We've been expectin' you."

All talk in the bar ceased and all eyes swiveled toward the bar. Larry's words are not being spoken softly.

Underhill can no longer contain his rising ire, like white hot molten lava. The big man stands, upending his stool, and grabs a handful of Larry's shirt, drawing his fist back to punch this ass into tomorrow. In a flash, Larry reaches across the man's arm and backhands him across the mouth, knocking his ball cap spinning. Underhill loosens his grip on Larry's shirt. He spits blood on the floor, draws his fist back to punch Larry but a larger fist grabs his and spins him around. He looks first at a thick muscular neck at eye level, then up into the cool gray eyes of a larger and stronger man with a lightly scared face. It's George Blake, one of the bartenders and prime-time "trash hauler." George hits Underhill in the middle of his face and the lights in the big man's eyes go out. His body careens off of the upended heavy metal bar stool. His face bounces when it hits the barroom floor. Part of a tooth lay in the small puddle of bloodied saliva on the floor beneath his face.

Larry comes from behind the bar and goes through Underhill's pockets for ID and removes a very sharp stiletto with a spring release. George pours the remainder of Underhill's beer on the brother's head, then they haul him to his feet by his jacket. George jerks him to-and-fro, like a dead goose, his head showering beer all around. Clutching his jacket with both his large fists, George shakes him completely awake while rattling his teeth.

George pulls Underhill's face up close, George's eyes clear and calm, glancing from Underhill's eyes to his bloody mouth. "You ever come back here, sir, you will spend a long and very painful time in our very fine hospital." With a hard, calloused hand, George slaps Mr. Underhill's face, putting emphasis to his words and slinging more droplets of beer around. "…And should you come back after that, you will not need a hospital." He slaps the man again. "—You'll be able to hug your dead rapist brother in person—you got that?"

Larry stuffs the man's change and ID back into his jacket pocket, rams the ball cap tight but wonkie on his head. With the entire bar watching, George grabs the seat of Underhill's pants and his jacket collar and vigorously rushes him through the batwings, Underhill's feet barely touching the floor. George flings him out onto the gravel drive.

Bar customers scramble to the windows. The whole thing is almost as good as Friday Night Fights on TV, except the show on TV lasts longer.

Simon Underhill gets slowly to his hands and knees, shaking his head to dissipate the effects of the punch and painful 'exclamation marks.'

With authority, George puts his size 13 brogan broadside to Mr. Underhill's butt and he is once again performing The Bitter Root's acclaimed 'gravel sprawl.' He rolls over on his back, arches up, and grips his painful backside. He gets slowly up and rushes George, throwing an overhand right which George catches in his mitt-sized hand and punches Underhill in the jaw, knocking the big man out a second time.

Several regular customers of the bar, coming in for drinks, look down at the limp, supine body. They walk around it as though it's giving off an offensive odor, look at George, nod curtly, and enter the bar, unfazed by the trash or its hauler.

The End

CHERRY'S COLT

"Nice Colt. Looks like it's been used some. Is there a story behind it?"

"I won this Colt single action .45 at an estate auction. It was got rid of by the family whose grandfather, named Cherry Reeling, owned the weapon back in the late 1800s. He was a cowboy and worked for a ranch outside of Cody, Wyoming. A lot of men during that time carried Colt pistols because they were lighter than a rifle and it was easier on a horse you might be riding all day or on a cattle drive for a thousand miles or more—apparently, Cherry won the Colt in a poker game one Saturday night. It was a fine looking Peacemaker and brand new at the time. The stakes were high. A cowboy named Joe Three Toes Jones saved up and bought it from the factory. Cherry put up three months' wages he'd saved. His opponent, Joe Three Toes, could not cover the bet and so put up his brand-new factory engraved, silver plated colt with ivory grips to cover the bet. Cherry had two queens and won the pot and the Colt."

"What's the story behind the marks and notches in the grips?"

"Well according to the family, the first notch was a reminder that a critter snuck into Cherry's camp and was rummaging through Cherry's kit with its wet snout. Cherry, being a light sleeper, was awakened by the noise, sat up, Colt in hand and shot that ugly critter right in the head. He grabbed the sneak thief by a leg and dragged it a hundred yards from his camp and left the mangy critter for the other hungry beasts. He didn't care nothin' for the dead, for dead anything… two legged or four. …Those were the days!"

"What about the moon shaped marks on the grip end of the frame? The square bracket marks next to the moon marks and overlapping the same?"

"Well, as the story goes, while Cherry was working for various ranches, he often needed to use a hammer now and again and so, being without one, began using the butt end of this colt. He tried real hard not to hit the ivory grips. But you can see there were a few misses. Apparently, he got pretty good using that Colt as a hammer for regular nails and horse-shoe nails… and whacking other things that didn't need shootin'. He was a good shot with it too.

"What about the marks on the barrel where the silver is scratched and torn away?"

"While a cowboy, he was often far from the ranch, working cattle and such like. He might come upon a stretch of fence that needed its strands tightened. He would use the barrel of that Colt to twist the wire taunt—thus the marks.

"As for the second notch in the grip… well that notch marks the death of his very close friend and partner of several years. His friend's name was Steve. Steve and Cherry were between Cheyenne and Laramie. They were chased by a couple of braves. The chase went on for nearly twenty miles. Both were dripping with sweat and nearly exhausted with the effort. At last the Indians gave up and Steve and Cherry slowed to a walk to cool off. Steve took a very bad fall, stepped on a rock wrong and 'snap!' broke his leg in two. Rather than see his friend and partner suffer, Cherry pulled out this here Colt and with much grieving, sadness, and apologies to Steve, put a .45 bullet in his head.

"And there you have the notches and torn silver plating and marks on the butt end of this Colt."

"How did he get away with that? Seems someone might be missing Steve, a wife, a mother, a sister? …To my thinking, Cherry should have been hanged for the killing. Those must have been wild, lawless days. Steve's leg could have been fixed, good as new, for God's sake!"

"The first notch was for a prowling Coyote he shot. The second notch was for his horse, named Steve."

"…What? …Who in their right mind would name a horse Steve?"

"Cherry Reeling."

The End

1,2,3 TURKEY-NECK

CHARLES DIMPLE, DRESSED IN GRAY SLACKS, A BLACK LEATHER JACKET, AND A white turtleneck sweater, smelling of JOOP! eau de toilette, hurries down the alley shortcut on his way to the 13th Street bus stop to meet Lola. Traffic noises on the cross street behind him make him an easy mark. Something hits him on the side of his head, and he's out cold.

He comes to and panics. His mouth is taped shut, he has a mammoth headache, and there's a bag or sack over his head. His hands are strapped down to the arms of a metal chair and his legs are strapped to the chair legs. He begins making loud, pleading nasal noises and rocking his body violently, trying to break free. The straps bruise the flesh of his wrists and his ankles, but the chair doesn't budge. Two voices are talking in hushed tones off to his right. He quiets himself and listens.

"You're sure you want to do this?"

Raymond nods. "I'm positive." He looks at the short, square, powerfully built man with thinning hair. The man is wearing coveralls totally zipped up and fastened at the neck. On his head is a black watch cap; thin leather gloves cover his hands. Raymond knows the man only as Marvin. He found him through the want ads in the local birdcage paper. The ad read, 'Home Owners, Apartment Dwellers we can solve most problems. Give us a call. If we can't— we know someone who can.'

Raymond observes how careful Marvin is not to brush or touch anything in the empty machine shop, with the exception of the contemptible figure strapped to the chair in the center of the shop.

"I'm certain." He continues, "I'm gonna extract payment for even attempting to spoil my little girl."

"That's fine. Whatever you say. I don't wanna know nothin' else. But remember this. If you attempt to describe me to anyone, especially the cops, I or one of my associates will find you, and you will not ever be normal or pain-free again, nor will anyone you care about remain in one piece. Understood?"

Raymond looks into the man's cold gray eyes and shudders. He momentarily considers that maybe he should let the authorities deal with this. But he's always felt like a bumbler and coward dealing with confrontations. He was picked on, smacked and punched by school bullies as a teenager. His whole life he's been afraid to fight back. He has never had the confidence to defend himself against antagonists or in any situation requiring a physical response—he feels he must do this himself.

"This is a Beretta 92, 9mm pistol," says Marvin. He ejects the magazine from the weapon, showing that it is fully loaded, then re-inserts it in the grip and smacks it firmly into place. "The serial number has been removed with acid. How you ditch it is up to you. I recommend deep water with no witnesses. Keep your finger off the trigger until you're ready to shoot it. Again—should I have unwelcome visitors, you will be found, wherever you are, and you will pray to have your throat slit from ear to ear." He draws a gloved finger across his throat in emphasis. "Am I clear?"

Raymond swallows, looks Marvin in the eyes again, and nods.

"Say it. Tell me with words that you understand what I've just promised you."

Apprehension and anxiety is clearly visible in Raymond's expression and in the gloss of perspiration on his upper lip and forehead. "Yes, I understand completely. You've no cause for concern. My word is good."

"As is mine." Marvin cocks his head at Raymond. He holds out his hand, and Raymond, with a slight, involuntary trembling, counts out fifteen $100 bills. With a gloved hand, Marvin turns Raymond's hand over and slaps the pistol onto it. Raymond looks at the pistol then up as the zipped-up man disappears through the door.

He looks again at the pistol in his hand then to the figure once again trying to break free of his restraints.

"You know why you are here?" asks Raymond, standing in front of the captive.

"Mm, mm!" then in a higher and panicked pitch nasal, "Mm, mm, mm!" while violently trying to tear himself free from his cable ties.

Raymond looks down at the perverted lump of seeping human waste. He's angry for what this fool had planned to do with his daughter and also for the years of his own abuse as a teenager. A lifetime of rage is concentrated on this thing quivering and fouling itself in front of him.

The Beretta is cradled in both hands. It feels heavy, a solid solution to the problem. How remarkable, he thinks as he looks at the pistol. It feels more comfortable in my hand than I imagined. I hate guns and know absolutely nothing about them. I wonder why I didn't choose a hammer, or a screwdriver, or a knife, or a baseball bat? Any of them would accomplish the deed. He shrugs. Then it comes to him. Those tools are extremely personal. The pistol makes me once removed. All I have to do is pull the trigger.

Even with my eyes closed.

"You were gonna sexually abuse my daughter. She's only fifteen. My Lola is not your Lolita. How many other girls have you defiled? No, forget that, I don't care. It all stops here, you piece of monkey dung. Why didn't you pick on a mature woman who can say 'no' and defend herself? Why pick on an innocent child?"

He points the Beretta at Charles's head. Closes his eyes and jerks the trigger. Click!

It didn't go off! It didn't fire! Raymond yanks on the trigger two more times with his eyes still squeezed tight against the noise and the recoil he knows will come. Still nothing! He screams to himself. He opens his eyes to look at the damned thing while pulling the trigger repeatedly. Finally he calms down a little and looks more closely at the pistol in bewilderment. What's wrong with this damned thing? It ought to go off when I pull the damned trigger!

Charles is frantic—waiting to have his brains splattered everywhere and then nothing! He's bobbing up and down as much as his restraints will allow and rocking from side to side and twisting to free himself. The ties cut into his wrists, and they begin bleed.

Looking at the pistol, Raymond tries to remember Marvin's instructions but his mind is complete white noise, his brain has turned into tapioca. Then he remembers Marvin smacking the butt of the grip. He slams the bottom of the grip, points and pulls the trigger again and again—click, click! "Nothing!" he screams. "This piece of shit is bogus!"

Charles is hearing the clicks and he rocks and twists and makes Hmmmm sounds as loud as he can until he can't do it anymore. The wrist restraints cut more deeply into the flesh of his wrists. Blood is running off his fingertips. He rocks back and forth trying to break loose or at least tip over. The chair won't move.

Raymond stares at the pistol. Drops of his perspiration plink onto its blued surface. Sweat stings his eyes. He wipes the sweat from his face with a shirtsleeve. His brain still refuses to engage. He's never fired a Beretta—or any damned gun, for that matter. He's never had interest or experience or desire until now. He fumbles and finally ejects the magazine by accident, which clatters to the concrete floor. He retrieves it, and with shaking hands, tries to insert it but the magazine is facing the wrong way. He corrects it and slams it home. He jerks the trigger a couple more times, still no bang, bang! His heart is racing. Then it dawns on him that Marvin had pulled then released the top of the pistol. He draws the slide back a bit, looks into the opening and sees nothing in the hole at the end of the barrel, but further down he sees the bullets in the end of the magazine. He pulls the top cover all the way back and a bullet springs up. He lets the slide return slowly and watches it skim the bullet into the barrel opening. The slide does not close all the way so he hits the back of it hard and it closes.

He glances at Charles. His rocking and struggling has almost ceased. He appears exhausted. There is blood on the floor around the chair.

There's a red dot by a lever on the side of the gun. Raymond pulls the lever down to cover the dot. The weapon's hammer drops. Not understanding, he pulls the trigger again pointing it at Charles. Nothing happens. Mush, mush, mush. In complete rage and frustration, Raymond growls and screams. He takes the pistol by the barrel, kneels down and smashes and hammers away at Charles' right foot, determined to turn every damned bone to pulp. He hammers through the shoe like a madman. His sweat is splattering all round as he pounds away. Charles, all the while, is screaming through his nose as his foot is crushed over and over again.

Raymond notices that Charles has stopped moving and making noises. His head has dropped to his chest. Raymond prays he will be limping the rest of his life and with each painful step will remember why it happened. He stops smashing when he sees blood oozing from around the shoelaces.

This is better than blowing his brains all over the place. He cuts the cable ties at Charles' wrists and legs.

Back at the bench, he tries the trigger again and nothing happens; the hammer will not stay pulled back. He moves the lever so that the red is visible again and now the hammer stays pulled back. He holds it and decides to keep the damned thing since he has not shot Charles with it and paid fifteen hundred dollars for it. He walks to Charles who is still slumped and checks his pulse, avoiding the blood. He is alive.

He looks around. He's touched nothing. As he walks toward the exit door he shoves the Beretta into the waistband of his pants and the damned thing discharges. The bullet cuts into his groin and left leg. He hears the bullet ricochet off the floor and bounce around the shop. The shock and pain is excruciating. It knocks him to the floor and takes his breath away. After several panicked moments, he just knows he's shot his dick off and blown his leg apart. He remembers Marvin reminding him to keep his finger off of the trigger until ready to shoot.

With herculean effort and in enormous agony he staggers to his feet and looks down at his crotch. Blood is everywhere. The pain is breathtaking. Tears stream down his cheeks. He feels lightheaded. His knees buckle and he nearly goes down again. He curses out loud at his stupidity. It's like listening to someone with a kid's string-and-tin can phone. He grips the edge of the nearby table and nearly loses consciousness. He forces himself to hobble out to his scooter. His pant leg and crotch are drenched in blood.

Nancy? He hopes he can get to her without passing out, wrecking his Vespa and further wrecking himself—and what about the police?

"Oh my God! What have you done?"

"I shot my dick off! And blew a hole in my leg!"

"What? How in hell did you do that? Drop your pants; let's see what you've done."

"My leg is not my concern!" He lifts his un-tucked shirt, releases the belt buckle, unzips the fly, and un-fastens the button, and they slide to the floor along with the pistol.

Her eyes open wide at his bloody shorts and Nancy covers her open mouth with her hand to stifle an astonished gasp. She raises her eyes to his. His are wide with fright and pain. He is deathly pale and white around the mouth. He looks down at all the blood. He is trembling. His nose is running and his mouth is drooling. He backs up with steps restricted by his pants, cradling the Beretta.

The moment his blood-smeared fanny finds the mattress, his eyes roll up and he passes out, starting to fall to one side. Nancy pushes him onto his back.

She looks at her phone in panic and considers calling 911 but decides against it for now. She sees no spurting blood. Instead, she retrieves her scissors from a kitchen drawer and cut his shorts away. She gently lifts his penis. The bullet has ripped a fleshy furrow about an inch from the base of it and looks to have been deflected, glancing against the pelvic bone, then tearing through his pants pocket and driving a coin-shaped object just beneath the skin of his thigh about eight inches in length. The coin or coins deflected the bullet again away from his leg.

She returns from her medicine cabinet with several items. She gets a towel under him, as best she can, then blots the oozing rut with gauze. The bleeding had nearly stopped. She can't help smiling to herself. He won't be humping and bumping anytime soon. She sprays hydrogen peroxide on the wretched trough and watches it foam as it performs its germ-killing action. With saline solution, she washes the ragged entry wound in his thigh where the bullet impacted the change in his pocket. Then, after sterilizing a razor blade with a match, she slits the skin across the leading edge of the item and perpendicular to its path and wide enough to allow the coin shaped object to slide out from just under the skin. She presses the back edge of the disk forcing it from its channel and her incision. She draws a finger back along the coin's path and discovers two more coins still in the ugly red- and blue-colored tunnel. These she will leave for a doctor. She uses saline solution followed with Polysporin and a lot of gauze to pack the ragged entry wound and her incision. More gauze and tape finish the thigh patch.

She scissors hair away from the ragged bullet graze, another spritz of hydrogen peroxide then Polysporin, gauze, and tape completes the surgery. She is not a doctor or a nurse, but she looks with satisfaction at her handiwork. She feels she owes him this much. The patches will have to do until he sees a doctor. Coins are filthy with germs. Infection will happen, no doubt at all. He needs to have the remaining coins removed soon.

She wonders what kind of story he will tell the hospital staff. Not to mention his estranged wife—and the police?

He must have left DNA at the scene. He's a cooked turkey. What about fingerprints? What about the pistol? She looks for it. It's folded in his bloody pants, nearly under her bed. What should she do with it? She doesn't want to touch it. She will let it be.

Now, she thinks, would be a good time to visit my mom in Texas. She's had enough of the hump and grind with Mr. Raymond Jules. That pistol is none of her business. She'll pretend she didn't even see the damned thing if he asks about it.

Raymond groans, rolls his head from side to side. His eyes flutter open.

She watches him until he appears alert, then asks, "How did you manage to get shot?"

He looks around then finds her. He seems unsure of where he is. He then focuses on her. "Oh my God, it wasn't a dream!" He shakes his head then groans and squeezes his eyes closed and covers his eyes with a still-bloody hand. "What did you say?" he asks from behind his hand.

"How did you get shot?"

He pauses, shaking his head trying to wake up his memory then every detail floods back. He frowns. "Easy, by not knowing a damned thing about guns!"

She hands him two aspirin.

"I'm in major pain here—aspirin? Aspirin? Shit! Anything stronger than aspirin?" he says. He tries to sit up then cancels that idea. The pain brings tears to his bloodshot eyes.

"You think this is a pharmacy? What did you do to him?"

"Did I shoot it off?" he asks in a terrified voice. "That's all I wanna know."

"What you did won't be between us ever again," she says, keeping a straight face.

His mouth drops and he looks like he wants to die. "Then it is gone! I did shoot it off!"

Feeling a bit heartless, she hesitates then, "No, no. You missed it by a full inch. Both of you are lucky turkey's necks."

She shakes her head in disbelief at the whole sad affair and hands him water. He swallows and chokes a little on his good fortune and the aspirin.

"What'd the bullet do to my leg?"

"It shoved this dime under the skin." She hands him the coin.

"How in hell did you get it out?"

"I cut it out."

"You did what?"

"I cut it out it out with a razor. It was your leg—I didn't feel a thing. There are other coins in the same channel. You'll need a doctor to remove them."

There is a long, pain-filled silence. Nancy just looks down at him with a faint smile at her lips. For once, he is on the bottom and she's on top. She turns quickly and walks to the bathroom to wash her hands of the entire thing. Then realization comes to her, loud and clear. Did she know what he was going to do?

There is loud and violent hammering at the front door. The door shakes from locks to hinges. "OPEN UP! Bellevue Police Department! OPEN UP!"

"Just a minute!" she shouts back. "I'm coming! Don't break my door!

Charles covers his eyes with a blood-encrusted hand and wishes he were elsewhere or maybe even dead.

Nancy walks quickly to the door wiping her hands and face with a towel. She shoulders the towel, and with a degree of foreboding and brusqueness, frees the dead bolt, drops the security chain, and steps back, as quick and smooth as saying 1, 2, 3.

The End

THE PENTHOUSE

THE DAMP AND WRINKLED SHEET LOOSELY ENTANGLES DAVID'S LEGS AND LOWER body. Across his forehead and about his ears his black hair lies in sweaty curls. He is spent, for the moment, having shared in the fulfilling of their recurring sexual fantasies. Sherry, often aggressively, initiates their lovemaking, and he follows. Then he catches fire and she follows—eagerly, hungrily.

David clasps his hands behind his head and stares up at the ceiling. His thoughts are only of Sherry, her incredible responsiveness, her desire to please him, and her remarkable silence.

David is reticent also—to the extreme. Like his father, expressing and sharing his deeper feelings is not possible. Deep within his heart and mind, he may wish it were otherwise. His need for such expression is, however, beyond his reach. David may want someone, but he does not need anyone. This has often caused the women in his life to cling to him, to pull at him, to plead with him, and to want and need more of him. When this happens he needs some space or he'll suffocate.

Sherry clings to David as a ripened apricot clings to its source of nourishment. She, however, is totally unaware of the incredible power she exerts on their relationship. She fears abandonment and she cannot read him. She, like her Mother, is oblivious of the innate feminine power she possesses. Sherry's fear and blindness result in debilitating pain and obscures all her reasoning.

There has been no verbal intimacy between them, none at all. David's need to leave, though temporary, is a bewildering and toxic stain on her psyche, and it is cumulative. She cannot understand why he must leave. She cannot express her feelings of abandonment. The more she clings and pulls at him, the stronger and more urgent his need for space becomes.

When he leaves she is awash in unbearable agony.

Their difference and sameness are such that David and Sherry fit perfectly together, like two mated puzzle pieces. They are isolated, stuck within their relationship's concretized margins—day-to-day external influences, at this juncture, do not and can not exist for them.

She lies beside him, her hand resting lightly on his chest. Across his body she watches the curtain lift gently away from the window, stirred by a gentle breeze. She observes the sunlight pour across the velveteen couch containing his clothes and splash out across the oak floor. Tiny specks drift on the same currents, sparkle for a few moments in the light, and are swallowed again by the shadows of the room.

She watches him staring at his clothes on the couch. She focuses on one, damp, dark curl that lies against his temple. She touches it with a timid and trembling finger. A tiny muscle at the corner of her right eye twitches. She is startled at the internal sound in her left ear of a brittle twig snapping. Her expression appears to droop momentarily, to lose strength or spirit.

Out of habit, David's eyes are still on the velvet couch and his clothes, but his thoughts are of Sherry.

She holds her breath. The performance repeats again, as an endless loop, in high definition, against the screen of her mind. As he leaves, she will embrace him, press her body against his, trying desperately to entice him to stay. She will make faint whimpering sounds and cling to him as he unlocks and opens the door to leave. He will gently unclasp her arms and hands, not hurting her. Then he will tell her that he will call her later, close the door, and be gone. She will then slump against the door, and her world will become empty except for the incredible ache.

She mentally stops the replay and says, "I'll make juice for us. Is pineapple ok? It'll be refreshing before you leave."

"Pineapple sounds great."

She stands and, still self-conscious at being naked even after all these months, slips into her pink satin robe with large, sumptuous, brocade apple blossoms covering it, and walks gracefully into the kitchen. He watches her move to the kitchen and he does not feel smothered this time. Maybe she finally understands. Maybe he'll even stay a bit longer this time if there's no clinging.

She pauses in the doorway, with the juice tray, watching him for a moment. He watches her and is not staring at the couch as he usually does. She places the tray on her end table. He looks at her and smiles, marveling at her radiant femininity and how perfectly the brocade apple blossoms suit her. She hands him a champagne flute of pineapple juice. He rises on an elbow, raises the stemmed glass toward her, thanking her, toasting her, and then drinks it down. It is cold and refreshing.

She takes the goblet and places it back on the tray. While still in her robe, she lies down beside him—puts her hand on his chest. His eyes open very wide. He arches upward slightly—his whole body convulses briefly and trembles as though an icy hand has seized the base of his spine. He turns his head toward her, with a questioning expression forming on his face. A trickle of frothy juice makes a tiny rivulet from the corner of his mouth to his ear.

She smiles and nods at him and pulls the sheet away and caresses his languid organ, still moist from her body's own fluids, enjoying the warmth of it in her hand. She smiles at how quickly she has changed his mind. She becomes ecstatic. She marvels at the simplicity of it—he is going to stay after all! Her spirit soars. The branch has shattered! She is free from it. She stands, removes the apple blossom robe that she loves, and while holding it, drinks her juice quickly, and lies down again drawing the robe across their feet. She traces the lines of his body with her hand and lays her warm thigh over and against his cooling, flaccid member, places her cheek against his shoulder, and drapes her arm across his chest.

The apple blossom robe slips softly to the floor, finding a more comfortable resting place. A single tear slips down her cheek to bridge onto his shoulder. A breath of fresh air moves against the gossamer curtains at the window. Warm, life-giving sunlight touches the feet of the sleepers on its continuing journey across the room. Dust motes spin and dance merrily about on blind, fragrant currents. Curtains inhale and exhale against the open window.

The End

TRILLYA

I CRANK OUR FORD INTO A U-TURN, INTENDING TO FOLLOW IN THE WAKE OF THE Toyotas; the maneuver is not easy, as our beast has no power steering. As I swing by the red Harley, we hear a commotion coming from amidst a group of abandoned hulks off to our right. It's an angry, strident voice.

"That's a woman's voice, Cob!"

Of all the situations to violently resist, topping our list is: abusing women, children, the elderly, and the infirmed. There are many who rail against all that. Count us in. "I'll take a quick look-see, Cob, then we're out of here." Sticking one's nose where it doesn't belong is a good way to get it bobbed, or worse. I park at the outer edge of the maze, close to an unobstructed exit. Being blocked in is not healthy.

"I've got your back, Mal."

I shut it down, step out of our gas-guzzler, holding my 1911 next to my right leg. It's cocked and the safety is off. My trigger finger is pressed against the leading edge of the trigger guard. Being startled and pulling the trigger in reflex to a sudden noise is for the knucklehead who shouldn't be alive today anyway. That kind of fool is a wasting fresh air and good water. All I need is to shoot off my kneecap or blow off a few toes.

It's a warm morning that's amplifying the stench of human waste. I walk in a crouch among the hulks, trying to locate and sneak upon the commotion. I'm trying to avoid the putrid fluids oozing from some of the hulks. Nearly all of these vehicles are sitting on their hubs. After several minutes, I come up on a heavily sun-cooked and oxidized blue Ford van. The woman's strident voice fills the air. The van's been totally stripped. The brake light bulbs and reflectors are gone. The seats are gone, and the radio—even the mirrors and sun visors.

Its windows have been shattered. It's empty except for a heavily stained air mattress in the cargo area. I ease my head around the back of the van and find the ruckus.

I hope Cob has been able to track me. I raise my arm to catch his eye. He pokes his Winchester up in response. He's crouched in the bed of our beast with a good vantage point, perhaps fifty yards away, using the cab as a shooting platform.

I slowly ease from behind the van. Two young guys, gang bangers, maybe in their twenties, wearing chambray shirts and faded black cargo pants, are watching a third, similarly dressed 'zero', holding a young woman on the asphalt. The left side of his thick body has pinned her right arm. His left arm is under her head, holding her left wrist in a tight fist. His right leg is across both of hers. With his free right hand, he's slapping her, trying to shut her up. Her face is red from it. Blood from a nostril is smeared across her face. She's cursing, thrashing, and bucking to be free of him. There are no tears.

"Let go of me! I'll kill you bastards if it takes years! Marco's gonna hunt you down, Pico—all of you!"

She's fighting against what will happen to her by these three.

The guy holding her down is having trouble unbuckling the studded belt of her jeans. He slaps her again real hard, and blood and saliva from her mouth splatters his shirt. He'd already ripped open her jean shirt and pulled her bra up exposing her very lovely, darkly rippled breasts.

I point with my left hand at the fat sap, to my left. He's holding a shotgun with its stock resting on the overburdened belt at his hip. His round face is sweating, and he's grinning with sheer enjoyment at the spectacle on the ground. Ancient sweat deposits stain his shirt, probably from similar, strenuous days. The shotgun, a Remington 870, could be a stolen police weapon. I point with my .45 at the guy to my right. He's slender, with a head and face full of red hair. His eyes are close-set and small. A lustful leer dominates his face. Foamy green saliva occupies the corners of his mouth. A crown tattoo adorns his upper arm. He's holding a Smith & Wesson or Taurus .38 revolver in his left fist. He shoves the wheel gun into a hip pocket. One of her boots has been unzipped and removed. All three of them are totally focused on the day's menu special.

"Damit Jude. Hold the bitch still!"

"Whack 'er again, Pico! I'm tired holdin' on to 'er. She don't know when to give up! I'm doin' all the work—You guys're just grinnin' an' droolin' about getting' a piece of her!"

"Just hold 'er Jude! I'll strip 'er. Then I'm gonna fuck 'er an' I want her fightin' it!"

Pico licks his lips in anticipation, then kneels to strip her. That's when he sees my boots where there were none before, at the ass end of that striped and violated van. "What?! ...Who the hell?!" He says in a startled voice. "Damn it, Roy!" he barks, looking at Roy while pointing at me. "Pay attention Dumbo!" The scattergun starts to come down as Roy is surprised. His eyes flair wide—the shotgun's single eye starts looking for me.

The redhead, Pico, stands while reaching for his back pocket. Cob's Winchester speaks twice. I hear both bullets striking flesh. Cob's first round takes the scatter gunner above his right eye. He drops the scattergun and it clatters beneath the dead Chevy Blazer next to him. His head rocks back with the force of Cob's hollow point round as it scrambles his brain. He drops like a bag of wet sand into some empty cans scattered on the asphalt. Cob's second bullet snaps past my right ear causing me to flinch and wince at the same time as that lead whistler passes very close and smacks into the right armpit of the redhead. He shrieks and goes down as though someone has cut every piece of safety wire holding him upright. His weasel eyes widen in surprise, hate, and pain. He looks from the muzzle of my .45 to my eyes. I know what he wants, but he's sitting on it. He stands with pained and staggering effort, while trying to get hold of his armpit. His eyes are squeezed tight against the pain. Blood is pulsing with considerable force around his hand, flowing down his arm, off his fingers onto his boots. He's trying to stop the flow. Cob's round has apparently blown the artery on the inside of his upper arm. With contempt dominating my expression, I'm wondering just where they'll place the tourniquet. Better yet, maybe I'll shoot him where it really hurts to give him more pain while he bleeds out. One of his blood brothers will have to apply pressure directly on the wound to stop the bleeding. And then, how will he get out from all these ripe hulks, and to what hospital?

Most of the hospitals have been looted, nearly destroyed, conceivably by these very three 'shit for brains' gang members. Where are the doctors and the nurses? Even considering his mortal predicament, I can see in his eyes that he desperately wants to have at that revolver in his butt pocket. I'm sure he understands his chances of survival are zip, zero, not gonna happen. Well, "a man's gotta do what a man's gotta do," John Wayne said in the movie *Hondo* when a brute wanted to shoot Wayne's dog. In the movie, the guy was no fool;

he wanted no part of Hondo, Wayne's character. I arch my eyebrows and nod my head and say "A man's gotta do what a man's gotta do. Go for it!" Well I'm not the Duke and this is no movie set.

I sound flippant about this situation, but I really don't give a flop how it sounds. These three are sub-zeros. I guess I'd rather leave them in pain and suffering than make it easy for them, considering what they've probably done to others and were about to do to this young woman.

With effort, he pulls that revolver out of his hip pocket with a blood-slippery hand. I shake my head and shoot him in the knee and then his groin. His revolver clatters to the asphalt, under the vehicle behind him. He is down again, cursing, moaning, and rolling around among the same cans as did Roy. He looks at me with pure hatred. It all happened in seconds.

Jude, the one holding the woman down, has turned his shaved head and is looking up at me. He releases his grip on the girl. She yanks herself free, sits up, and quick as you can think, plants a backward elbow strike in the middle of his face. She really leans into it. His head bounces off the blacktop. He grimaces in pain and puts both hands to his face and head. She pulls her bra down covering her breasts, and quickly snaps what's left of her shirt. She catches me kinda lookin' and admirin' her. "What are you looking at?!" Her eyes are narrow angry slits. I can see her thinking, what kind of shit I'm gonna give her. She stands up and kicks Jude real hard in the ribs with the boot not yet removed. He howls in pain. Then she spits on him.

"You through?" I say.

"Give me that pistol, then I'll be fucking through," she says, tossing her hair out of her eyes and holding out her hand and waggling her fingers for my .45.

"Forget it!" I yell, "It's time to go! There might be other snot eaters about!" She reaches into red's front pocket as I'm gathering my two empties. He's nearly out from loss of blood. I hope she avoids the blood and the pee. She pulls out a stiletto, pops the blade and shoves it through Jude's cheeks side to side then turns back to red and shoves the blade into his neck and wipes the blood on his shirt. She stomps her socked foot into the removed boot and zips it up.

She's maybe five-eight or nine with a trim, lean body. Her black hair is cut short with copper highlights. Her nose is a little turned up, her eyes are a light translucent brown. I can see right down to the pupils. Incredible! Her lips are split and swelling from being punched and slapped. Her complexion is olive, her two front teeth, protruding slightly, give her face a sensuality that is startling. The flesh over her right cheekbone is swelling where she had been hit really hard. It will be badly bruised for a while. Blood is smeared across her mouth. With all of this surface damage healed, she would be very easy to look at. I've always liked easy to look at, just like my murdered wife, Sharon, and my beautiful dead daughter, Melissa.

She and I back out of that maze of deadbeat men and vehicles. Once clear, we run, skirting the resident, rancid hulks, to our Ford. Cob has it running. He's covering our retreat and feeding more .25-20s into his pride and joy. It's an original engraved Model 1892 Winchester, manufactured in 1905. True, it's a diminutive caliber and an antique, but in his hands, I can cover a three-shot group, at a hundred yards, with a dollar—a silver dollar, that is. I wouldn't insult such a fine, tight group with a 'clad' dollar—even if I had one. A 'clad' is a minted coin, bright and shiny on the outside and totally worthless throughout. Yeah, our current U.S. coinage is totally worthless. Just like many 'clad' politicians in D.C. An Oreo cookie with a creamy filling. One of these revolting hulks has more value.

"What's your name?" I ask her.

She turns to face us. I can see that she's wary about what's coming next.

"Trillya." There is a faint accent to her voice.

This is my brother, Cobre. We call him Cob. I'm Malo, Mal for short."

She nods, and our eyes meet. Her expression is not friendly; her gaze is suspicious. There is no sweetness there either. Any sweet, warm, and soft, even thankful words are long gone. She's wiping blood from her face with a licked corner of her torn shirt. Many men and women have that same look. Considering what we face today, cold untrusting eyes and a quick trigger is what's often required to continue breathing—to see another sunrise.

"Do you need a lift?"

"That's my Harley," she says, pointing a thumb over her shoulder to the red motorcycle, not taking her eyes from us. I reach into the cab, and from the bracket on the dash I pull a backup revolver. I walk to where she stands near her bike. She is tense. Her weight is evenly spread on both feet, a sort of boxer's stance. She holds that stiletto down by her right thigh, her thumb on the release. She's all set for the second pit of snakes to make their move. And she has a "no" in her right fist. She throws a quick glance at Cob who is looking all around for possible threats, then again at me. I hold the Smith & Wesson 442 by its grip. She glances from the piece to my face. I raise the pistol and in the same motion, flip it, neatly catching it by the barrel and reaching it out to her.

She's tense for an instant at my motion, then reaches out and takes it from me.

"Ok, Trillya, if you ever get to AJ, Apache Junction, just ask for the Penny brothers and folks'll point the way. That's not going to fit in your hip pocket by the way, maybe your boot."

"You let me worry about where to put it."

"Its loaded with hollow points," I continue. "It feeds on .38 special ammo, no +p loads or .357 magnums, they won't fit anyway, they're too long. You can trade for specials anywhere. Rule number one: Don't ever leave home without it. Rule number two, don't ever hand it to anyone so they can look at it. Rule number three, the first two rules apply to that stiletto. How you could even think about going anywhere unarmed and alone boggles my mind."

Her expression relaxes a little. "I was armed. I had Bill's knife, but they took it after Pico hit me—they were supposed to be friends."

I shake my head in disbelief. "Nice thing about that 442 is that its hammer is shrouded. You can shoot from a pocket, a purse, or a paper bag and the hammer won't hang you up." She glanced at it. The fewer who know you have it, the grander the surprise if you have to stick it in some fool's ear. We'll wait till you leave before we go—who the hell is Bill? What manner of 'fool' lets you come here alone?"

She opens the cylinder of the Smith, checking the loads. She flips the cylinder closed, like in the movies.

"Don't close it that way. It's hard on it." She ignores my bewilderment, at least she knows how to open it. She nods at me, and not turning her back to us, moves to her Harley. Suspicion no longer the dominant part of her expression, but still in play. She shoves the Smith into her right boot top and the knife into her right hip pocket. Mounts, keys, and fires that chunk of hard candy to life.

"You've got to be kidding!" She laughs. "Bad Penny? Copper Penny?" Now she's laughing and shaking her head. She steps it into gear, and rips out of the parking lot, fishtailing a bit as she guns it, still laughing, her short hair, blowing behind, and then she is gone.

"She's thinkin' we're a couple of 'fruit loops' with the names we have. Shit, Cob! Will the jeering at our names never end?!"

"Whoa, she's sweet!" Cob says with raised eyebrows and a nod, as he slides behind the wheel.

"Forget it Cob, you'd be lucky if Tomiko only skins you and doesn't remove a smaller organ with that heirloom she keeps close. Besides, Trillya's got a definite "No" in her boot."

"Yeah, I wouldn't touch. Don't think I'd skin-out all that well. I have no tats so ending as a lamp shade is out of the question. Happily married I might be, but my eyes aren't rusted shut from all those years in Seattle."

"We'll keep a sharp eye out for chambray and black colors. If they show, we'll kill 'em and quick, no walkie 'n' talkie. The redhead's dead, he's bled out by now. You blew the artery in his upper arm and I gave him a taste of what he's probably been dishin'.'"

"Yeah, he flinched at the first shot. Think we'll see her again?"

"Who knows? Let's make tracks or we might take incoming from some other boogers. I wonder how many are in that gang."

"Ever heard of that black and blue bunch before, Mal?"

"No. I'm guessing they're out here from Phoenix. Not much left there. Stores and homes looted. Many buildings burned. Most folks have left for other parts or are dead. Easier to get food and water further north. Speaking of water, we need a good rain to cut this stink."

"Forget the rain, Mal. In this heat the humidity will only make it worse. Why do you suppose that gal wasn't more shook up with what they was trying to do to her? I saw her torn shirt and they smacked her around some."

"Ya can't judge that book by its cover. Healed up, she'll be very nice to look at, but there's a tough, hard person underneath, and now, with that .38, she's loaded for rabid coyote. Anyone with designs to get in her pants had better check her boots at the door! Times have changed folks. Some just give up, lie down and die. Others, their bad comes out, loud and clear cause who's to stop 'em? Others just get tough and hard… anything goes, to keep living. That's Trillya and that's us. If she'd had my pistol, she'd have killed 'em all and not blinked. Maybe I should have given it to her for closure and all that psychology BS." As it was, she used that stiletto on both of 'em. I recalled the look she'd given me as I was sort of admiring her breasts. She would have put a round in me too, for sure.

"Her man, Bill, or whoever, can take care of revenge on whoever is left. Let's make tracks, Cob. Engage!" I say, pointing the way while pulling on my goggles.

Cob grins, "Aye, Captain." He pulls his goggles down then gives me an elbow.

The End

THE SPARROW UNIT

FOR EACH PERSON THERE IS A MOMENT IN TIME, A LINE DRAWN IN THE SAND, BEYOND which his mortal life will not continue. James Penny's entire being was screaming that his time had arrived. He'd thought he was ready for his final moment—had he deceived himself? Was anyone ever entirely ready to give it up—to die?

He shivered as eight targeting lasers danced on his chest and neck. He could almost feel them crawling across his flesh beneath his shirt. He carefully pulled the bill of his ball cap low, thinking to protect his eyes. Beads of perspiration trailed down the small of his back, bled through his shirt, and soaked the waistband of his Levis.

The Arizona sky was a cloudless, dusty blue slashed with crisp aircraft contrails. Maybe he should have been on one of those planes.

The air was still. He was alone and isolated. Life around him was moving on—oblivious to the mortal confrontation about to occur on this diminutive patch of the Arizona desert.

The ringing phone woke James from a deep sleep. He rolled over and squinted to read the clock. 4:03 a.m. Early morning phone calls had always brought bad news. At 82, he thought he'd be used to bad news, that he could handle it with mature, calm detachment.

He let it ring three more times, sighed uneasily, swallowed hard, and then answered. "Yes?"

The computer-generated voice said, "Is this James Penny?"

"Who is this?"

"Never mind who I am. You've got a little more than an hour to fade into the desert or wherever. Serious federal folks are comin' for your bang-bangs." The line went dead.

James wiped a palm down his instantly sweating face. He had known this day was coming—that an obscene and vicious force would kick in his door and put an end to him.

He recalled the Homeland Security directive spread across the valley on radio, television, and in print. All firearms and ammunition must be surrendered for destruction on a specific day and in a specific place. The penalty for non-compliance will be extreme. James had purposely ignored the mandate. Surrendering one's means of security and defense was unthinkable. He would surrender nothing.

Lying there, staring at the phone, he grimaced and shook his head as he questioned the wisdom of his failure to comply with the order. At the time, his anger and frustration at what was occurring on the streets and building entrances in town made his blood boil, caused his hands to tremble. He sat up on the edge of the bed and eased his right leg with its swollen knee over the edge. He knew the fluid in it would have to be drained again. He hobbled into the bathroom and looked at the worn-out face staring back at him in the mirror. He scowled and shook his head. "What were you thinking, Wrong-Way?" It was a name his wife Marci used for him when she felt he was on the wrong path. "You're not too damned wise for all your years. This is gonna be the end of you. They might even lock you away for keeps. If you're lucky, maybe you'll just stroke out!"

He showered, shaved, and dressed in Levis, boots, and a cream-colored shirt. He put on a kettle of water for coffee. His trembling hands spilled coffee grounds on the countertop. While the coffee steeped in the French press, he picked up the kitchen phone and pressed a speed dial number. He cradled the phone between shoulder and ear while it rang, and carefully poured coffee into a mug.

"Hi … I've had better mornings. Look, do you remember what we talked about at the last turkey roast? … If you could text me a list of the nine or ten spices you used to marinate your turkey jerky, I'd be grateful. Oh, I need the list ASAP, I'm going shopping within the hour … Yes, that would be fine. No, you don't have to drop it off, just text it to me. Good. Hopefully, I'll talk to you later in the day. And thanks. Bye." He made no mention of the pack of butterflies now in residence in his gut. He smiled—what did butterflies have to do with marinating turkey jerky?

He opened the drawer of an end table near the front door and retrieved his .9 mm Beretta 92FS. It held eighteen rounds. Pushing the safety off, he pulled the pistol's slide back enough to verify that the eighteenth round was in the breech, and set the hammer on half-cock. He liked the solid feel of the weapon; fully loaded, it was not a lightweight. The heft of it was reassuring, because he knew what he could do with it. His advanced age had nothing to do with shooting it, but everything to do with knowing when to use it. He pushed the *on* switch at the base of the left grip and held the piece firmly, activating the Crimson Trace laser. He slipped a spare magazine in the watch pocket of his Levis and stowed a second magazine in the mag pouch in front of his left hip. He kept the safety off.

All he had to do was to put the front sight on the target, pull the hammer all the way back with his left thumb, and press the trigger. He preferred this single action for the first shot, as opposed to shooting it double action, which was a bit quicker. He preferred accuracy over speed. This worked for him. The large knuckle of his trigger finger had been aching from rheumatism for several years, but it had not hampered his shooting.

He carefully slipped the weapon into his waistband. With his coffee, cordless phone, his swollen, aching knee, butterflies, and one of the family albums, he waited at the table on the shade porch of his single wide mobile home in Arizona's Apache Junction.

As James waited, he heard scratching noises coming from his roof. Damned birds dancing on my roof again! He thought, I'm gonna put an owl silhouette up there one day—and soon! I wonder how they'd taste as turkey jerky.

He speculated what Marci would have said if she'd still been alive. She was never far from his mind, but in times of stress and uncertainty he thought of her as though she were standing right next to him. He wondered what had become of their daughter, Shana.

Hurtful words had passed between him and his daughter, about politics, mostly. Shana had stormed out angry. He hadn't heard a word from her these past three years, nor could he find a trace of her on the internet. Marci could have healed the estrangement—assuming Shana could be found. He wondered if she'd changed her name.

At the table, he opened the album and glanced through some of the pages. It took an effort to allay the loneliness and sadness that engulfed him now, in his final years. To ease the fear and trepidation of what was about to occur, he looked at the portrait of Marci and Shana. Remembering the argument was bitter. In spite of their differences, he loved his daughter.

He should have paid more attention to her education. She'd come by her political beliefs in school. The changes had been gradual, subtle, at least to him. Maybe other parents had been more attuned to what was happening, and more alarmed.

At first the Pledge of Allegiance was suspended, deemed irrelevant. It took time away from other more important classroom matters. In many schools the morning prayer and Pledge of Allegiance were cancelled. They made some students uncomfortable because they didn't believe in God or the goodness of their country.

The Nativity scene at Christmas time was also removed.

One school administrator determined that a certain child's lunch from home was not wholesome enough. The lunch was taken from the child. The school said it could better look after the nutrition of the children than the parents.

At the time, James considered these to be freak anomalies, only in the news for their entertainment value, and nothing more.

Shana had asked: "Why are we killing the bears and their cubs at the North Pole? They're drowning! The ice is melting! Our SUV is killing them—you're melting the ice driving our SUV. Why do you drive that beast when you know you're killing those animals? We need an electric car!"

He shook his head at the remembrance. He blamed himself for her conversion. Not only her body, but her mind was being fed school lunch. The National Education Association gave schools money. In return, the schools were obliged to follow the Federal education guidelines. He added it all up as a seditious plot to change the country into some other form of government. He was not liking the smell of it.

His mouth felt as dry as his desert front yard. The coffee provided no relief. His stomach was knotted. The thought of eating breakfast was not pleasant.

James frowned and looked up at the sound of two heavy vehicles approaching his circular drive. He closed the album. The lead vehicle was a Rapid Deployment Vehicle, used by SWAT teams. The huge, heavy machine made crunching sounds as it came up his graveled circular drive, stopping just beyond his walkway. The second vehicle was a municipal rear-load waste collection truck that backed part way up his driveway. The driver got out and began setting up a chop saw at the rear of the vehicle.

James walked carefully down the cement path to the edge of the driveway; he was going to position these intruders where he wanted them. He felt unsteady, hyper-stimulated with adrenalin, and his right knee was stiff and very painful, even from sitting just a few minutes. He tried not to limp. Limping would only signal weakness.

Eight heavily armed members of the Enforcement Unit aggressively exited the RDV and lined up before him on the drive, their weapons at the ready, shouldered, but pointing at the ground. All eight were dressed in matching coyote tan Battle Dress Uniforms. Two embroidered patches rode the left sleeve of each BDU shirt. The top patch was the Homeland Security emblem. Beneath that was a bold, powerful bird, with its talons clutching a limp garden snake. The snake's head was held tight in the bird's beak. Each Unit member wore body armor, the latest in flack vests, a black Kevlar helmet, a Camelback hydration unit, and several double-loop flex cuffs threaded beneath their black duty belts. Their eyes were concealed behind mirrored sunglasses. Their faces were expressionless. Not a grin, not a frown. They were blank, clay-like death masks, dispassionate, unresponsive—locked, loaded, and ready.

An officer walked in front of the Unit. He was a tall, strongly built black man, a first lieutenant, judging by the silver bar attached to the lapels of his BDU. His uniform was starched, pressed, and bloused into his highly shined assault boots. You could cut your fingers on the creases, they looked so sharp. He, too, was wearing body armor and a Camelback hydration unit. An MP 10 submachine gun was draped across his chest. Attached to his duty belt and strapped to his left leg was a tactical holster holding a .9 mm Beretta pistol. He was holding a clipboard of official-looking papers.

He stopped in front of James and glanced over his shoulder. His unit spread out so he would not be in their line of fire.

"My name is Lieutenant Bloom. We're an enforcement unit with the Department of Homeland Security. You are Mr. James Penny?"

"Yes."

"We are charged with confiscating and destroying all firearms and seizing all ammunition in your possession. You will also pay the penalty for each firearm and each round of ammunition. This is the result of not complying with mandate SB-99-3, which demands the surrender of all weapons and ammunition. We'll start by taking the pistol in your waistband and the spare magazines." The lieutenant pointed his finger toward James's pistol and continued, "I have a warrant allowing us to search the rest of your property for all the weapons we suspect you possess, and any others in your charge. Should you profess to have sold any firearm, we will need confirmation of that sale and the name and address of the buyer. The consequences of such a ruse will be met with arrest, detention, and we are authorized to use force if necessary. Am I understood, Mr. Penny?"

How do you know what guns I have? James thought. Then he remembered all of the paperwork he'd filled out and signed when purchasing each weapon. He wondered at the threat imposed on the Federal Firearms License holders to get them to release their paperwork. It was probably simple. "Give 'em up or go to jail!"

James nodded that he understood.

"You have three handguns, two long guns, and a shotgun." Lieutenant Bloom glanced toward the dump truck. James followed his glance. "That is where we will chop each weapon at its breech. No one hunts with pistols," Bloom said, pointing to James's Beretta, "or assault weapons. The National Health and Safety Guidelines have declared all firearms a safety hazard, not only to your family and neighbors, but to local and federal governments."

"The Bill of Rights gives me the right to possess firearms," James replied.

The lieutenant grimaced and shook his head, "No one has the right to possess any firearm—period. They are safety hazards. This is the law, and you would be wise to accept it, sir."

James cleared his throat, took a breath, and glanced down at the machine gun strapped across the lieutenant's chest. He spoke, his voice a little higher in pitch now. "There is no mention of hunting in the Second Amendment, or any place in the Bill of Rights or Constitution, for that matter. It's an irrelevant, ignorant, and childish argument. Our founding documents are still the rules by which this republic is run. No amendments have been ratified to replace any portion of our founding documents. No one in this Government is worried about citizen safety. The recent mass shootings are just an excuse to rally public opinion against gun ownership. In truth, you want to be able to sleep at night. Your greatest fear is an armed population, tired of being arrested, detained, tortured, and dictated to, coming for you in the night. If we surrender our guns, we're surrendering our rights, our freedoms, and our country."

"Debating you is not why we are here, Mr. Penny. Present that case at our Phoenix field office. We are here to destroy your weapons, collect your ammunition, collect the penalties and/or arrest you. Should you persist in delaying tactics, you will be taken into custody under the New Patriot Act as a suspected terrorist. You will be detained indefinitely, questioned for as long as needed to determine your threat potential, and that of your friends and family."

Lieutenant Bloom could see that Penny was physically uncomfortable. His old body is giving him pain, he thought. He's favoring one leg. There's pain there. Perspiration is streaming down his face and soaking through his shirt. Make him sweat. Let his body soften his resolve and we can end this without further delay. The lieutenant thumbed slowly through the sheath of papers, looking occasionally at Penny. As he did so, he was thankful that he had his youth, his health, and his dream of becoming an important spoke in the new political wheel in spite of his race. He felt only a slight twinge of discomfort performing these tasks. He had been at the bottom of the food chain most of his life. This job had to be done and it was his to accomplish. He'd not completely believed in the increasing brutality with which forces were pushing the country into a new political age. He felt fortunate however, that for once in his life, he was on the power side of the curve. The right or wrong of it was not important at this point. Once he'd proven himself worthy and capable, promotions were assured. He hoped that future assignments would be less unsavory. Successfully dealing with these situations would liberate him, and then he would be free to let his ambitions soar. Petty confrontations like this would be behind him. He opened his stance a little, squared his shoulders, and proceeded to stare at James with authority.

James tried to hide the physical discomfort of his body, but he could not. His swollen knee ached, and the toes on that side had gone numb. He watched the lieutenant thumb slowly through the clipboard of papers and looked again at the mirrored sunglasses of the Unit members—they were just waiting for the signal to pull their triggers. Not a sound, not a movement of air. He very subtly shifted more of his weight to his good leg. Asking to sit down was only a thought. He silently cursed his 82-year-old body for betraying him. He would not give in. He would not go quietly into that good night. If he were to drop dead or be shot dead here and now—so be it. He would die facing the betrayers of his country, these messengers of doom. "It ain't over 'til the fat lady sings," he muttered to himself, his voice barely audible.

"I can see that you are in pain, sir, and would probably like to end this. So let's end it now. Carefully hand over your pistol and the magazines. If you continue to stall, I'm going to have to arrest you and take you in. And we'll still get everything we've come for." The lieutenant reached out with his left hand, waggling his fingers for the pistol in James's waistband. "Hand over that sidearm, sir, and stand aside."

James's blue-grey eyes narrowed. In a firm voice he said, "No. You're on private property, lieutenant. I reject your authority. You and your sparrows should fly away, and I mean right now!"

Lieutenant Bloom shook his head, cocked an eyebrow, turned his head toward his Unit, and gave a nod. James now found himself marked by eight lasers, and looking at the business ends of eight automatic weapons. He heard their safeties come off.

The lieutenant looked James in the eye, shook his head again as though admonishing a wayward child, and smiled with contempt, showing a set of extremely white teeth. "Okay, we'll do this the hard way. This is what we get paid top dollar for. You are marked, sir." Showing the measure between thumb and forefinger, he said in a measured tone, "You are this close to being shot dead. Do you understand? You will lose everything."

James slowly raised his left fist.

The lieutenant looked down to find a laser playing over his chest. He now saw ten armed and masked figures aligned across James's peaked roof, where there had been none before. They had the high ground advantage and were within easy rifle range. He glanced over his shoulder at his Unit. Each of them had a laser crawling over his body. There was some uncomfortable shifting among them. Each was now lasered while lasering … an Arizona light-show standoff.

"The laser on your chest, Lieutenant, is from a Barret 44, a .50-caliber sniper's rifle. Your vest won't keep it from blowing you apart, and anyone standing behind you." There was a slight movement behind the lieutenant. Out of the corner of his eye, James noticed the municipal worker trot quickly to the far end of his dumpster, out of the line of fire. He continued, "I may die here and now—so be it. Should you have your way, only the dead will be free from the oppressive cruelty I've been seeing for the last couple of months. Check points manned by riot-gear-clad individuals, possibly TSA, checking IDs against a database. Citizens being flex-cuffed and loaded into a bus, headed for a detention center somewhere? A local military base?" He paused and scanned the Unit's faces … no change in expressions. "Have no fear, because all of you," he swept the Unit with a finger, "are going to die here, today, with me. You'll be free and out of the game. Your deaths are as certain as sunset." Then he added, "My family is dead and long gone; I know I'm dead for this.

All of you may have years to live, families to make, loved ones to be with, and dreams to fulfill—oh, and lots of luck to you in fulfilling those dreams should they not run parallel with your master's plans."

He paused and looked Bloom in the eye. "It's your move, Lieutenant. Do what you need to do. Let the hammers fall as they will." James slowly raised his left fist again. There was a sharp series of clicks as safeties came off weapons, which was followed by a silence so profound that a dropped pin would have been heard. James realized that his anger and adrenaline had incinerated the butterflies in his gut. All the aches and discomfort in his body had faded.

The lieutenant looked again at the laser marking his body, and at the masked riflemen facing him.

There was only unblinking resolution in James's face. He stared at the lieutenant, "Your side gets one, me. Our side gets nine. We win. You lose."

"You're charged with noncompliance, and now with threatening the lives of federal agents. Wanna add to the list?"

"You're a breath away from the Philippine Communist Party's Sparrow Unit. That was the name of their death squad. They murdered the party's political opponents."

Bloom lifted one eyebrow. "Fine, let's add hate speech to the list."

"Hate speech my ass!" James said. "You can shove all that political correctness up that part of your anatomy where, unlike Arizona, the sun will never shine!"

Bloom apparently had no intention of dying this day. "Stand down," he said over his shoulder, as he raised his arm and lowered it. His team turned off their lasers, locked their weapons, and stood down. However, lasers remained on the Unit. "Mount up!" he said, and they turned to leave.

"Hold up there, Lieutenant," James said. "We're not through here. Place your weapons on the ground in front of you. Do it now!"

James drew his Beretta and placed its Crimson Trace laser directly on the lieutenant, his old, watery eyes expressionless. "There are no options, Lieutenant, no back-up, no back-down, and no further discussion."

"And if we don't comply?" The lieutenant asked, looking down the barrel of James's Beretta.

"Then the nine of you are dead, here and now, before you can get your safeties off. And I will shoot you in the mouth and blow out the back of your head, Lieutenant. Let's not forget the Barrett 44. You'll be the first. Live or die, Lieutenant, it's your choice. You have five seconds to lay 'em down, or I'm going to kill you." From a distance of about eight feet, James kept the laser of his Beretta on Bloom, and began slowly counting.

"All right! All right!" Bloom said, holding up his hand to stop the count. "Lay your weapons on the ground!"

Several very tense seconds passed slowly. James noticed that expressions had cracked the Unit's stoic masks. James held his breath while following the lieutenant's every move with his pistol.

Finally, Bloom laid his submachine gun slowly on the ground. Dutifully following orders but marked with some hesitation and glances toward their lieutenant, his Unit followed his lead.

"Don't worry about it, men! We'll be back and set this right!" Bloom faced James, feet apart; his powerful shoulders hunched forward, his fists clenched, and his face compressed. With a thick forefinger he stabbed at James. "You'd better grow eyes in the back of your head, 'cause your life's timer is fast approaching your ending bell!"

"I'll be right here, Lieutenant. I'm going nowhere."

The Unit turned to leave.

"Now your body armor!"

Bloom came up short, turned, and took a half-step toward James, giving him a look of hatred.

James calmly thumbed back the hammer of his Beretta, putting the hammer on full cock, giving the pistol a very light trigger and the single action James wanted.

Bloom paused, squinted his eyes, and in a husky voice, "Okay. Do it!"

The Unit members threw their hydration units to the ground in disgust.

"We're gonna strip you of all your equipment. Now your side-arms, spare magazines, and clips—don't forget your knives, and any hideouts … and your helmets," James continued.

There was more grumbling and cursing and throwing equipment to the ground. "What, you don't want our boots, too?" Bloom muttered.

"No one I know would want to walk in your boots," James said with contempt.

The entire Unit looked to their lieutenant for an order.

"Hesitate or refuse any part of this," James said, "and you're all dead in less than three seconds. You lose absolutely everything. We win."

James sensed that several of the Unit were tempted to take up their weapons anyway and fight it out to the last man. Doing so would be suicide, and he prayed they'd make the better choice.

"Some of you pat 'em down," James said over his shoulder. He waved his left hand.

Three masked patriots crawled from the roof to conduct the search.

"Your days are numbered, old man," Bloom said, again poking his finger at James, trying to smother the ache in his belly. "I'll have your head—and every one of yours!" he drew a finger along James's roofline.

"You know where to find us. By the way, we're making several videos of this little episode," James announced, with a pained grin. "I'm certain your superiors and the American public will appreciate your official commentary when they watch it on the internet. By all means, keep talking for the camera. Many will draw courage from what's happened here. They'll know exactly who and what you are. Your confiscating and taxing chores might be a bit more difficult from here on." James bent his bad knee a little to ease the pain, which was surfacing again. It was little help.

Bloom's eyes lost their focus for a moment. How could he have botched this simple task? It occurred to him that there must be a traitor in his own organization. Penny had been warned and Bloom's Unit set up. Their tactical advantage had been lost when he ordered his people to stand down. It flashed briefly though his mind that the administration might be overconfident in its assessment of a passive citizenry. This rabble had been willing to kill and die for their beliefs.

At least we could have died fighting, he thought. He was sick at heart. How was he going to remove this blemish, this—this grotesque and oozing pustule from his mind, his gut—and his record? His hopes for his future were disappearing like water spilled on the hot Arizona sand. He felt faint. Bile burned in his throat. He was forced to swallow several times. There was a time, he thought, when such a failure required the commander to fall on his sword. He didn't have even a penknife to slit his wrists. Not to worry, he thought bitterly, someone higher up in HLS will do it for me.

When the Unit was relieved of its equipment and was prepared to leave, James noticed that one member, at the end of the line, was a young woman.

She purposely removed her sunglasses and looked straight into his eyes. It was his daughter Shana.

It was as though he was slugged in the gut with the butt of a rifle. He now knew why he couldn't find her. She had changed her name.

Bloom saw a look of bewilderment and pain cross Penny's face, and he followed Penny's eyes to Sergeant Davis. He was nonplussed. He wondered at the connection. Had he known what it was, maybe he could have used it to his advantage.

James saw Bloom's expression turn, momentarily calculating, before it was replaced again with an angry grimace. His daughter—a member of the Unit! He struggled to recover. "Now get the hell off my property!" he barked at Bloom, but his voice was weak. He saw that the chop saw had been stowed and black diesel exhaust issued from the exhaust of the waste collection truck.

One of the Unit flipped off Penny and his ten patriots. Someone shouted back at him, "That's either your IQ or your number of legal parents! Which is it?"

The Unit filed into the RDV and slowly exited James's drive. Lieutenant Bloom stood on the rear platform of the vehicle, staring at the rejoicing of James and his associates. The Unit's own camera had also captured the entire fiasco, and several of the rebels had carelessly removed their masks. That could prove unfortunate for all of them in the near future. He smiled as he and his Unit receded into the distance.

The rest of the resisters came from the roof and there was sniggering, cheering, handshaking, and backslapping over the victory.

James's and Marci's long-time friend, Rita Snapp, gave James a hug and whispered, "We saw her, too. It breaks my heart that she came back into our lives like this." Marcus, Rita's husband, congratulated James, and shook his head in sympathy. Mal and Cob Penny, his nephews, members of the rooftop, consoled him. They too were stunned at seeing their cousin a member of the Unit.

James set the safety on his pistol, backed up, and sat on his porch steps. He stretched his right leg out, hoping to ease the ache. He laid the pistol on the step next to him. He was trembling from adrenalin, pain, and exertion; his age had caught up with him. He was exhausted, and in agony and shock at finding his daughter a member of the Unit. She'd been willing to kill him. She'd marked him with her laser! Her father apparently counted for nothing. And yet, unknowingly, he would have participated in her slaughter, also. The others were unaware that the young woman in the Unit was James Penny's daughter. Now he understood how families must have felt during the Civil War—fathers against sons, brothers against brothers.

The equipment and arms were gathered and loaded into a van to be stashed against future need.

One of the hooded figures wondered aloud who owed the tax on the surrendered weapons and ammo? "Maybe the lieutenant for having lost them?" Chuckles followed his suggestion.

Sitting on the stoop of his home, many thoughts crossed through his mind. Maybe it was time for another Declaration of Independence from yet another group of tyrants, homegrown this time. Word had it that more than a dozen conservative talk shows had been shut down by the government. Good-bye, First Amendment. Many of the employees had been detained for railing against the administration. Their whereabouts were unknown. Some even speculated that they had been executed. Other folks across the country, who'd been criticizing the administration, were disappearing, and their family members closely watched. Tom Rush had trashed and refuted the policies and politics of the Left over the radio for 27 years. His following numbering in the millions. He'd been out of the country when the shutdown occurred. The hope was that he would be continuing his enlightening theater by shortwave broadcasts from Saint Elsewhere.

James looked at his co-conspirators. Some of them had removed their masks. The Unit could have filmed the scene also, and if so, facial recognition would put all of them in danger. Torture would not be out of the question. Maybe, James thought, now is the time to strike back rather than be stricken into inaction, giving this Socialist government the opportunity to do whatever they damn well pleased, without consequence. He caught Rita's eye, pointed to Marcus and his two nephews and waved them over. Maybe now, he thought, is the time to have another turkey roast.

The End

THE OMEN

In my waking dream
    I am a freight-train of 79 baggage cars, being pulled
    by two powerful locomotives
    with open throttles
    down a line of track at 90 miles an hour.

I can see the end of the track in the distance
    The two rails end abruptly, snug against the base of a granite mountain
    My uncle used to say that "speed doesn't kill, it's the sudden stop is that kills."
    The coming collision will not kill this new-me
    however, every earthly, joy

every frustration, every regret
    every misunderstanding, painful occurrence
    every slight, every accolade, every accomplishment
    every failure, every should-a-would-a-could-a
    will be completely obliterated—

so completely destroyed that absolutely nothing will remain!
    Each of the 79 box cars represents one year of my life
    Chock-full of my life's stuff
    —add the two locomotives, One, this-me the other new-me and you have
    my age
    —and a good night to you.

ABOUT THE AUTHOR

I am the oldest of two, crumb cruncher, in an Air Force family. We lived many places, mostly on the East Coast and in the South. Attended several high schools and graduated in Japan in 1957. Served in the Air Force '58 – '62. Degreed in '67 from West Texas State University with a BA in English and just shy of a BFA as well. Lived and worked in NYC for ten years, a terrific post-graduate experience. Copy writer, briefly, office manager for a mail order catalog, then as the advertising manager for a company in the South Tower. I built and worked my own pottery studio and sold planters to florists on Manhattan and in N.J. I have other stories in progress.